Tales from
Russet Grange

by Crispin Aldrin

ISBN 978-1-80352-399-6

Printed in the United Kingdom

ISBN 978-1-80352-399-6

9 781803 523996 >

From the Family and a Friend...

"Nowhere near as funny as he thinks it is."
Author's Wife

*"The perfect book to read when
you're sat on the toilet."*
Author's Brother

"Can't I just wait for the film?"
Author's Son

"Sexist Drivel"
Author's Son's Girlfriend

"Fucking Brilliant"
My Mate Malcolm

Tales from Russet Grange

Printed by Mixam (www.mixam.co.uk)
Publisher: Independent Publishing Network
Publication date: 31st July 2023

~ FIRST EDITION ~

ISBN: 978-1-80352-399-6
Author: Crispin Aldrin
Email:hello@russetgrange.co.uk
Website: www.russetgrange.co.uk
Twitter: @RussetGrange

Presented on eco-friendly, recycled papers certified by FSC

Disclaimer

**This book *'Tales from Russet Grange'*
is entirely a work of fiction.**

The characters described here,
whilst being influenced by the author's experiences
at a number of golf clubs as an employee, freelancer or
member, are not in any way based on specific persons.

**Any similarity to actual persons, living or dead,
is purely and entirely coincidental.**

The golf club *'Russet Grange'* is a fictional golf club.
It is not based on any golf club that the author has ever
worked at, played at, or is otherwise aware of.

**Any similarity to an existing golf club is again
purely and entirely coincidental.**

Foreword

There isn't one.

To Jan and James.

Introducing *'Tweety Snippets'*

You've paid for over 300 pages and by Haaland's Hammer you'll get over 300 pages.

I can't be arsed to write that much though so I've chucked a few choice tweets from *@RussetGrange* in some of the blank spaces as an easy way to pad out the pages.

Here's one to get started:

Our latest innovation at Russet Grange is making us an absolute fortune. A premium rate "How was your round?" line.

Nobody else gives a toss, so pay £1.50 per minute to tell some kid on minimum wage about a putt that lipped out on the 16th.

#golf #innovation #cash #businessidea

p.s - Since writing most of this nonsense, Twitter seems to have become **"X"**, but we shan't worry about that.

The Card of the Course

In keeping with the golf theme there's a
'Card of the Course' entry at the start of each chapter.

I provide a chapter title, a par figure
(3,4 or 5 relating to the chapter length), total wordage,
and a *'Joke Index'* with an index of 1 being the least
bad chapter and an index of 34 being the worst.

THE TALES

THE TALES

There are some very sharp minds
in our greenkeeping team.

Referencing the current disquiet among some
of the working population, our young intern
Ryan just said "Lucky we don't go on strike,
that grass won't mow itself".

Three words son: "Flock of sheep".

An Introduction to Russet Grange Golf Club

The winding private drive through one of Cambridgeshire's finest orchards to Russet Grange Golf Club more than hints at an establishment of good standing, a place where the traditions of this finest of sports are preserved, as they have been for generations.

A place where all those who love the game of golf are welcomed on the unwritten and unspoken expectancy that the club's rules and regulations will be observed and respected, and that a proud 120-year history merely represents the first 120 years, with many more decades still to be written.

One can easily imagine a Professional's shop under the charge of a humble fellow named Kenneth, well into his sixties, who once took Arnold Palmer to 18 holes, and whose father guided Russet Grange through the toughest of times during the Great War. Equally easy to imagine is a spikes bar adorned with memorabilia and a private lounge where deals are brokered over a fine malt or a vintage port, ably served by Hopkins, the Club Steward, who knows everything but tells nothing.

The elegant curves of tree-lined gravel, which have surely witnessed the whispers of Bentleys and Jaguars driven by brigadiers, captains of industry and Harley Street surgeons, do nothing but add to the expectation of a club where they just might have considered filming a 1960's spy thriller, or perhaps applied to host The Open in days gone by.

Leather Chesterfields, a hint of Cuban cigar, lockers labelled with the monikers of peers of the realm. These leaps of imagination are short leaps indeed.

But then, as the clubhouse moves into view on the last of those gravelled bends, the mental picture that has been perfectly framed over the last half mile gets shredded like that most famous of Banksy's efforts.

What should have been a majestic building of Bath stone, fronted with oak doors and fluted columns, manicured lawns, tinkling fountains and with snowdrops peeking into the promise of Spring, turns out to be an abomination that has surely adorned the pages of Portakabin Monthly's *"How to Fuck Up"* feature. A tired and unloved carbuncle, perhaps built from plans rejected for a 1970's comprehensive, bereft of any redeeming feature other than a partly collapsed banner offering half price bacon rolls with any green fee. In golfing parlance you expected a pristine sleeve of Pro V1s, but instead you discovered a dozen Argos Commandos.

A glance across to the seemingly well-tended 8th and 17th greens, adjacent to this abomination, does at least give some hope for the course, but not much as evidenced by a sign that warns: *"Do not retrieve balls from the pig farm"*. (Yes you read that right, the course designer, Major G.P. Bosworth-Minecraft esq. was known for his non-conventional style. Thus, the 9th and 18th holes, a pair of 500 yard par fives, give golfers the chance of a decent stroll following their game).

There is also what can only be described as a mating pair of knackered shoe cleaners, clearly well past their working days, probably having last spun their mud-caked and woefully-worn bristles when Ben Hogan was on The Tour.

Further clues to the status and standing of Russet Grange are not hard to spot. The Ladies' Captain's parking spot (nicely done on the apostrophes there I thought) is occupied by a burger trailer, still sporting a sponsor's banner from a long-since cancelled Pro-Am. The buggy shed is covered in more pigeon shit than Nelson's Column after a three-month stint of avian diarrhoea, and peeling paint, missing tiles and drainpipes clinging on to the clubhouse for dear life suggest that the last time there was any money for maintenance was when Double Diamond flowed freely on Club Nights.

But fear not. There are 18 tees, 18 fairways and 18 greens. The clubhouse and Pro-shop, such as they are, remain well supported by six hundred members, many of whom have neither a criminal record nor chronic personal hygiene issues. There are willing volunteers, regular visits from golf societies to boost the coffers, and almost half of the staff know what their actual job is.

This is Russet Grange Golf Club, a club owned by its members, and these are just some of its many tales.

Twitter would be many times better if every other fucking tweet wasn't a picture of a packet of biscuits from the 1990s asking: "Who remembers these?"

Yes we know the sausages only cost us 10p wholesale but it's 99p if you want an extra one. And no, you can't swap the beans for an extra rasher of bacon.

We are this close to becoming a "Staff and Societies Only" venue.

Introducing:
Kevin 'Cardiac' Pudgett (56)
Full Member
Nationality: English

Kevin Pudgett

*5**6 years old and just a Big Mac away from a cardiac arrest, a cider drinker through and through, Kevin Pudgett looked 50 when he was 30 and now he looks 75. He is a typical farmer though, absolutely minted, most of which came from EU subsidies for growing fuck all. Strangely he sports a rather fetching mullet but doesn't have any hair on the top of his head.*

Pudgett owns a very shiny Aston Martin and when it doesn't start, which happens surprisingly often, he drives to the club in one of his eight tractors.

Despite an immense frame, which wouldn't have looked out of place at the 1977 World Darts Championship, he's a single figure golfer and once won a bet that he couldn't down an 18 can slab of Strongbow during a round and still break 80. He drank the lot on the front nine and shot a 76.

Kevin Pudgett has been married to wife Claire for 35 years, and she's pretty much as obese as he is. Her liking of checked shirts and country music is why Pudgett refers to her as "My little Daisy Duke". Ironically she looks more like Boss Hogg in a wig, but he loves her to bits. He once heard a member say that she "…looked more like a Nissan Juke than Daisy Duke". Pudgett floored the aforementioned member with a 'Prescott Right Hander'.

Other than the above incident, he's the least confrontational or aggressive person anyone will ever meet, the archetypal 'big old softie', loved by all. There's already a place reserved for his commemorative bench when that final fatal burger drops into his immense gut and calls time on his left ventricle.

Plus:

Ray 'Oddjob' Pullman (66)
Full Member
Nationality: English

Ray Pullman

Pullman is a member (and to be honest there are a few of them) who isn't what could be described as a workaholic. Indeed there's only one thing he likes less than working, and that's paying income tax.

Despite claiming that he's known as 'Oddjob' because he is bald and once played at 18 holes at Carnoustie with Sean Connery (he didn't), the nickname is purely because he derives all of his income by working cash in hand for gullible old ladies. How he gets away with this skulduggery really is anyone's guess but get away with it he does.

Pullman plays golf a couple of times a week, less if he's busy ripping off a particularly wealthy senior citizen. He does a nice line in insurance assistance too. "You might as well claim for a new carpet love, I can easily knock over a tin of gloss".

He was a decent golfer until he broke both of his legs, falling from a roof whilst repairing a gutter that didn't need repairing. A subsequent attempt to sue the homeowner, because the decking supporting the ladder gave way, backfired when it was pointed out by the defendant's solicitor that Pullman had himself fitted the decking just eight months before. The case, just like the decking, collapsed.

In 1979, Ray Pullman appeared on the TV show 'Mastermind', scoring just six points on his specialist subject of 'Naval Battles of World War II'. How he ever got accepted on to the show is anyone's guess, but he progressed no further, completely embarrassing himself in the general knowledge round, the lowlight of which was suggesting that a Dachshund was a type of freshwater fish.

Also introducing:
'Uncle' Andy Biggs (58)
Clubhouse Assistant
Nationality: English

Andy Biggs

*O*ne or two people at Russet Grange truly have their finger on the pulse of the club. 'Uncle' Andy Biggs however takes things considerably further. He has it hooked up to an ECG machine and MRI scanner. If it has happened, is happening, or is going to happen, Biggs knows about it. He's no busybody though, far from it. He watches, he listens, he reads and he keeps it all to himself.

You know that bloke who worked with your Dad, the fun one who you had a big shed full of home brew, motorbike engines and jazz mags? The one who you thought was your uncle but it turned out he was just a bloke married to someone that your Dad fancied and kept making excuses to visit? That's Andy Biggs.

You want someone to come in at 6:00am and churn out breakfast for a society of 40 hungry Cornishmen? Biggs'll do it. Looking for someone to run the bar because a recently-employed floozy just changed her Facebook status to 'it's complicated' and stayed in bed and cried? Biggs is your man. Perhaps you need a volunteer to drive around in a buggy and sell beer and pasties at a charity golf day? Biggs will come in on his day off and put in a 14 hour shift.

We begin...

Kevin Pudgett and Ray Pullman arrived in their *'home from home'*, the Russet Grange clubhouse bar, having just finished a very pleasant nine holes on an equally pleasant spring morning. The pair had been good friends for many years and members at Russet Grange for almost as long.

"Cider please Andy, one for yourself, and I'll have a bacon bap. Ask Royce to chuck a couple of sausages in it too, gotta look after this bad boy". (Tony *'Bacon Rolls'* Royce is the current Chef, he's woeful and we'll meet him later in another bang-average chapter). Pudgett grasped his stomach and gave it a wobble as men do, its immense bulk rippling in a slow, almost hypnotic fashion. *"What you having mate?".*

"Just an orange juice please Andy, going to have a couple of weeks off the booze. Doctor reckons I've got high levels of something or other, you can't be too careful."

"Christ, that's a bit worrying, you sure?" Pudgett's concern was beautifully misinterpreted by his golfing buddy, and with his resistance broken in under five seconds, he turned back to Andy Biggs and gave the smile of a chubby man. *"Oh go on then, I'll have a Stella".* (We shall encounter Andy Biggs many times as we progress through these tales, he's one of the good guys.

As the drinks were being poured time seemed to stand still. The pair of them, both all too aware of their mortality, gazed at the walls of the Spikes Bar. Walls that over the years had been adorned with the photographs of a myriad of Russet Grange's former Club Captains. Most long since having holed their final putt, and all, until a case of indecent exposure in 1979 started the rot, fine gentlemen of good standing and moral fortitude.

Yes, as many of his fellow members had previously concluded, those from the last few decades were, to put it mildly, a mixed bunch. Whilst the Wentworths and Sunningdales of this world display portraits of men of achievement, dignity and dedication, the mugshots on display represented something more of a cross-section of society. Included in varying degrees of photographic splendour were at least one convicted sex-offender, an arsonist who specialised in failing restaurants, two local fraudsters (captains 1987 and 1988 respectively) and a bloke who once ended up in hospital with some *'Dove Original'* roll-on deodorant lodged deep inside his anus.

The deodorant episode is one of the worst kept secrets at Russet Grange and a suggestion to have the incident noted in the members' handbook *'notable milestones'* section was only defeated by a small number of votes at the 1998 AGM. At that meeting it had been well argued by Ray Pullman that there probably wasn't a golfer in the county who didn't know that one of Russet Grange's former captains had rather embarrassed himself in the personal hygiene department, and that an official acknowledgement might help put the matter to rest. Nevertheless the vote did not pass. (unlike the Dove Deodorant with the assistance of some industrial-strength lube and the deft right hand of a trainee nurse at the local A&E who drew the short straw).

(Readers might also like to know there is an unwritten tradition at Russet Grange that visiting groups should place a Dove Deodorant on the club professional's shop counter in recognition of this sorry episode. On busy days it feels like a re-enactment of the pen scene in *'A Beautiful Mind'*).

Out-voted by a similar margin at the same AGM was the suggestion that whichever poor sap got tasked with taking the new Captain's photo each year should also provide a black and white version to be replaced and displayed upon their death. Ray Pullman was a staunch supporter of the plan, it made perfect sense to him. Indeed, his speech to the assembled masses (31 in total, including those who had to be there and the cleaner who hadn't been told about the meeting) is the stuff of legend:

"We've got pictures of bent coppers, third rate gangsters, corrupt Councillors and 'Roll-On Bobby' hung on the wall. They say you shouldn't speak ill of the dead, so under the circumstances it might be nice to know if the bloke you're currently moaning about has already vacated his place in the buggy shed".

Pullman's speech from the day was still etched in the memory of many a member, and Kevin Pudgett was always keen to take the opportunity to mock his mate.

"Full colour, every one of them, real shame that your idea got the thumbs down all those years ago." chuckled Pudgett. If truth be told both men were still shocked at the 16-15 defeat of the proposal, the cleaner's *"nay"* ironically making the difference. (Someone told her she was voting for a new Henry vacuum cleaner but rules are rules and her vote counted). *"It would certainly be good to know which of those*

old buggers entered his last bunker in a box". (That's three euphemisms for dead golfers already, and the book is only a few pages old. Marvellous stuff).

"Right I'm off for a slash, same again please Andy". Pullman went to answer the call of his bladder and as Pudgett continued to gaze around the room he could not help but be impressed that the four frames for the 1974 to 1977 photos were identical. They stood out like perfectly groomed soldiers in a regiment of otherwise ludicrously varying styles, size and design. *"Someone was really looking to the future back then"* he mused, impressed that many years ago a committee member had shown initiative and bought more frames than were needed at the precise moment in time. From his experience, pretty much every club official he had ever encountered had possessed the kind of foresight that might normally be expected from a bunch of Haribo-powered toddlers with ADHD playing in a Harvester Inn ball pool.

And yet, for all that it was and probably ever would be, Kevin Pudgett, just like so many of his fellow members, loved Russet Grange Golf Club. He especially loved it on days when his Aston actually started.

Big celebrations at Russet Grange this evening, the #marketingteam managed to create a clubhouse poster with only five grammatical errors.

A Tale of San Miguel and Chips			
Chapter	Par	Length	Joke Index
2	4	1,718 Words	20

Introducing:

Bob 'Ronnie Biggs' Cheese (56)
Full Member
Nationality: English

Bob Cheese

*O*ne of life's under-achievers. In a career that spanned almost 12 years, Cheese rose to the ranks of 'Chilled Aisle Assistant Supervisor' at an Asda superstore before his career was cruelly cut short. In early '91 Cheese slipped on a bag of frozen sweetcorn, and whilst an early diagnosis of nothing more than a sprained ankle suggested a swift return to work, a more detailed analysis by the family doctor revealed he might never walk again.

Subsequently the same family doctor did ten years inside for malpractice, gross negligence, and insurance fraud but not before Britain's second largest supermarket paid out a cool £600,000 in compensation.

Cheese found his feet again, soon after the money hit his bank account in fact, but he remains bitter about the accident which he claims cost him a prime position at his local Budgens. "They thanked me for my interest but said I wasn't suitably qualified. I reckon they had me down as a troublemaker, so I took them to court. Another five grand, easy money."

In 2010 Cheese was convicted of benefits fraud, having claimed a carers allowance for his ex-wife who had moved to Whitby some five years earlier to work as a pilates instructor. A six-month suspended sentence meant he could carry on with his golf, and his criminal activities did have a positive outcome as his nickname of 'Nob' was swiftly changed to 'Ronnie Biggs'.

Plus:
Ellie Carter (24)
Barmaid
Nationality: Southern Irish

Ellie Carter

Part time barmaid, full time hottie, Ellie Carter really is quite the girl, bringing in minimum wage when serving behind the club bar, and (until they banned the more 'fruity' stuff) also bringing in around £4k/month from gullible saps on her 'Only Fans' web page. These days the figure is closer to £3k, still a tidy sum for spending an hour a week doing fitness videos in your pants.

Carter is fully loaded in the brains department too, with a PhD in astrophysics to her name.

As is compulsory for young females in this field, she has an 'I Love Cox' coffee mug, adorned with the face of Britain's most famous pop-star come space scientist.

Revealing a little bit more cleavage when leaning over to collect glasses, accompanied by "same again gents?" delivered in a soft Southern-Irish accent, never fails. Bar takings are 30% higher when Ellie Carter's impressive breasts are on duty.

It's a case of "look but don't even think about touching" though, because her Scandinavian boyfriend Kurt is a man-mountain cage fighter and bodybuilding coach. His YouTube channel is called 'Pain and Gain from Kurt the Dane'. Upset Kurt and you get hurt.

And:
Steve 'Marge' Simpson (57)
Club Manager
Nationality: Scottish

S teve Simpson is a former army major from the Scots Dragoon Guards who takes no shit from anyone, and who, incredibly, isn't aware that he's known around RGGC as "Marge".

Steve Simpson

Previously married to Barbara, who represented Scotland at curling at the 1988 winter Olympics, they divorced when she put on around six stones of blubber following her sporting demise and new-found love of fried chicken, earning herself the rather cruel nickname of "Bargain Bucket Barbie".

A member once had a drunken rant on Facebook about Simpson, claiming that "My Labrador could do a better job, and as Labradors go he's fucking stupid". The dog-loving member was in the office at 8:30 the next morning, could be heard crying at 8:32 and was kicked out of the club by 8:35.

Simpson speaks fluent Russian and has a black belt in TaeKwondo. Upon leaving the army he was recruited to the security staff at the Ukrainian Embassy in Glasgow but left after five years for a quieter life in golf, taking a job at the Scottish PGA.

He maintains a delicate balance of management style that he describes as "A subtle mix of hard bastard and really hard bastard". If anyone is stupid enough to question how Simpson runs things at Russet Grange they receive the sort of reply that he was about to give to Bob Cheese, after which they always wish they hadn't questioned his methods in the first place.

We begin...

It had been a shitty morning following a shitty weekend in a shitty month for Bob Cheese. At the best of times Cheese wasn't what you'd call *"upbeat"*, far from it, he was a miserable human being, but having just been dumped out of the Summer Knockout by *"A lezzer who knocks it further than Bubba fucking Watson"* he was grumpier than usual and looking for something to moan about.

This month, just ten days old, had already seen a six hundred quid vet's bill for a cat he hated, his daughter in tears over yet another failed relationship, and a burst pipe in the loft that destroyed most of his bedroom ceiling and all of his Val Doonican albums (one for the youngsters there…). The only glimmer of joy on the horizon was a place in the knockout final beckoning if he could just bring a hint of his best golf to this Monday morning's match. Cheese was a bandit, he knew it, most members knew it, and whilst his handicap had been massaged more than Thom Hankey on a trip to a Thai brothel (we'll meet him later), he hadn't broken any rules. So Bob Cheese reasoned that the handicap committee could, in his own words: *"Go fuck themselves"*.

Trouble was, he did bring his best golf to the match, but it wasn't even close to good enough. A sound thrashing by *"Bubba Lezzer"* took just over two hours. His miserable loss was made even more miserable by the match finishing on the 14th hole, meaning a walk of shame measuring just over a mile, a walk punctuated by insincere comments such as *"Good luck in the final"* and *"You'll be in single figures soon"* when what he wanted to say was *"You've obviously got a cock, a pair of balls, and the testosterone levels of a prize ram"*.

"Ah fuck it" thought Cheese and he strolled to the bar, safe in the knowledge that a few seconds of looking at Ellie Carter's epic breasts would cheer him up and provide more

than enough material for his afternoon self-pleasuring. *"San Miguel and Cheesy Chips please Ellie"*. He wasn't keen on saying *"please"*, but Cheese reasoned it was a small price to pay for a cheery smile to lift his mood, even though she, like his drive on the eighth, was miles out of bounds.

Cheese handed over his bar card and awaited the satisfying *'ping'* of suitable funding being in place, but like a monetary dagger being stabbed into his wallet, Ellie looked at Cheese, gave him her best apologetic smile, and said: *"Sorry Bob, you need another 50p"*.

"What the fuck?" thought Cheese. A pint, four quid. Chips three quid. (Discounted prices, visitors pay a little more if you're thinking of popping by to check out Ellie Carter). Cheese was no mathematician, but he knew that he had at least seven quid on his card. *"The beer and food went up yesterday, sorry Bob, but I do need another 50p"*. Cheese wasn't going to get angry with Carter, far from it, this wasn't her fault, but in his mind a two-foot putt to beat Bubba Lezzer had just lipped out and someone was going to get a gobful. He looked around. No bar manager, no clubhouse manager, no cleaning lady deciding to hoover round at lunchtime. In fact there was nobody in the clubhouse who didn't hate him for his golfing life of banditry and therefore not a single person to offer even a hint of sympathy. There was only one thing for it, and it involved a trip to the *'Inner Sanctum'*.

As luck would have it, Steve Simpson was in a good mood. He'd just heard that Bob Cheese had been dumped out of the aforementioned knockout, an event that only added to the joy of hearing news just two hours ago that his ex-wife had been refused a gastric band by the NHS. Happy days indeed for this self-styled hard bastard, and when Cheese stormed into the office the promise of a minor conflict that he knew he would win and that Cheese would lose, only served to sweeten his mood.

"What's going on Steve?" enquired Cheese, *"How come it's now £4.50 for a San Miguel and £3.25 for chips? The club is taking the fucking piss. I can have the same thing in Spoons for three pound fifty and that's without a members' discount."*

"Hi Bob, and a very good afternoon to you". Simpson loved this kind of discussion. *"That's a very fair question and I could give you an equally fair answer, but I know you're grieving from this mornings' loss, so I'll be brief. Have you ever run a golf club, Bob?"*

"Not as such." A tsunami of fear washed over Cheese. He knew he was about to be on the receiving end of Simpson's infamous *"bad cop, bad cop"* routine.

"Well, I have. So you can either fuck off to 'Spoons, where I assume they don't have the cost of maintaining 100 acres of countryside and paying chefs in gold bullion, or you can pay the money like a good boy, have another gaze at the lovely Ellie, and then go home to crack one off whilst she's fresh in your little mind. How does that sound to you?"

No reply was needed, Cheese had been destroyed before the verbal jousting match he had hoped for had even begun. With his tail between his legs, suitably bollocked and generally pissed off that he had been served another soft scoop from life's ice-cream tub of misery, Cheese left the *'Inner Sanctum'*. Deflated and defeated for the second time in an hour. Cheese's shitty month to end all shitty months had just got even more shitty.

Twelve days later the metaphorical icing on this particular cake of shit would be complete, when Cheese had his handicap cut under the *'general play'* rule by the golf committee. (look it up, it was a thing when I started writing this bollocks) Oh, and as you'll no doubt have guessed by now, *'Bubba Lezzer'* won the final on the very same day.

We've just introduced our Premium Golf Membership scheme.

An extra £500 per year for which you get absolutely nothing, other than when you pay for drinks with your membership card, the clubhouse PA system proclaims: "Look at me, I'm enormous".

Introducing:
Pete 'Balcony' McTorry (69)
Full Member
Nationality: Scottish
(Special Forces Clan)

Pete McTorry

*E*very golf club has a Scottish member with a moustache who claims he was part of the SAS team which stormed the Iranian Embassy back in May 1980, and our man is Pete 'Balcony' McTorry. Despite the secrecy surrounding this crack team of elite soldiers, McTorry has no problem telling anyone who'll listen that he "...threw in the first flashbang and shot two of the bastards before they knew what hit them".

With such a successful line of bullshit so entrenched, it is no surprise that McTorry also claims he was approached to be a consultant on the Lewis Collins film 'Who Dares Wins', and that he "...drank Bodie under the table night after night, and then taught him how a real Professional deals with Johnny Foreigner".

When questioned a little more about his antics with British Special Forces, McTorry simply points to a third-rate tattoo of a dagger on his arm, gives a Glaswegian wink (same as any other wink to be honest) and says:"That'sh all you need to know shun."

Decent golfer, great company too, though on May 5th, 1980, he was, just like almost everyone else, watching the snooker final.

Plus:

Timothy Bleauchamp (79)
Club President
Nationality: Surrey

Timothy Bleauchamp

B leauchamp is the classic golf club President. A captain of industry, local planning officer, big cheese in the Rotary Club (because the Freemasons rejected him in under five minutes) and as corrupt as an Estonian prison guard. He's his number one fan and talks like he bathes his bollocks in Bollinger. Bleauchamp is universally despised by pretty much every member, though those currently seeking some sort of planning permission are more than happy to suck up to him. (Five grand in used twenties sees pretty much anything agreed).

In 2002 Bleauchamp had a 'relationship' with a representative of the County Golf Union over a table in the halfway house which came to a less than happy finish when the two of them were discovered by Greenkeeper Alex Barnes (who we shall meet later in the book). Barnes knows that his little secret will come in very handy one day, very handy indeed.

He once served as a local magistrate, but was kicked off the bench (or whatever they sit on) when he got done for drink driving after an epic afternoon session on the Bacardi at a county cricket match. Blowing three times the legal limit after having stuffed his ageing Mondeo estate into the disabled children's enclosure, was not a good look.

And:
Mark 'The Fesh' Herreng (43)
Full Member
Nationality: Local

Mark Herreng

*M*ark Herring is really, really stupid, and worse still, he resides at the end of a very short fuse. A potent personality mix which has often resulted in needless confrontations, such as when, following a lunchtime on the sauce, he was thrown out of WH Smiths for trying to pay for a 'top shelf' magazine with his (expired) organ donor card.*

He has been at the club for more than a decade and still hasn't worked out his nickname. The truth is nobody has the balls to explain it for fear that they'll be swiftly listed on the Daily Mail website as one of his victims in the ensuing acts of senseless violence, little more than clickbait next to images of some Love Island imbecile.

Not that he is without fear either, as anyone who has spent more than five minutes in his company will testify. If he's not furtively scanning the clubhouse for faces from a past he probably doesn't have, he's head-down, hoodie covered, and feverishly typing on what many assume is a 'burner' phone.

Herreng resembles that bloke from 70's band 'Sparks', not the one with the Kevin Keegan perm, but the Hitler-esque chap with the slicked-back hair and limited motor functions. It's not a look that the lady members find unattractive, but that's hardly a compliment when the bar isn't set much higher than the ability to not need a piss after two minutes of line dancing.

As to golf, well he's always a little bit lethargic for the front nine but following a flushless visit to the halfway house bog he'll be positively buzzing as he lines up his first drive on the journey home.

We begin…

When tee times were introduced at Russet Grange, as you can read about in a later chapter, concerns were expressed by the President of the *'Gusset Rangers'*, Pete McTorry, that such a radical change would mean an end to the group's Saturday gatherings. These gatherings involved an extraordinary bar spend from dawn to dusk by the most inclusive and joyous bunch of golfers that ever graced the tragically worn carpets of the Russet Grange Spikes Bar.

In truth *'concerns were expressed'* actually means that a pissed up McTorry told the actual Club President, Timothy Bleauchamp, that fifty members would be telling him to shove his golf club up his arse and taking their combined £20k spend and £45k fees to the nearest club that would have them unless they got their ninety minutes on non-competition Saturdays.

The conversation that followed between Bleauchamp and Club Manager (our very own hard bastard, Steve *'Marge'* Simpson who you met the last time you sat on the toilet) was brief. *"Of course they can have their tee times, I'm not a fucking idiot Tim"*. Simpson continued with fiscally-driven enthusiasm: *"In fact, tell McTorry that we'll stick a grand behind the bar for them as long as everyone is welcome to play"*. Simpson of course knew that anyone who wanted to be part of this particular group already was, himself included, so with a disaster averted he pulled a litre bottle of tax-free Glenmorangie from his desk and settled down to a well-deserved Friday afternoon tipple.

And thus, with Saturday mornings saved, the Rangers continued to meet, to be the life and soul of Saturdays in the clubhouse, and to chuck money behind the bar like there was no tomorrow. Indeed, for former Rangers President Nigel Whelk, there really was no tomorrow following one especially boozy Saturday some time ago.

Three pints of Guinness before playing, five cans of Stella during his round, and then more pints of the black stuff chased down with a whisky or two meant that Whelk was in no state to call a taxi or walk home. (By the way, it's satire, if this kind of thing bothers you then you're not going to enjoy the next 280 pages much). Thankfully nobody else was hurt when he stuffed his transit van into a Beech tree, but Whelk met his maker that day. On the Saturday following Whelk's untimely demise the *'Whelk Wheel'*, complete other than the Ford badge still lodged in Whelk's chest, became another trophy for the Gusset Rangers to play for.

And so we move to the present day, two years having passed since that fateful accident, with the *'Whelk Wheel'* up for grabs. The Rangers began to arrive from 8:30am, most certainly not a coincidence as this was the weekend opening time. Proudly placed on the bar was the new *'prize to rule them all'*, mounted on part of a branch from the very tree that Whelk had uprooted as he took a bend that wasn't there. The previous year's winners Mike *'Plough Boy'* Smockman and Keiran *'Mullet'* Doors (both of whom we will introduce in another chapter, yada yada...) would later turn up, eager to challenge for this historic prize, but the early attendees consisted of many Rangers regulars. Golfers (in the loosest possible terms) sporting nicknames such as *'Club Foot'*, *'Oscar Pisstorius'*, *'Dildo Baggins'*, *'French Harry'* and the current Rangers captain Mark *'The Fesh'* Herreng. (I have no idea why I chose him to be honest, he doesn't seem like the right sort, but it's done now.)

Drinks and banter flowed, as did baked bean juice and budget ketchup, both gravitationally attracted and appropriately dribbling to the carpet, adding yet more provenance to a knock-off Axminster that had been patterned with all manner of foodstuffs over the decades.

The draw for teams was made amid the kind of noise, confusion and general disorganisation that was a mainstay of these wonderful events. Some names appeared twice, some not at all, and those who had multiple nicknames derived from many years of service had no idea what was going on. Everyone loved it this way.

There was *'Cock Out Dave'* (self-explanatory) and *'Fritzl's Locksmith'*, also known as *'Officer Dribble'* (Former Traffic Warden with a particularly weak bladder), who was listed to be playing twice. *'Tapeworm'* (not what you'd think), also known as *'Anal Alex'* (exactly what you'd think) was not listed at all. But it all got sorted, 36 golfers, 12 threeballs, lovely jubbly. Then the door opened and to everyone's subtle and not so subtle disdain, *'Stain Devil'* announced his arrival. This fucked up the numbers beyond belief, and sausages were thrown. *"You're faaaacking late, faaaack off home"* suggested, nay demanded, *'Honorary Human'* (Don't, just don't. It's worse than you're imagining). It was a suggestion that *'Stain Devil'* laughed off in the way that only someone oblivious to their own universal unpopularity could ever manage.

Groupings of eleven threeballs, and a fourball which would go out last, was the solution to the numeric conundrum, sorted, as ever, by Julian *'Brains'* Ditcher (Not especially clever but he likes faggots). The format remained both undecided yet somehow agreed (I don't know what that means either but it builds a picture). Cans of cider, bottles of lager, packets of Jelly Babies (courtesy of a job lot from the bloke who worked in a Texaco garage) and some herbal tobacco were loaded onto trolleys and into bags. *'Darth Bader'* (no legs, collapsed lung, always wore black - why the hell didn't I write a profile of this guy?) grabbed his buggy and attached bottles of gin and rum to the onboard optics.

Slowly but surely the games got underway. Some had a long wait in the clubhouse, some would have a long wait after their game, but all would have a bloody good time, because the Gusset Rangers were the very definition of sociable golf.

Indeed, it goes without saying (but I'm going to say it to pad out the chapter) that there is nothing more sociable in the world of sport than competing for the steering wheel from a Ford Transit, a car part which had become a major player in the final drive that Nigel Whelk took to the pearly gates.

We shall revisit this tale of the Gusset Rangers later in the book where we report from the course in a game that once more descends into a farce. Then we shall turn our attention to the post-golf shenanigans which include the sacrificial burning of a golf bag and a pseudo-religious ceremony involving a well-known brand of savoury snacks.

> *If any of you lot with the orange paint fancy coming up to Russet Grange and having a go at the 18th green, fill your boots. We could do with the publicity.*

A Tale of a Threesome			
Chapter	Par	Length	Joke Index
4	4	1,733 Words	12

Introducing:

Guy 'Forty Shades' Potton (40)

Club Professional
Nationality: English

Guy Potton

Club Professional at Russet Grange, loved by all, adored by divorce lawyers. If astrology were a proper thing, Potton would be a Shagetarian. At just forty years of age he cheekily admits "I've been married three times, but I've had at least a dozen wives". Remarkably two of those he was once married to are club members who are now in a relationship with each other. Potton proudly suggests that his woeful attitude to women "...turned two of my exes into shrubscouts".

The classic lovable rogue, Potton pretty much idolised by anyone at the club he hasn't slept with, and some that he has, but his marriage record means that despite a decent income as a professional golfer, he has equally decent outgoings which include supporting five children and a workshy wife with a designer handbag addiction.

A fellow Pro, who was aware of Potton's fiscal strains, pointed him in the direction of some lucrative work in the adult entertainment industry. His appearances in some rather low rent 'specialist' movies provoked much merriment at the club, but also earned him a few quid and a suitable nickname.

Plus:
John 'Virginia' Conrad (61)
Full Member
Nationality: English

John Conrad

A friendly looking soul these days but Conrad liked to think of himself as a hard-core punk rocker "back in the day". Indeed he played bass guitar in the band 'Damage' which enjoyed a couple of minor hits and were once on the bill with 'The Exploited' during a brief UK tour. (He's unlikely to forget his punk days as he sports a misspelled tattoo reading 'Danage' on his right arm, testament to the stupidity of youth and the incompetence of an unlicensed and self-evidently incapable Spanish tattooist).

His less than promising music career gave way to a relatively successful career as a cleaning products salesman during the late 80s, which was also the time when he took up golf. He wasn't half bad either, winning the club championships in 1989, though this

*was a year when the club's best players were either a)
representing the county or b) in prison. He's not keen on
people referring to him as 'Virginia' though, a reflection
of the tennis legend's '77 Wimbledon win, a tournament
noted for its near-absence of quality players.*

*Conrad is teetotal but his wife Doreen likes the odd
Pina Colada. She used to sell Tupperware and won
a trip to Barbados for the two of them in a company
competition. Sadly, one too many at the airport left
her in a bit of a state, and the subsequent tumble down
the plane's steps left her with a broken ankle and no
holiday. The Gusset Rangers still like to sing "Oh, I'm
not going to Barbados" when Virginia is on the tee.*

And:
Mike 'Top Gun' Parris (58)
Full Member and Club Captain
Nationality: Jock

Mike Parris

*Club Captain,
and therefore an
ex-copper and
Freemason. Mike Parris has
had a morbid fear of flying
since watching 'Airport
77' as a ten-year-old kid.
Thus he never plucked up
the courage to go on a plane
until he was 50, when he flew with the world's second
favourite airline (EasyJet) to Madrid.*

Within two minutes of take-off most of his stomach contents were in his lap, and Parris describes the remaining ninety-six minutes of flight time as "The worst of my life, and I've been shot in the bollocks".

Parris came home from Madrid via a two-day train journey, a cross-channel ferry and a £240 / five hour taxi ride (tip included).

His abject hatred of flying earned him his nickname Top Gun. Truth be told he's a good sport, wearing a flying suit to his Captain's Drive-In with his wife (who most members agree is a fit as fuck) dressing as an especially slutty air hostess to act as his caddy on the day.

A native of Scotland, a popular figure at the club, scratch golfer. His striking good looks make him the envy of many. Two of Potton's ex-wives (the shrubscouts) once turned up at the Summer Ball wearing 'I'd go straight for Parris' T-Shirts.

We begin...

Guy Potton liked Tuesdays. Not only was Tuesday his day off from his duties as club professional, but it was also the day that his current floosie's husband spent away at head office, leaving Potton free to pop round and, in his own words, *"Ride her like a Derby winner. Five minutes in the saddle and a sloppy photo finish for Instagram"*. And they say romance is dead.

In fairness, the floosie in question knew Potton's reputation and she cared not one jot. He was a lot more fun than her hubby and a bit more fun than *'Buzz Lightyear'*, a *very* close friend who lived in a bedside drawer, so she enjoyed Tuesdays a lot. Wednesdays however… well let's just say she was rarely in a state to attend her spin class.

For now though we hop over to Russet Grange mid-morning, where Potton had arranged 18 holes with two of his best male mates at the club. Mike *'Top Gun'* Parris and John *'Virginia'* Conrad. Both decent sorts whose company would ensure that no matter how bad the golf was, and sometimes it was very bad indeed, it would be an immensely enjoyable few hours.

The banter started on the first tee. *"You look fucked Virginia; Doreen keep you up all night did she?"* Potton's reference to Conrad's ragged appearance was nothing less than expected, and as he smacked his second-hand Yonex 'Big Dog' down the middle of the fairway his retort was equally sharp. *"Yep, eight hours solid mate, I had to imagine your ugly mug a couple of times to steer clear of the vinegar strokes".*

Potton wasn't sure if being the person his friend imagined in order to delay that most intimate of marital moments was a good thing, but having given it some thought he decided he was happy to help. So happy in fact he planted his three wood just 80 yards from the pin, with the grace that only a professional can manage, and a rank amateur only dream of.

Next up, Mike Parris. A lot of women and men lose their looks as a natural part of getting old, but proper men like Mike Parris often go *'full Clooney'* and mature like a fine clarinet. (That was meant to be *"a fine claret"* but I left it in for a laugh). Our third member of this threesome was better looking at 58 than he was a 28, and at 28 he'd shagged Miss England, a well-known BBC News presenter, and most of the pre-menopausal totty in his village.

Parris was currently serving as Club Captain, a popular choice, particularly among the ladies, and as befits a scratch golfer with a raging hangover, his drive was more off the mark than Gary Glitter in a stairlift advert. Mulligans were allowed though, but Parris managed to find the pig farm once more and conceded the hole before he'd left the tee.

Scratch golfer, single figure golfer, professional golfer. Nothing but pride was actually being played for, and of course whilst Potton would expect to win every hole, nobody cared one jot. This was about being in the moment, as it always had been whenever these three had played together, including the infamous '98 Pro-Am when Conrad had ended up bollock naked in a bunker on the 18th, Parris had ended up bollock naked inside the Pimm's tent during a midnight raid, and Potton had ended up bollock naked inside the girl from the county golf association who was supposed to be running the show.

Drives went straight and true, or not. Wedges found themselves just a few feet from the pin, or not. Putts from twenty feet were sunk, or not. The laughter however hit the mark every single time, and as the front nine turned into the back nine, the hip flasks took the kind of pounding that Potton normally reserved for the more accommodating and suitably discerning ladies of Cambridgeshire and beyond. (Let's be honest, this book is basically a 1990s *'lads mag'* on a golfing theme).

Parris's fear of flying was exploited on every tee. *'Come Fly With Me', 'Leaving on a Jet Plane', 'On the Wings of Love'.* You name it, Conrad sang it, full Bublé, and on each and every occasion his tunes were met with joy. *"Fuck you and your fucking songs...."* exclaimed Parris on the sixteenth tee, *"...have some of this".* Nine iron in hand, 140 to the pin, pond in the way. *"Fuck".* No matter how good you are, and Parris could certainly play, eight cans of Stella will often steer a golf ball to an aquatic demise.

"Water landing, your worst nightmare mate". Oh the dry wit of Potton. Neither playing partner could conceal their sniggering, like a pair of schoolboys who had happened upon some hedge porn on their way home from football practice on a Saturday morning.

Parris had in fact been out of the game since the tenth hole. Having not reached the ladies' tee with a drive which, had it been breathalysed, would have resulted in a five-year ban, he had been required to complete the remaining 488 yards with his cock hanging out. Embarrassing at the best of times, downright tragic when you do it on the longest hole on the course with a ladies' match progressing its sorry way down the parallel seventh and eighth. Even more of a disaster when said match is being played between the county and the neighbouring county, contested by women for whom child-bearing age is a distant memory and for whom a big dollop of joy left their lives on the day that Margaret Thatcher got ousted.

Anyway, no need for any more golf description here, you'll get bored with it by chapter eight at best. So Potton, Parris and Conrad completed their game, having long-since stopped keeping score. Golf in the company of friends was the real winner, as it always is, though a late lunch and a few more little tipples came a close second.

Potton of course couldn't stay too late. *"These ladies don't shag themselves you know, at least not when I'm on speed dial"* he joked as his taxi arrived.

Parris looked at Conrad and smiled. Guy Potton really was a legend in their eyes and they were proud to be involved in his golfing life. As to the other parts of his life, well that was where they knew to leave things to the professional.

To the member who did something of a "toiletry nature" behind the Chairman's Range Rover, we've got you on CCTV son.

Drop him a letter of apology and you'll hear no more about it, otherwise Adam Bobble's posting the video on Facebook.

Introducing:
Trevor 'Surf 'n' Turf' Bishop (64)
Head Greenkeeper
Nationality: Cornish

Trevor Bishop

*T*revor Bishop is Head Greenkeeper and he's a man who really never left 1968, despite being only 10 at the time. He drives an absolutely fucked VW camper van ('The Pussy Wagon') which is adorned with such quality stickers as 'Sex Wax', 'Huntin' for Beaver' and 'Atomkraft Nein Danke'. Being a surfer he regularly makes a stupid sign with his thumb and little finger, accompanied by ridiculous sayings such as "I was really stoked out there dude" as he gestures to the 18 inch waves off Cromer beach in Cornwall.*

Like many surfers he has actually never been surfing, but he does have a surfboard and a CD of the Beach Boys Greatest Hits in the passenger footwell of The Pussy Wagon. Like Brian 'Tex' Hanley, who we shall meet later, Bishop desperately wishes he was American so he could have refused to serve in Vietnam. This rather overlooks the fact he would have been nowhere near n-n-n nineteen at the time of that particular conflict.

A native of Truro, Bishop has the compulsory long hair, a bit too long in fact. He thinks this makes him look like Brad Pitt, but it actually makes him look like a Cornish tramp whose last visit to a barber shop was when his mum took him. (Like the author he was probably given a lollipop for not screaming the place down).

He's harmless enough though and a fairly decent golfer, though he does tend to take a few cans out with him, meaning he's usually drifted into speaking 'full hippie' by the time he reaches the sixth hole.

And:
Dean 'Worzel' Watkins (39)
Greenkeeper
Nationality: English

Dean Watkins

Dean Watkins is loved by all, especially the local charity shops where he not only buys all of his wardrobe, but anything else that he perceives as being a bargain. Along with countless 'pre-loved' T-Shirts, pairs of jeans and, unbelievably, second hand boxer shorts, he has also amassed eight copies of 'Bravo Two Zero' and quite the menagerie (it means 'collection') of pottery figurines.

*Known (quite rightly) as 'Worzel', he's one of those
people who always looks dirty, but he doesn't care
and he doesn't smell. Just like his boss, you won't find
Worzel in a barbershop either, his thinking is that his
hair will just grow back, so what's the point?*

*A trophy win in 2012 meant that Watkins attended
Presentation Night, though the Chairman was not
impressed that his one concession to the dress code was
to wear a club tie over a second-hand Iron Maiden
'Number of The Beast' T-Shirt. (British Heart
Foundation – St Neots Branch).*

*Watkins is not one for relationships, with the love
of his life being an orange Renault Megane. This
masterpiece of Gallic engineering is, as you might
expect, a complete shitbox. Its habit of depositing
various fluids wherever it is parked led Chris
Hazzerd to mastic the doors shut, paint a confederate
flag on the roof, and 'General Leak' on the bonnet.*

We begin…

The greenkeepers' shed at almost any golf club is a
Holy place, the Holiest of all some might say. An
agricultural church where mortal men fear to tread,
and where mortal woman is terrified go within 100 yards of.

Not that greenkeepers as a whole are a scary bunch, but
there are few places left in England where *'nudey calendars'*
are still considered *'de rigeur'* and the merest suggestion of
sexual equality is met with well-practiced derision.

As Trevor Bishop once said *"Women working as greenkeepers is like having men working as nurses. Has never happened, never will"*. Nobody had ever wanted to ruin Bishop's day and point out that male nurses have been around since the invention of medicine itself, so he lived in blissful ignorance, believing that a bloke spotted in a hospital was either a doctor, a surgeon, or a patient.

Let us get back on track though, before I upset anyone else with this line of reasoning that should, I'll be honest, have been left in the early 1970s.

The *'Holy place' at* Russet Grange was of course no exception. Wall to wall coverage of young ladies standing semi-naked or completely naked next to chainsaws, mowers, those machines which eat tree branches, and that most wonderful of inventions, the hollow tining machine. Also, there to be spotted by the keen-eyed, or those who specifically came for a gander, was a signed photo of the gorgeous Sarah Shaw (a veritable *'Page Three Stunner'* of a pin-up. We shall meet her later, it will be worth the wait).

Anyway, by and large, the members and staff at Russet Grange cared not one jot about what went on in the shed as long as the fairways were cut, the greens ran true and the bunkers had actual sand in them.

A quick word about bunkers (this is a new bit as a result of in-pub-editing): You non-golfers would not believe just how challenging it is to put sand in a big hole. Greenkeepers the world over make it very clear that it takes far more than a shovel, a hole, some sand and a bit of physical effort. The author is not convinced, but they are experts and I am not. Also, having alienated 50% of the population in the first paragraphs, it is probably better to keep greenkeepers on my side.

Anyway, Trevor *'Surf n Turf'* Bishop led a team of four, which also included Alex *'The Taxi'* Barnes, Freddy West (yes really, both of whom we will be introduced to later when we take to the course), and Dean *'Worzel'* Watkins who was, by some margin, the most educated of this particular mowing crew.

"Christ, are you reading again mate? Haven't you finished all of the books by now?" Bishop never did understand why Watkins preferred books to *'Youtube'* or *'Pornhub'*. In truth his mockery was more than tinged with admiration for his workmate and good friend.

"Yep. Shakespeare's Romeo and Juliet at the moment. A tale of two lovers who died too young."

"Great tune, who doesn't like a bit of Dire Straits? Not read the book though. You know me, Andy McNab, Chris Ryan, Jilly Cooper. Much shagging in it?"

Watkins responded with an exasperated look which spoke volumes, but could be briefly summarised as: *"You fucking ignorant fucker."*

Right moving on, that's enough about books for now, time to get on to the food and this barely adequate chapter's *'raison d'etre'*. (French, but nothing to do with raisins).

What would be a breakfast break for people who worked office hours was lunchtime for these four low-rollers, especially during the summer when a 3:00am start was, well, par for the course. So here we are at 8:00am with lunch being munched to the pages of Shakespeare's finest, *'Strimming Monthly'* (published bi-monthly for some weird reason) being skimmed through, and a five million hits Youtube video of tree-felling disasters including multiple limb-losses being laughed at hysterically.

Freddy West however was a bit sleepy, and his sleepy state meant that he relaxed rather too far on a chair that he knew could barely stand his weight when supported by four legs, let alone two. The chair gave way and time almost stood still as a Sweet and Sour Pot Noodle tub (King Size, obviously, these boys work for a living) spun a few times in the air and then dumped its content all over West's *'St Neots Strimmers - Because Every Bush Needs A Tidy Trim'.* sweatshirt. (That, right there, that's going on the merchandise website along with the RG logo pitch mark repairers and the Sarah Shaw calendar).

"Fuck my life" laughed West as he tried in vain to scrape the sweet and sour noodles and accompanying pseudo-vegetables off of his chest, but the more he moved, the more everything spread. The slowly-congealing sauce and bits of noodle slid onto his neck, up his sleeves and into his groin.

Alex Barnes, who was sharpening his precious chainsaw and thinking about the shower scene from *'Scarface',* could not contain his merriment, but Watkins, on returning from a particularly satisfying dump (on company time), stood in shock. For a split second he was in a slasher flick and had he not just paid a visit, and a good one at that, he would surely have shat himself.

West was helped to his feet by his exasperated boss, for whom this incident was no less than the kind of thing he had got used to over the years.

Blokes were like this, women weren't, but in the unlikely event that one of the fairer sex should ever consider a job that involved mowing seventy acres of grass at three in the morning, he knew full well that an interview in an office wallpapered with laminated jazz mag centrefolds and chainsaw-wielding bimbos would persuade the applicant to consider a different career, probably in nursing.

Well that was a mercifully short chapter wasn't it, which conveniently leaves space for another one of my frighteningly accurate Tweety Snippets:

Absolutely perfect conditions here at Russet Grange today, it's fucking pissing down.

No members anywhere near the place so it's time for the staff and social media team to get drunk as fuck and charge it to the bar account of some poor sap who won't notice for a month.

85 degrees and unbroken sunshine forecast for our fictional #golfclub in #cambridgeshire.

We've let the members back on to the course today, they've spent long enough on the naughty step.

£1.99 for #fullenglish #breakfast, 10p a pint.

The Pro was on #tinder all week. He looks rough.

Got to love the younger members of our clubhouse team. Here's a choice quote:

"Any dietary requirements?"
"No"
"Amazing"

Oh to be so easily impressed. I draw the line at "good" in any situation, unless you once walked on the moon.

A Tale of Egg Mayonnaise			
Chapter	Par	Length	Joke Index
6	4	2,060 Words	5

Introducing:

Tony 'Bacon Rolls' Royce (45)

Head Chef

Nationality: Half Tibetan, Half English, raised by Sherpas

Tony Royce

There are little bullshitters, there are big bullshitters, and then there is Chef Tony 'Bacon Rolls' Royce who reigns supreme when it comes to telling big fat porky pies.

Claridges? He's worked there. Gordon Ramsey? He taught him all he knows. KFC? His granddad fought beside Colonel Sanders. Royce's CV is basically a photocopy of the Michelin guide, and indeed if you were to replace "worked at" with "delivered groceries to" then it is not a million miles from being factually accurate.

So why the drop from the highest echelons of the catering industry to churning out a seven item breakfast for a fiver? Royce will say that the hours at a golf club are more social, which is true, but also that after upstaging "That snake Blumental" on one too many occasions, none of the other top chefs would go near him. Unsurprisingly this isn't true.

Tony Royce does live up to his name though, and on the fat-stained wall, besides chip fryers brimming with month-old cooking oil, you'll see a certificate presented by "Golf Society" magazine in 2014: "Best Bacon Rolls under £1.99 - 3rd Place - Southern Region".

Plus:
Katy Pleaser (46)
Full Member
Nationality: English

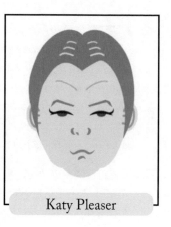
Katy Pleaser

The woman for whom the expression "resting bitch face" was invented, and appropriately enough, behind the expression lies an actual bitch. Pleaser is most certainly the member with the least appropriate surname. She was once upgraded to Business Class on a transatlantic flight, and moaned at the check-in desk "Could you not have told me before I left home? I would have brought more luggage".

Naturally she's universally disliked among her fellow lady members, though tolerated by many of the men as she has what Chris Hazzerd described as: "Body of a Porn Star, brains of the Daily Star".

Indeed it was those very same attributes that launched her career as one of Bruce's "Dolly Dealers" in the mid-1990s though her TV stardom ended fairly abruptly when she slapped a fellow airhead during post-show hospitality because: "She was looking at my boyfriend as if she wanted to sleep with him."

Pleaser doesn't play a great deal of golf, she prefers spending time having her hair and nails done, or downing a bottle or two of fizz at her Aunty Doreen's tanning salon (you can guess the name, it really isn't difficult). When she does play though she treats the game as more of a fashion show, with shorts skirts, too-tight tops and a pony tail hanging through her baseball cap. A cheerful look, and one which belies the fact she's a miserable cow.

And also:

Keiran 'Mullet' Doors (56)
Full Member
Nationality: Zummerzet Ooh Aar

Keiran Doors

*I*f you were in a room with Keiran Doors you could easily be forgiven for thinking that the door was a portal to the 1970s, because that's the time he last spent any money on clothes*.

He's a native of Somerset and whilst he's no longer a "local yokel", he has never really moved on from the three litre Capri, Bridgwater Carnival, and an all-too embarrassing erection at the Young Farmers barn dance.

Back in the old county he was brought up by his Auntie Betty. His mum couldn't function with or without a pint or two of scrumpy on board, and his dad, Dave "Massey" Doors, lost his left arm in a hay bailer on the day he went back to work after losing his right arm in the very same machine. Whilst "drinking cider through a straw" is the lyrical preserve of The Wurzels, it's not so funny when it becomes the only way for you to get apple juice into your 'limb-compromised' torso. Poor dad.

Anyway, let's return to Doors, it's his bio after all. This 'Son of Somerset' sports a quite superb mullet, and for the best part of 30 years he has been telling anyone who will listen that said hairstyle "is coming back into fashion". (Author's note: In the two years since I wrote Doors' bio I can report that he was right, the Mullet is back, at least it is here in Somerset). On the golf course he drives a ball 300 yards, very occasionally in something approaching the right direction.

*He did buy a knock-off Miley Cyrus 'Wrecking Ball' T-Shirt from a local pound shop, but following an all too predictable need for regular washing, it lasted less than two weeks at the hands of the Zanussi spin cycle.

We begin...

It can be hard for golf clubs to recruit chefs. Apart from the relatively short and highly sociable hours, elevated salary, free parking, countryside setting, lack of any real pressure, and a very favourable working environment there is virtually no appeal. Thus, when Tony Royce agreed to join Russet Grange, the Board of Directors were delighted.

Royce was hired on the basis of a mightily impressive track record. His CV listed countless roles at many catering establishments, though sadly (and as time would prove, unsurprisingly), said CV was a near total fabrication. The only grain of truth on the document, (apart from giving his correct name plus his date of birth to within a couple of years), related to eight days at the Strensham Services Wimpy franchise. A job from which Royce was sacked for gross misconduct (yeah, exactly what you're thinking), narrowly avoiding a criminal record in the process.

In fairness, the Board didn't solely rely on the work of fiction that supported his application. He did in fact cook a perfectly acceptable cheese omelette (flat, not the sort you see proper chefs make on Youtube) for Julie Boseman. She was acting as the Board's chosen culinary expert on the basis that she was at Russet Grange, and almost sober, on the day of Royce's trial shift.

For the first couple of weeks things went reasonably well on the catering front. Pasties, sausage rolls, assorted pastries, chicken nuggets, fish finger sandwiches. You name it, Royce reheated it perfectly from frozen (pressing the correct button on the oven, *'pasty-auto'*, *'bread defrost'* and so on, each and every time).

There were perhaps a few occasions when members (Pam Cleaver, I'm looking at you) questioned the amount of ale and vodka required for beer batter when nothing on the menu mentioned this particular coating, but neither Cleaver nor anyone else was going to rock the culinary cruise liner when chefs of Royce's falsified experience were so hard to recruit.

And then came the Captain's Drive-In, the springtime event which heralded the start of the golf season (a season which ran from April to October, conveniently coinciding with the maximum stench of the porcine ordure drifting in from *'Shady Glade'* next door). In an ironic reminder of why he got sacked from Wimpy, Royce was going to have to pull his finger out and actually prepare *'proper food'* for around 150 all-too-expectant Russet Grange members.

Posters for the Drive-In (lovingly prepared by the marketing team via the power of Microsoft Word '98 (knock off version), featuring a third-rate scan of the Russet Grange logo, generic golf clipart, and copious use of 'Comic Sans' font) referred to *"a high quality buffet served throughout the day"*. The entry fee of £10.00 to include said buffet, twos competition, prize fund and a charity donation was certainly seen by many as on the steep side, so the assumption was that the buffet really would represent the very best of Russet Grange's new Head Chef.

Royce would probably have described his *'modus operandi'* as *"old school"*. Not perhaps so much a reference to traditional cooking methods or hitting sous chefs with a stout ladle, but more because he believed food hygiene regulations were something dreamed up by jobsworths who *"...knew fuck all about cooking and everything about unnecessary rules"*.

Thus, along with various salad leaves, pork pies, vegetarian quiche, *'locally-sourced'* cheeses (from an Asda Megastore three miles away) and pretty little ramekins of catering chutney, an egg mayonnaise that was about to make club history was served. All of this, in a warm clubhouse, four hours before it was due to begin being eaten. (Royce, as well as being a bullshitter, was as thick as Eskimo's winter anorak, and did not understand that first tee time of 10:00am did not indicate the time when eager diners would want to start stuffing their fat little faces).

Right, time for a bit of golf. It's what you paid for unless I sent you a free copy. The crack team of Katy Pleaser and Keiran Doors (I think we meet them earlier, I've lost track) were the first to finish. After 14 holes they had recorded precisely nine points. They had lost the will to live, their playing partners had fared little better, and as the halfway hut was closed due to yet another staffing fuck up, they were flagging from hunger and gave up. (That's the golf bit done, you can relax again).

Pleaser was not one for smiling, Doors the opposite. Both strolled into the clubhouse, gazed lovingly at the buffet table, and set about getting their five quid's worth (or thereabouts, neither had mentally broken down the entry fee into constituent parts, unlike some we could mention).

"Fucking lush". Pleaser didn't mince her words. *"Lettuce and everything, just like on Masterchef"*. Doors was equally impressed, *"Bloody marvellous, I haven't seen a spread like this since my mum got remarried again to my Uncle Brian"*.

Their golf had been woeful, as evidenced by having woven an eight mile path around just two thirds of a four mile course, but they'd paid their entry fee and with two groups making their way swiftly down the 18th hole, it was time to strike at the once-chilled but now lukewarm fodder on offer.

Plates as full as plates could be were swiftly dispatched, with not a thought about the frankly dangerous temperature of the offerings, and whilst a bit of limp lettuce isn't going to trouble the digestive system, the same couldn't be said for warm (and unwittingly out of date) eggs swimming in a mayonnaise of a similar provenance. Sadly, the human process of turning criminally unsafe food into an urgent need to dispose of it via various bodily functions is not an instant one. Nobody had indicated that this was a *'one visit only'* lunch, and our sporting pair dug in, blissfully unaware of the culinary time-bombs they were incubating.

Thirty minutes passed before the first tell-tale gastric rumblings and another five before Doors, presumably due to the four pints of cider agitating the semi-solids in his gut, leapt from the table and tried in vain to get to reach the clubhouse bogs. He didn't get close. Pleaser looked on in horror, wondering what the hell was happening, but thirty seconds later she too was an unwilling competitor in the race to park her lunch in the toilets, a race that, given the imminent demands of her digestive system, couldn't be won.

Andy Biggs looked on in horror. Brian Handley almost threw up in sympathy despite not having been anywhere near the egg mayo. A rather delightful young couple who were being shown around the club with a view to becoming members decided on not becoming members in an instant. As for Royce, well he was blissfully unaware of his part in the ensuing commotion that was entirely of his doing.

It was sheer good fortune that Doors and Pleaser had come in early (though not in their eyes of course). Had play progressed as planned, and the (petri) dish of egg-mayo delivered its payload to schedule, at least a dozen poor souls would have been right in the firing line. Luckily Doors and Pleaser were the only victims of what we shan't call *'MayoGate'*, and a nice little bribe/bonus on their bar accounts meant that the incident produced considerably less fallout that the two of them had experienced during that fateful day.

Tony Royce was not so fortunate. He had lasted longer than some, but even at Russet Grange you can't expect to give people food poisoning of a projectile nature (at both ends) by not following the most basic of food safety regulations and expect to keep your job.

Having said that, the whole sorry affair meant another entry on his CV, and in a world where chefs remained in such demand, his experience of *"re-imagining the catering operation and at a prestigious golf club"* was surely worth another couple of grand on his salary expectation.

Just drove through #Dinnington in South Yorkshire, a town famous of course for the "Minsters of Rock" festival.

The chap who cleans our clubhouse carpets does so in the middle of the night.

With no lights on at all, he is guided by a well-trained, small bird of prey that he keeps as a pet.

Yes, our kestrel man hoovers in the dark.

Earlier today one of our intermediate members came into the clubhouse and said: "Greens were super quick today."

Bar manager didn't hang about. Told him the word was "very", called the Chairman, bloke got his marching orders.

We don't put up with that kind of crap at Russet Grange.

A Tale of a Pro-Am (Part One)

Chapter	Par	Length	Joke Index
7	5	2,393 Words	16

Introducing:

Lionel 'Darcey' Lewis (82)
Full Member

Nationality *"Anything you want it to be sweetie"*

Lionel Lewis

*T*here are those who say that the 80's sitcom 'Hi de Hi' was based on Lionel Lewis's book 'Redcoats Getting Shafted' which his cover notes described as a "genital warts and all" look behind the scenes of Butlin's Skegness during the 1950s. The truth will never be known, but what is certainly true is that our hero spent many a night dancing with the girls and eyeing up the boys as he gave foxtrot demonstrations on a ballroom floor swimming with Double Diamond and piss.

"I was a real-life Patrick Swayze" claims Lewis, and that would be true if it weren't for a near total lack of dancing ability, a complete lack of abdominal muscles, and the fact that he is as gay as a banana blancmange in Brighton, wearing a pink tutu.

Despite his homosexuality Lionel Lewis got married to his childhood friend Deirdre Niall in 1970. Only when they divorced a few years later did he confirm his sexual preference to a few close friends "For five years I was in denial, but never in Dee Niall". (Yes, it's a weak gag, but I doubt Charles Dickens would have done better).

Shit golfer, great bloke, always first at the bar.

Also introducing:
Ken 'Benefits' Christie (55)
Full Member
Nationality: English

*W*here there's Ken there's a claim, and he gets the fucking lot. Broke your finger in a lift at John Lewis due to your own stupidity? Twenty grand out of court settlement. Found a piece of bone in one of those funny

Ken Christie

tins of ham that's impossible to open? Five grand. Mental trauma from Diana's funeral because his dead wife was also called Diana? Fuck all, but he claimed.

A brand spanking new Jag every few years courtesy of Motability (mild gout when it gets a bit damp) allows him to transport his clubs, 'dole pole' and the occasional prostitute in comfort. (A pole which he seems to need in the clubhouse but not walking with quite the spring in his step for five miles around a golf course).

And let us not forget the golden ticket "carers allowance" he receives. Christie's mum is 70, enjoys hill walking, swimming and Mecca bingo on a Tuesday, but £400.00 a week from you and me to look after her because she once left the gas on and got diagnosed with the early stages of dementia by a corrupt doctor is taking the piss.

As you might expect, Benefits bores his way around a golf course, wandering aimlessly from fairway to fairway, just hoping for that stray golf ball to come his way. As he once said to Cardiac Pudgett: "Get smacked in the chest by a wayward drive, nice bung to a bent medic and you're looking at six figures. That's the 'Srixon Jackpot' right there. One of those and I could give up this fucking game".

Plus:

Sophie Pasqualle (24)
Full Member
Nationality: Russian/Italian

Sophie Pasqualle

Sophie Pasqualle has a Russian mother and an Italian father, so not only has she got shatteringly good looks and the luscious accent of a Bond 'femme-fatale', she really knows how to cook meatballs in vodka.

Pasqualle is a looker all right, and when it comes to men she knows what she likes. Five million in the bank, at least one yacht to their name, and a clothing allowance. Such men don't exist at Russet Grange, but given that jobs are for other people, and you can't shop all day every day, golf is her sport of choice.

Despite not being of the 'loves other ladies' persuasion, Pam Cleaver has a photograph of Pasqualle as the desktop wallpaper on her phone. "I'm not gay, but I could be tempted" she once muttered to Lionel Lewis after one too many Bacardi Breezers.

The older ladies are none too keen on our Russian/ Italian Goddess, referring to her as "The Italian Boob Job". The nationality is half right, the cosmetic claim is completely false, the wonderful rack that young Sophie gloriously flaunts at every possible opportunity is entirely down to the Glorious God of genetics.

We begin…

The Russet Grange Pro-Am made its first appearance on the Cambridgeshire golfing calendar way back in 1997, on the day that Princess Diana died. (Two mentions in the chapter, it's what she would have wanted).

Thus, the mood at the inaugural event was somewhat mixed with Martin *'Trotsky'* Sykes (we'll meet him in the next chapter) pretending not to care one jot (he's not what you'd call a *'Royalist'*) and Lionel *'Darcy'* Lewis, barely able to hide his sadness at the loss of someone he had never met, and was now certainly never going to meet. But as Lewis himself would have said, had he been able to stop blubbing *"The show must go on"*, and go on it did.

The '97 event was actually a reasonable success, and during the next decade the Russet Grange Pro-Am established itself as one of the top eight such events in West Cambridgeshire. Edible food, a good atmosphere, respectable prize money and the support of some local drinks companies helped things along nicely. There is no question however that the regular appearance of Hadyn Duke's two *"fit as fuck"* daughters (I'm quoting greenkeeper Freddy West here), dressed in Baywatch swimsuits and handing out free Magnum ice-creams, was quite an attraction for what was always a male-dominated occasion.

There were leaner years though. In 2008 a drinks company went bust two days before the competition owing the VAT man millions, and after the 2013 event a local prestige car dealership invoiced the club for £20,000 for repairs to some very precious metal which ended up in a pond. The invoice would have been for £30,000 but Adam Bobble knew a bloke who knew a bloke, and with some handy welding, and to paraphrase the Spice Girls, *'Two Became One'*.

But let us move on to this year's Pro-Am. In fairness the marketing team at Russet Grange had done a good job for once, with all forty tee times filled by teams of three amateurs (some of whom had as much experience of golf as they had of being astronauts) and one professional Mars Bar salesman.

Sponsorship had been gleaned from various local firms (proper businesses in most cases, but there was also a grand in cold hard cash donated by the Satchell Brothers, a local *'firm'* of the criminal variety who were trying to keep things sweet with two members from the local CID).

Tony Royce had long-since been sacked (last chapter, but a few months have probably passed, I'm not that fussed about chronology here) and an agency chef was on duty to churn out a buffet to impress. At a cost of £500 per day, top-notch grub should have been a given, but you'd be surprised at the reluctance he showed in providing any offerings which required what most in the catering trade would call *"preparation"*. Having said that, the bar had been set pretty low by the aforementioned Royce, as testified by a perspex sign on the kitchen wall which currently read: *"23 days since we last gave anyone food poisoning"*.

Ken Christie was one of the mid-morning starters, having been one of the few club members, along with Lionel Darcy, who had actually paid the £100 entry fee. (The Ladies' section, Seniors' section, Junior section, five committees and a staff team had all been given complimentary entries). Christie and Darcy liked a bit of value, so they arrived four hours early to make the most of the bacon baps, barely-thawed Danish pastries, and unlimited coffee before their rounds. Christie even had the gall to ask for a takeaway coffee and bacon roll *"to tide me over for the first couple of holes."*

"Almost didn't bother entering this year Lionel". Christie's miserable drone never changed, even on this most glorious of days. *"Mum had an assessment at the clinic and it was touch and go, really worrying"*.

"Is she not well then Ken?" enquired Darcy, *"Sorry to hear that, your Margaret is such a sweetie"*.

"No she's fine but they've tightened the rules for getting a carer's allowance, and the stupid cow forgot to pretend she has the

Big-A". Christie frowned and continued: *"It was only when I pointed out that forgetting about it was all part of the illness that they signed my ticket for another six months. Lose that money and I'm fucked"*.

"Well I hope she pulls through..." replied Darcy, as confused as he was compassionate, *"...must be difficult for you mate"*.

"You're not fucking wrong, I was up at six to drop her off at the airport, she's flying to Tenerife for a month with her friend Betty. Lovely old bag, no family..." Christie made that 'money' gesture with his thumb and first finger and continued *"...should be leaving me her house in the nice part of Huntingdon with a bit of luck."*

The chatting continued and the clubhouse gradually filled, golfers ebbed and flowed. Laughter, banter and a general feeling of wellbeing blossomed among what was basically a collection of committee members, businessmen, farmers and entitled baby boomers enjoying a Friday off work, just like they did every week.

There was however a moment of heated exchange when a visiting *"Right-on millennial wokey twat."* (The words of Keiran Doors) objected to a conversation that he overheard between Martin Wagstaff and Chris Hazzerd (both to appear later in the book): *"Have you seen the news about the Olympics Chris? The beach volleyball birds don't have to have their arses on show any more, they changed the fucking rules. Who the fuck's going to watch that now? No fucker cares about the volleyball, they just want to watch fit birds getting sand in their snatches"*.

"Couldn't agree more..." nodded Hazzerd, mildly annoyed that yet more very soft porn would be disappearing from TV screens. *"...first it was the dolly birds on the motor racing, then the darts, it'll be the boxing next. If you want to see any top totty on telly these days you've got to watch 'The Price is Right' on UKTV Gold. Absolute fucking joke."*

The *"wokey"* that Doors had identified took objection to this perfectly well-reasoned discussion that was taking place between a pair of intellectual heavyweights, and made his feelings known to Wagstaff.

"What a disgusting attitude, you should be ashamed of yourself. It's not 1970 any more and women should be able to play sport without being regarded as sex objects."

Wagstaff, who was halfway through his fourth large Bells (and having, unusually for a man of his age, *'pre-loaded'* via a few snifters before leaving home) was almost as pissed as he needed to be before even considering hitting a golf ball. His retort was as brief as it was to the point.

"Fuck off".

Hazzerd had also been on the sauce for quite some considerable time, and he was not slow to wade into the verbal jousting match between his friend and someone who was, by virtue of what had been quite a well-reasoned comment, an outsider and also a twat.

"Yeah, fuck off".

The incident blew over soon enough, with the wokey man hopping over to what both Wagstaff and Hazzerd rightly assumed was the vegan section of the buffet, before heading out to enjoy 18 holes of golfing fun or misery.

At this point Sophie Pasqualle appeared, a vision of utter loveliness in a sea of receding hairlines and impending erectile dysfunction. A last-minute replacement to join the team of Christie and Lewis, she gracefully wafted her way to the bar and enquired to Andy Biggs, in an accent that would have charmed the nuts off a Topic bar, about her playing partners.

"Hello Andy, I'm playing with Mr Christie and Mr Darcy, but I don't know who they are, could you point them out please."

Biggs smiled, he had already seen the look on Ken Christie's face. A look that said *"Holy fuck, thank you Lord, thank you"*.

Introductions were made, Pasqualle was all kinds of lovely, Christie was a dribbling wreck, and Darcey went full-camp exclaiming *"Oh I just luuuuuve your shoes"*. A team of golfers, though they didn't know it yet, soon to be joined by Ryan Framley, a professional golfer to make up their team of four and about to play the round of his life.

Framley would break the course record that day, and our three amateurs would also play the rounds of their lives, but more of that in the second chapter about the Pro-Am. (I might have forgotten about this in the second Pro-Am chapter, it doesn't really matter though, much of this nonsense was written whilst half cut on Ruddles at £1.49 a pint. This has since gone up to £1.71 and will probably have topped £1.90 by the time you're reading this bollocks).

Also, it should be noted that Framley makes Potton look like a rank amateur in matters of the physical act of love, and if you readers were to assume that he *'got jiggy'* with Pasqualle after the competition's prize giving, well let's just say that Framley peaked twice that day.

For now though things were in very good order at Russet Grange. Merriment in abundance, the Gin & Tonic van ready to refresh those on a freebie and those who had been unlucky enough to have to pay. Prizes to be won on every hole including a box of pasties from Hogg's Meats, your height in Amstel Lager (maximum height 5' 10" - golf shoes to be removed for measuring) sponsored by a local driving school, and a set of saucepans, original source unknown, but provided by a competitor who had won them at this very same event one year earlier.

Imagine also the scene on the first tee. Flags flying, courtesy of the main sponsor *'Biddies Gutter and Drain Services'* and four somewhat ageing vehicles of various brands, washed specially for the day in Tesco's car park and supplied by *'Brain Simpson Autos - Cambridgeshire's Leading Independent Vehicle Specialists'* (Yes, the banner printers spelt *'Brian'* wrong). Cars supplied in haste because right at the very last minute, the local Mercedes dealer heard about the pond incident from yesteryear and decided that sticking £300k worth of E-Class and S-Class on the elevated first tee at Russet Grange, and giving both sets of keys to a part-time barman and full-time drunk was probably a very bad idea.

Anyway the Pro-Am golfing fun continues later in the book, I bet you can't wait.

A Tale of a Trotsky Lecture

Chapter	Par	Length	Joke Index
8	3	1,867 Words	26

Introducing:

Martin 'Trotsky' Sykes (62)
Full Member
Nationality: Scouse

Martin Sykes

*E*very golf club has an ex-docker from Liverpool who hasn't been employed for 20 years or worked for 40. At Russet Grange Martin 'Trotsky' Sykes is the go-to guy for tales of abject misery, "management scum" and the highlights of the 1974 Communist Party election manifesto.

He despises capitalism with a vengeance, but not enough to stop him owning five houses which bring in a pretty penny in rent from the countless dealers, addicts and assorted scoundrels who the local Council is legally obliged to provide shelter for. An estimated £60k every year keeps him in Che Guevara T-Shirts, with plenty of change to spend at that bastion of the revolutionary worker, the private members' golf club.

Like so many of his ex-colleagues, he claimed he was "sacked by Thatcher". The truth is that he took voluntary redundancy when Blair was in office, and then spent six months cruising around the Med, helping to "protect the jobs of the working class slaves who build the ships".

Sykes is pretty well despised and liked at Russet Grange in equal measure. Those who despise him do so because he's a miserable leftie who only seems to speak the language of misery, whilst those who love him do so because he's a working class hero, even though his life has been pretty much untainted by doing actual work.

Plus:

Liam 'Flange' Heron (21)

Intermediate Member
Nationality: From the Land
of the Stud

Liam Heron

With a birdie surname you might think that Heron could play a bit of golf, but far from it. Out of all of the members with any degree of bladder control, he is by far the worst player. It isn't for lack of effort or investment though, he's spent thousands in lessons and equipment, so Guy Potton adores him.

One of the reasons for his lacklustre performance on the course is that he's normally spent the previous night "in flagrante" with his partner of choice, of which there have been many. In other words, far from leaving it all out on the field, he's left it all in the bedroom (or hot tub) with nothing left for the field.

Indeed, our Liam lists "shagging" as his main hobby on his Facebook page, and he's not what you might call "fussy". Plenty of Fish, Grindr (yes really), Match.com and countless other dating sites have young Heron's profile in their library.

And as is always the case in stories like this, our hero once left his unlocked phone on the bar for all to see, and see it they did. Many, many pictures of various young and not so young ladies, some single, some betrothed or married to others, including a rather fruity image sent to him by Julie Boseman, accompanied by a not-so-subtle caption about "losing his balls in the rough".

Liam Heron. Crap Golfer. Good Lad.

And also:
Pam 'Cleavage' Cleaver (49)
Bar Staff
Nationality: Irrelevant

Pam Cleaver

A *barmaid nicknamed "Cleavage". Hmmm, it does appear that 1970 wants its chapter back, but there is no doubt that Pam Cleaver's moniker is well-deserved. When wearing her usual low-cut tops she looks like the semi-finalists in a Telly Savalas lookalike contest have taken up residence.*

In truth it's not all shits and giggles, at least not until she's had a little bit of Vodka with her cornflakes, and then life is one big party. In fairness though her love of the booze isn't allowed to get in the way of work, so she sticks with a rule of never letting a member buy her a drink before 10:00am (9:30am on weekends).

There is a general understanding that Cleaver has "got something on the chairman" otherwise her drinking would have seen her dismissed years ago. The fact is that "something" is that she's been banging him for the best part of a decade, and when he goes to his Masonic meetings he's actually off to spaff his beans at the local Travelodge for twenty minutes of all too energetic sex before rocking up slightly flustered at the Lodge.

Cleavage isn't entirely sure who her father is because her mum was one for "free love" in the 1960s and 70s, so chances are she's from the seed of a rock star, a roadie, or any one of the 300,000 male hippies who attended the 1971 Isle of Wight Festival.

We begin…

Martin Sykes and Liam Heron were unlikely bedfellows (though at Russet Grange, which once advertised itself as *"Better than the Rumours Suggest"*, anything is possible). But no, these two just found themselves at the bar on an April afternoon, enjoying banter with the likes of Biggs, Cleaver, Hanley and Carter.

Yes, it was a quiet day. There were no visiting societies, no lunches booked, no meetings of any description, so four bar staff were scheduled to work. Many readers will recognise this as an absolute minimum under the circumstances.

(In fairness to Brian Hanley, whose job it was to sort the staff rotas, he would balance out this over-staffing by having only Ellie Carter work on the following Wednesday at the Professional's Open Day when 150 golfers would be attending, and a Round Table business lunch was taking place in the Giblet Suite).

"Subs up again, not a fucking clue". A blunt opening gambit to Andy Biggs from Sykes, but a career based on doing as little work as possible and blaming *"Tory Scum"* for the ills of an entire planet had left Sykes well placed to discuss the finer details of how to run a golf club. A club, which it has to be said, represented a juxtaposition of everything he hated in life (most things), but also everything he loved (golf and moaning, not in that order).

Biggs cleaned another pint glass and nodded. As a barman of some repute he had long since learned that the way to deal with members was via a non-committal response, agreeing without agreeing, disagreeing without disagreeing. He should have been a politician, but, like Sykes, the fact that he had a background of working (and I use the term loosely in Sykes' case) in industry, he was massively over-qualified to hold public office.

"Another hundred quid a year, they say it's just two quid a week, but why not get in a few more societies, a few more weddings, some business meetings, lunches, that sort of thing… Look after the members, you haven't got a club without them, and don't keep screwing them for every quid."

Ellie Carter could not help but hear this comment, after all the clubhouse was near silent, lacking, as it was, in customers. She knew the score and she decided to have her say. *"Well we had a society in last week Martin and you sat on that very seat and moaned that they were using members' tee times. We also had the Rotary Table lot in, fifty quid a pop for a few sandwiches, coffee and a meeting room and I think someone, it might have been you, said "Why the fuck are we letting in a bunch of failed fucking Freemasons, we don't need the cash ", at least I think that's what somebody, who might have been you, said."*

Brian Hanley was a bit shocked at this frighteningly forthright and astonishingly accurate reply. Pam Cleaver remained confused, so she carried on with the essential task of rolling cutlery into napkins with the precision of the finest timepiece, blissfully singing a few Barry Manilow hits as she went about her work. Sadly the gentle sounds of *'Copacabana'* and *'Could it be Magic'* did little to diffuse Sykes's anger, and a request from Brian Hanley for a bit of John Denver fell on a deaf ears.

Sykes continued his mini-rant: *"Management here, not a clue, place could be a goldmine but all they are interested in is an easy life, little work as possible, fucking useless, same with the committees, the Pro and the Board."*

Liam Heron, at a mere 21 years of age would not normally have had the cojones to reply, but he was on a day off from whatever it was he did for a living, and having already been to 'Spoons for breakfast and partaken of a couple of pints of

Ruddles (well five to be honest, but there might be Police officers reading), he was in the mood.

"Have you ever been on any committees mate? Sounds like you know your stuff, bet you could shake the place up a bit…"

Ouch. The bar *'team'* (for want of a better word) stood well back at the lighting of this particular blue touchpaper, all four a little concerned about how Sykes might respond, but also in admiration of the young Heron's line of questioning (there's probably a word for a young Heron, but I can't be arsed to look it up so I'll guess at *'Heronette'*).

"I probably could son, I probably could. Simpson reckons he's the dog's bollocks but I'm not scared of him, Blarnham-Flink, or whatever the fuck he's called, is only interested in one person, Potton is probably taking back-handers galore and that knob Haydn Duke is just an all-too-cheerful prick with a permanent grin who likes to keep everyone happy".

The *'bravery juice'* continued to affect Heron, who was excelling himself. *"Well most members are happy aren't they? We're full with a waiting list, loads of golf being played, course in great shape, record green fees being paid. It's not the greatest club in the county but I wouldn't go anywhere else".* Hanley gave his five-penneth: *"The subs increase is to buy another fifteen acres and put in a nine hole course. Decent idea I reckon, we've not had any complaints."*

Cleaver carried on with wrapping knives and forks, she didn't like getting involved in highbrow discussions at management level, and anyway, Sykes was in full flow.

"Also, Parris can fuck off, the plane dodging prick". He was not one to mince words, or indeed put forward a well-reasoned argument, and it was clear that his hatred of *'management scum'* extended to a wealth of people who gave their time freely for nothing more than the occasional pat on the back and the gratitude of the vast majority of members. (Plus free entry to the Pro-Am as we've just discovered).

To the casual observer it would have appeared that Martin Sykes really did not like anyone who hadn't spent the 1980s at the literal or metaphorical (look it up) coalface, and this was really not very far from the truth. He loved his golf, but forty years of almost doing some work had formed the foundations of a bitter and twisted man who looked for an enemy where none was to be found, and there really were none to be found at Russet Grange. (Apart from Reg Bollard and Les Hamill, who we'll be meeting soon in a chapter which is far better than this one. Everyone hates those bastards).

Biggs just smiled, Hanley, Cleaver and Carter did the same, but the last word on this proletariat-smashing conversation fell to Liam Heron, a young man with a Grade 'D' GCSE in political science to his name: *"Christ Sykesy you really are a miserable fucker, don't you sometimes wish you had a nasty illness or a couple of limbs missing? At least you'd finally have something to moan about."*

A Tale of a Belgian Golf Society from Ipswich

Chapter	Par	Length	Joke Index
9	5	2,660 Words	1

Introducing:

Roger 'Muffin' Themulle (61)

Visiting Golfer
Nationality: Belgian

Roger Themulle

A native of Belgium, now living in Ipswich, Roger Themulle is a leading light in the 'Bellies Golf Society' (Belgian Exiles Loving Lager in East Suffolk). At sixty years of age he finally realised that life in Belgium consisted of nothing more than wishing you were Swiss or French, with an occasional smattering of pride when a new Jean Claude van Damme film is released or when Kevin de Bruyne once again doesn't lead the nation to football glory.

Thus, with plenty of his life ahead, and regrets "too many to mention", he packed up his prized collection of almost-vintage Scandinavian porn, grabbed his golf clubs, put some cheese and crackers into one of the dotted handkerchief things which he tied to a stick, put it over his shoulder, and started the long walk to his garage whereupon he loaded up his Volvo and headed for the Rotterdam car ferry.

It would be a number of weeks before his wife noticed he was gone, and many months before she cared.

A new exciting life beckoned across whatever bit of water separates Belgium from Suffolk, and as fate would have it, he was not the only one making a pilgrimage to the land of turnips, cheap lager, and golf courses as diverse as a Ku Klux Klan AGM.

So we also introduce:

Johannes 'Nutloaf' Steinberg (64)
Visiting Golfer
Nationality: Belgian with a
hint of German

*B*rought up in post-war East Germany *(well it had to be, he wasn't born until 1958), legend has it that Johannes Steinberg became a vegan in the days when it wasn't*

Johannes Steinberg

compulsory to tell everyone you were a vegan.

Steinberg's parents moved to Brussels in 1974, some would say "escaped", but Steinberg senior knew one of the guards at the Berlin Wall (he'd helped him with his tax return some years earlier, though not with tarring his roof) and the conversation went thus: (obviously this was said in German, but I'm not firing up Google translate for you. Please read it with a German accent though, I need all the help I can get here).

"Morning Hans, I am taking my family to Brussels, I know this is slightly breaking the rules but…"

"Brussels…" laughed the guard, "…fill your boots, you'll be back" and an unhindered passage was given.

We've lost the plot here a little bit but anyway, Steinberg went to the Brussels School of Waffles, got married (probably to someone named 'Maria' or maybe 'Trudi') played a bit of golf and like Roger Themulle, also got bored of his (adopted in this case) homeland.

Fate rolled dice, like it does, and when he met Themulle as a fellow member at Poddington Heights Golf Club, a friendship was immediately formed. Over the next few months, as the sheer scale of Ipswich's Belgian community became apparent, the 'Biggies Golf Society' came into being, with Themulle and Steinberg proud to have been founder members.

A quick note here to mention that with his steak-dodgery, a love of Rock 'n' Roll and a frame that could be described as "rather large", Steinberg quickly picked up his society nickname 'Nutloaf' (Which I grant you isn't as good as 'Muffin' but hey, he's Belgian and thus almost anything is hilarious. Also, these pages need filling and I want "An introduction to Golf Societies" to begin overleaf).

That's Johannes 'Nutloaf' Steinman, a more contrived story about a fictitious character you are unlikely ever to meet, but I believe you can never have too many Belgians in a golf book, or any book for that matter.

A Brief Explanation of Golf Societies

As a first for this book of complete golfing nonsense, let us make a comment about golf societies, on the very slim chance that someone reading doesn't know about such things…

Anyone who has ever been part of a golf society will testify that going to other clubs is far more fun than playing at your own place. There's often a coach picking you up from your house and returning you later, so people can get absolutely bollocksed. It's an all day event, none of this *'got to get home by six because the wife has got tea on'* nonsense.

Drinking starts at dawn and there will be prizes to be won ranging from *"Nearest the pin on the sixth to win a small shrub"* to *"Twat of the Day"*. There will be no need to spend mental capacity on food choices because you will be given a bacon roll followed by the *"Chef's Special"*. (Which, as we all know is what the Chef couldn't shift last week).

Plus, there is the chance of the *'Holy Grail'* for golf societies, visiting a club that doesn't offer tee times to members, but it gives them to your lot because there's more than five of you. Under such circumstances there is a cast iron guarantee that at least three members will be having a fucking good moan about this to the barman on your arrival, and they'll be double pissed off, because whilst you've having such a good time and are going to be on the piss until midnight, they have to get home by six because the wife has got tea on.

Anyway, the Bellies Golf Society, as fate would have it, had chosen to play Russet Grange…

We begin...

Golf books published since the dawn of time have covered, at length, the antics of Belgian golf societies from Ipswich, so my apologies to you dear reader if you've read it all before. I wanted to write a chapter about this particularly divisive topic and well, this is it. Feel free to skip it if you wish. It was your money, it's now my money, and I really don't mind as long as your review on Amazon doesn't say *"3/10. Over three hundred pages of bilge and he never once mentioned Belgian golf societies."*

Right then. It's mid-May, almost 40% of the members at Russet Grange have paid their subscriptions (*"Due 1st April or you lose playing rights."* Comedy gold right there) and we hop to a morning of glorious sunshine, a Friday of course, when those with actual jobs have taken the day off. This is a perfect chance to get in 18 holes of golf, the kind of day on which members say to themselves: *"This is why I joined, life does not get better than this".*

This would be the thinking of pretty much any member, at any golf club, throughout the land. It was not, however, the thinking of Tanya *'TK'* Maxwell, who was more than happy to take a booking for 40 members of the Bellies Golf Society to bring their business to Russet Grange.

Meanwhile, in the clubhouse, high-end debate and nuanced discussion is the order of the day: *"Who the fuck let 40 fucking visitors in on a Friday morning? Was it that wanker Simpson?"* Adam Bobble was seething and Ken Christie was in his corner. *"Fucking lovely day, early season, and some twat rents out our course to a bunch of fat inbreds from turnip county".*

(These two haven't had much of a mention yet, so this is a decent chance to put them into an irate pairing and let them have a good old moan at Pam Cleaver, currently on bar duty and working her way through the *'GCHQ Quiz Book'*).

"Well it wasn't me", said Cleaver, *"but I think they're French and they paid sixty quid each for a bacon roll, a game of golf, and whatever crap the chef needs to shift before it goes mouldy."* (Didn't know Cleaver could do humour did you? Neither did I, but we've had plenty of Biggs and Hankey already).

Even Bobble and Christie could see the sense in taking two and a half grand plus bar bill, and the chance to shift some dodgy chicken breasts to gullible foreigners, but not wanting to get stuck behind them they finished their beers and made their way to the first tee. (They'd probably booked a tee time, though we haven't had that chapter yet, so feel free to assume they joined a queue of fifty other members, all standing around moaning about the queue of fifty two members).

The coach carrying the BGS arrived at 9:30am, having taken over two hours to cover the relatively short distance from Ipswich. The forty souls on board had, on average, consumed two litres of generic Belgian lager each, plus a frightening amount of Nutella and waffles along the way. Three piss breaks had been scheduled and duly utilised, and as our visiting friends pulled into the Russet Grange *'Coach Park'* (basically the bit of the car park where the lines were most worn out). An array of bushes provided additional relief for those who could wait not a second longer to once again empty their little Belgian bladders.

Heading up the group was Dieter Flugel, a shellfish merchant from Belgium's most northerly city, nicknamed *'The Mussels from Antwerp'*. (Yep, entire chapter for that gag). He headed to the bar and introduced himself to Pam Cleaver (well to her breasts if the truth were known, but she's used to sixty year old foreign nationals rocking up mid-morning covered in what she hoped was Nutella).

Can we assume Belgian accents from our visitors please? As luck would have it I am currently supping a fine pint of Leffe in 'Spoons but it's not helping me to write with an accent. (If you can't imagine Belgian, do a mix of French and German. You could call it *'Frerman'* or *"Gernch"*).

"Good morning, my name is Dieter Flugel from the Bellies Golf Society…" (you're reading this is an 'Allo Allo' style in your newly discovered Frerman/Gernch accent aren't you?) *"…we have a booking for eleven thirty, eighteen holes of golf and then some dinner. Also, where are the toilets please?"*

Cleaver was most helpful, and she was particularly pleased when Roger Themulle introduced himself as Flugel's second in command, and the bearer of the Bellies GS Visa card.

"I would like to pay our balance. Could you add two hundred pounds as a gratuity for the Russet Grange staff and another thousand pounds as bar credit please".

Cleaver was used to having to get blood out of a stone from most societies, normally handing an invoice of semi-fiction to whichever of their number was least shit-faced after dinner, so the presentation of a credit card, a more than generous tip, and a grand for drinks was quite the result.

The squirty-cream topping on this particular financial waffle came next *"... and please feel free to put any drinks you wish onto our bar bill"*. Ker-fucking-ching!

Roger Themulle has now had his moments of glory as far as this book is concerned, both he and Steinberg were last minute additions anyway. Good chance they'll appear in the sequel though. (For which I'll be wanting a £250k advance, *"Go Big or Go Home"*, that's my motto).

Reg Bollard and Les Hamill had been out for their early morning round (we're meeting them in chapter 11 unless I piss about with the order), and as they entered the clubhouse to the sounds of the laughter of pissed Belgians, their combined misery went up another notch.

"What the fuck do you think they are so happy about?" asked Bollard to his mate in misery. *"Probably not members."* replied Hamill with a Neanderthal grunt.

Pre-game bacon rolls were served by Andy Biggs to the ever-increasing mass of Ipswich-based Belgian ex-pats. He was on duty as the agency chef was unable to work, having written off one of his Ferraris the night before. The clubhouse became livelier and livelier as members of the Biggies drifted in through whichever door they had been able to find. One of the Biggies even came in via the loft hatch, nobody knew why, but he had got his foot caught in a string of Christmas lights and dragged them down with him, like a pissed-up Caesarean Santa, seven months early for the festive season.

Johannes Steinberg (oh he's back) was one of the last to appear in the clubhouse. He'd been on the phone to his wife to let her know that he had arrived safely at Russet Grange. (She worried about him, quite rightly to be honest, the last time he'd been on a day's golf trip it ended up him trying to bribe the captain of a Spanish trawler with a job lot of Waitrose chorizo, requesting safe passage to Bruges).

"Let the games commence" cried Steinberg (in a Belgian accent of course) as he burst his way through a door marked *'Staff Only'* before falling flat on his face, another victim of generic lager followed by more generic lager, taking the hastily produced *"Russell Garnge Golf Club welcomes the Fatties"* sign with him. (Maxwell really had done herself proud with the flipchart and magic marker, a multi-coloured affair including a drawing of golf ball plus what we assume was meant to be a sketch of the Belgian flag, but which was, by means of a rotational error, actually the flag of Germany).

Who knew Belgians residing in Ipswich could be such fun? I certainly didn't and I'm the bloke who wrote this nonsense.

Steve Simpson appeared, shocked at the sound of people enjoying themselves on a Friday, but reassuring smiles from both Biggs and Cleaver told him all was well.

"This lot look like they're having fun Pam, you OK?"

"God yes!" smiled Cleaver, *"They've paid their bill, chucked a grand on their bar tab to start with, tipped the staff another two hundred, bought my drinks for the day and one of them had the decency to look at my face when talking to me, lovely people these Frenchies".*

Simpson looked up *"Fucking marvellous, couple of groups like this every week and we could tell the members to fuck right off"*. He was serious too. *"No moaning about the greens, or the fairways, or the bunkers, of the fucking rough, no competitions to piss about with, no handicaps, none of that shit"*. He smiled at Cleaver, he loved his job when things were going well and members were being inconvenienced. Spotting that Andy Biggs was also smiling he threw a question in his direction *"What do you reckon then Andy, change the sign at the entrance? 'Welcome to Russet Grange, Staff and Societies only'?"*

You've probably read enough about people actually playing golf by now. You know the score, it's basically angry/happy/pissed people hitting a small ball around a big field which has been mowed to different heights. Some of these people regard said field as a toilet, a facility preferable to that provided by the portaloos, and some of them just hate the place, usually not quite enough to leave, but when they do they are replaced by new members who were equally as pissed off with their own club. A sort of *'EasyJet->Ryanair->Jet2->Easyjet again'* Merry-Go-Round, with golf courses replacing budget airlines.

We can also assume that you've read enough about post-golf activities too, so we'll wrap up this chapter safe in the knowledge that the Biggies Golf Society had the time of their lives at Russet Grange. The highlights of their day being when Pam Cleaver got them out in exchange for one of those really huge jars of Nutella, and when Johannes Steinberg, via the miracle of his porn-infested laptop, accidentally streamed some borderline yet quite hilarious filth involving a troupe of midgets and girls who probably weren't real cheerleaders, instead of the day's leaderboard, to the big telly in the clubhouse.

As Dieter Flugel gave his thanks to the clubhouse team, and to the members who had not only tolerated but actually enjoyed the company of these stout fellows from Ipswich, it was a shatteringly pissed Martin Wagstaff who rose to his feet and applauded the Bellies: *"Thanks lads, it's been a fucking ples…, a fucking ples… it's been fucking great, come again soon… and bring more Nutella for Cleavage…"*

We're not a club that thinks small so we bought a few lions to provide a bit of added amusement for members and visitors.

Sadly nobody seems that interested, we thought they'd be a roaring success.

*If there's an account out there with
a higher "Tweet Quality to Follower" ratio
that ours I'd be very surprised.*

*This is artisan tweeting, not just uploading a
video of a baboon shitting on a tortoise.*

*24 feet of snow overnight at Russet Grange
Golf Club, which, until it thaws, will be
known as "Russet Grange Ski Resort".*

*Accordingly we have put some lukewarm red
wine on the counter in a bucket, chucked in a
couple of orange slices, and are churning out
'Russet Gluhwein' out at nine quid a pop.*

A Tale of a Tee Times Debate			
Chapter	Par	Length	Joke Index
10	5	2,148 Words	8

Introducing:

Robert Farnham-Blink (70)

Chairman

Nationality: Bomber Command

*Y*ou've only got to look at Farnham-Blink to know that he worked as a pilot for British Airways, but that won't stop him telling you. Indeed, he has never been known to engage in conversation with anyone he hasn't previously met without asking them

Robert Farnham-Blink

what they did for a living in the expectation that the question will be reciprocated.

You might think that someone who previously had the lives of others in his hands would have a degree of competence in general life, but you'd be wrong. He put petrol into an almost new diesel-powered Range Rover then drove it until it died, causing £10k of damage, he needed an air ambulance when he fell into a ravine on a ski trip, and he put a tree through his conservatory resulting in an admission that simply "Watching a box set of 'Axe Men' doesn't teach you all you need to know".

And:
Dr Haydn Duke (64)
Full Member and Board Member
Nationality: As British as a Spitfire Sausage

"Damned fine fellow, damned awful golfer" is how Timothy Bleauchamp describes this most charming man, and few would disagree with either opinion. Mr Duke is, like his father, an Old Harovian, a former club captain, and a stalwart of the medical profession.

Hayden Duke

Duke is about as close as you can get to aristocracy without having a title or an estate in Scotland. When he's not playing golf badly he's either armed with a scalpel working as a consultant heart surgeon (so he should probably be named "Mr" but bollocks to that) or with a shotgun sending game birds to meet their maker.

It is rare that you will find the boot of his Lexus bereft of something he has recently shot, a practical vehicles which shares garage space with his beloved collection of impractical British sports cars. To quote Duke: "Lethal weapons in the eternal hunt for pussy, every damned one of the buggers."

*Our Master of Medicine is certainly a lover of the
ladies, having confessed in a particularly drunken
speech during his Captaincy year that "Being single
means it's always totty chasing season". Duke's success in
this particular field of sport is undisputed due to what
he described in the same speech as: "Genetics, wealth,
and a chopper the size of a tube of bathroom sealant".*

We begin...

The flyers had been circulating for some time *"If it
ain't broke, don't fix it"*. A crossed-out hammer and
screwdriver over a photo of a golf ball, the latter still
bearing a Getty Images copyright watermark. *"No Tee Times
at Russet Grange"*. The message was clear, and whilst it was
true that those who objected to the introduction of booking
tee times were entitled to their opinion, they only numbered
24 souls, and that included the bloke who delivered pasties
who thought he was signing a petition objecting to the
expansion of the neighbouring pig farm.

Most at Russet Grange, as was the case on all manner of
subjects, really didn't give a toss.

Trouble is though, the objectors were very motivated,
they were united, they had a flyer and a Facebook page.
Furthermore, as a bunch of regular golfers who were used to
playing on a Friday morning in, they had most to lose.

The Board of Directors had long-since recognised that
moving from 19th century social attitudes and financial
security, skipping the 20th century entirely (especially the

1970s), and acknowledging that in the 21st century things were a little bit different was something that meant change. Their remit ,as they knew all too well, was to look after the best interests of Russet Grange Golf Club, even though it was a shithole, and that meant generating enough money to run the place, money that was never, ever going to be sourced from membership fees alone.

Farnham-Blink was a nob, but he was a nob that was both qualified and willing to hold the position of Club Chairman. The only other possible candidate had made the local news in less-than-ideal circumstances just two days before nominations for the post closed, and whilst there were suspicions that Farnham-Blink had tipped off the press about his rival's regular engagement in *'car park activities'*, nothing was ever proven.

The February Board meeting agreed that the issue of tee times was something far too important to let the members have a vote on, but Julie Boseman (we'll introduce her later) made a very important point:

"Fewer than thirty people, including the pasty bloke who I doubt is a member, don't want them. Give them a debate, make a few quid at the bar, put it to the vote, win by a landslide and have done with it".

Haydn Duke wasn't convinced *"You sure Jules, suppose they're the only ones who bother to turn up?"*

Boseman agreed that Duke had a point, she respected the man and had more than a soft spot for him. *"We'll let people vote beforehand then. Every member gets a voting slip and most will vote 'yes' because we'll ask if they'd rather have tee times or go bust. Job done, get on the gin."*

Remember that scene in *'Pretty Woman'* where Julia Roberts goes back to that clothes shop and says *"Big Mistake"* to the snooty cow who kicked her out? Yeah, it's that again.

The message about a vote on tee times went out. People could vote in advance or come along to a debate and vote in person. All lovely and democratic, but with one massive flaw. Most members really couldn't give a flying fuck.

The general opinion among the non-fuck givers was that they either came along and played golf, or they booked a tee time and came along and played golf. This wasn't ripping up the history books, this wasn't shitting on the grave of long-dead Presidents, this was a change no bigger than when a vegan section consisting of a Plant Burger and a Quorn Sausage Roll was added to the clubhouse menu.

The tee times debate (or *"foregone conclusion"* as Boseman kept calling it) was scheduled for a Thursday evening, and on the Wednesday morning a grand total of eight voting slips had arrived at the office. Four in favour, four against. Figures that could be interpreted in only one way. Boseman had rather misread the situation, the *'flying fuck'* scenario had reared its ugly head and chances were that the *"If it ain't broke don't fix it crowd."* were going to turn up tomorrow and legitimately win the day.

Boseman had Haydn on speed dial, Farnham-Blink reported the potential tragedy to Norman Naylor (another who we shall introduce in a later chapter, you'll like him which makes a change). Each knew that a disaster was unfolding before them, one of their own making (Boseman's if the truth were known). All thought the same: *"Why oh why did we agree to vote?"* The Board had been elected to run Russet Grange, why give the decision to people who have an opinion too? (You're thinking *'Brexit'* aren't you? Well don't, this isn't about passport colours and bent carrots).

Calls needed to be made, *'yes'* votes were needed. Boseman, desperate to dig herself out of the mud, had another brilliant suggestion. *"Let's just phone round the people who want tee times and get them to come along tomorrow."*

"Are you fucking insane?" Strong words from anyone, shocking from Norman Naylor. *"The 'Ain't broken' lot would have a fucking field day if they found out, and they would find out, because there's not a member here who can keep their gob shut"*.

Duke brought some sanity to what was becoming a heated little discussion. *"Send out a reminder about tomorrow, stick on a free buffet and churn out the beer at half price. You'll get easily two hundred turn up"*.

Boseman was in awe of Duke anyway, but he might have just saved her arse. What she wanted to say was *"Brilliant, take me to the spikes bar, whip out your love tackle, and do me up against the quiz machine"* but she felt it wiser to say, *"Good suggestion, I'll get to work on the begging email."*

Thursday arrived, the clubhouse was cleared again of *'Ain't broken'* flyers, and every available chair was placed, ready for the night of the free buffet and Wetherspoons-busting value. Steve *'Marge'* Simpson (Club Manager, you've probably forgotten about him by now) was well aware of the developments that had been taking place, and as someone whose bonus depended entirely on the club making a profit, he was more than keen to see tee times introduced. Indeed, when Farnham-Blink had told him of the vote decision his response was both simple and direct: *"You fucking idiot"*. He slipped on his club tie and prepared to open the meeting, now just one hour away.

Two hundred souls, or thereabouts, packed the clubhouse. The promise of cheap alcohol and free food enticed almost one hundred and seventy of them from the comfort of their homes, the *'Ain't broke'* crowd were of course always going to attend. Each of those objectors, for whom a defeat would mean that Fridays would never be *'their'* Fridays ever again, knew they'd been kippered.

Simpson opened the meeting, introducing his fellow board members to an audience who, at best, didn't know who half of them were. Boseman, Duke and Potton were widely recognised, for various reasons, but the old bloke who had something to do with finance, the equally old bloke who was apparently the Club Chairman and the Scottish chap who said he ran the place were men of mystery.

Martyn *'Trotsky'* Sykes (we met him earlier I think, I've been moving things around quite a lot) stood up. *"Mr Chairman, this club has survived for well over a century without tee times, so I am here to make a simple statement on behalf of many, many members. 'If it ain't broke, don't fix it'. I submit to you Sir that 'it' isn't broken."*

Farnham-Blink rose to his feet. Among the few who knew him he wasn't popular, and if more people had taken the trouble to get to know him they wouldn't have liked him either, but this was his time.

"How did you get here tonight Martin?"

"By car, the wife dropped me off"

"Not in a horse and cart then?"

"No of course not"

"Sit down and think about that. If you still don't understand, feel free to phone a friend. There's a payphone in the village unless you happen to have some kind of magical 'Star Trek' communication device."

Laughter filled the room, and chances are that even a few of the *'Don't Fix It'* mob changed their minds at that point, but the discussions continued. For not only was it right and proper to hear the opinions of those who didn't like change, but the longer that proceedings went on the greater the chance of the bar breaking even.

Ken *'Benefits'* Christie, another who was strongly opposed to tee times had his say, making what he thought was a decent case for the defence, but Farnham-Blink was better prepared than OJ Simpson's lawyer. (The real one, not Ross from Friends).

"Thank you Ken, your points are noted. By the way, did you and Margaret go on holiday last year?"

"Yep, two weeks in the Algarve. Why?"

"Where did you fly from?"

"Gatwick"

"Nice, I've been there myself. When you went, did you just turn up and expect to join a short queue, hop onto the next available plane and then once you arrived just pick any hotel you fancied?"

Uproar. Farnham-Blink felt a bit of compassion, Christie had walked straight into that one, but he knew he was in the right and more importantly, he knew that nobody can just roll up for a game of golf at a club that has long since gone out of business.

The meeting wound up with a moment of dignity and honest concession. Sykes stood again, and gave a brief speech which marked his finest moment at Russet Grange (though the bar hadn't been set very high, I grant you):

"Mr Chairman, it seems clear that a vote was not perhaps the way that this issue should have been decided. Could I suggest that instead there is a vote of confidence in the Board, one which my friends here will surely support. Then we all adjourn to finish the sandwiches, washed down with a glass or two of discounted Merlot, as we toast the future of Russet Grange, a future likely guaranteed by the financial boost which tee time bookings will deliver.".

The assembled masses drifted away, and as Julie Boseman got up she couldn't resist a cheeky little smile in Haydn Duke's direction. *"Good thing I suggested the cheap beer and free buffet. Fancy a go on the quiz machine?"*

Saw the #CerneAbbasGiant today, amazing piece of work. Reminded me of the "Russet Grange Midget" carved into a bank near the 8th tee by one of our resident caddies. Four feet high with a flaccid member.

Still that's enough about the caddy, and the bloke whose clubs he was carrying.

"Why are Red October, Crimson Tide, HMS Vanguard, U571, Kalvin Phillips and a Meatball Marina sleeping in the car park?" asked one of our members.

"Well…" says our Chairman, barely containing his laughter "…we're putting up subs this week."

A Tale of Miserable Men

Chapter	Par	Length	Joke Index
11	3	1,344 Words	14

Introducing:
Les Hamill (80)
Full Member
Nationality: Land of Misery

Les Hamill

*T*he archetypal
miserable fucker,
who leaves his home
for three reasons: To buy
food, to go to the golf club,
and to be a Community
Speedwatch volunteer.

Hamill took up golf in the mid-1980s, joining a low-rent municipal club, but he only lasted five months, receiving a lifetime ban for throwing a bacon sandwich at a member of staff. The ill-advised act of pork-product chucking was preceded by finishing a bottle of Stones' Ginger Wine before midday. Hamill joined Russet Grange in '97, wisely not mentioning his previous club or the sandwich projectile disciplinary on the application form.

Les Hamill usually plays with fellow 'Old Miserovian' Reg Bollard, though he does do the occasional nine holes with Gertrude Muller. Hamill can't stand Muller, but she lives on her own in a big house, she has no living relatives, and she is gullible enough to listen to his 'legal advice' in matters of will writing.

He makes no secret of his loathing for the young, and his suggestion that "We need a good war" is rarely met with anything but venom, though it did once result in a good slap from Pete Whittington whose brother died in the Falklands. (He didn't actually, Whittington just fancied smacking someone after a woeful back nine in a seniors' match). Nice one Pete, nice one. (He's another one we shall meet later).

Carl Doller believes that Les Hamill is Mark Hamill's cousin, often referring to him as 'Luke', though Les has no idea why.

And:
Reg Bollard (81)
Full Member
Nationality: Nobody cares

Reg Bollard

*I*f Reg Bollard were one of the Mr Men he would be 'Mr Horrible Bastard'. As you would expect he gets on well with Les Hamill. He's Geordie, so the misery does come fairly naturally, especially when you consider that he spent 45 years working on the shipyards of Tyneside before ill health forced him to retire. He tells a tale that this was due to "bone problems" and that's partly true. His gaffer told him he was a "bone idle wanker", gave him six weeks' money and told him to fuck off.

*Whatever tale of woe you can conjure up, he's got
a bigger one, and he usually blames Conservatives
for them. Whenever there's a wake in the clubhouse,
Bollard will be around, feeding off the grief like an
Ethiopian seagull ravaging a discarded fish supper.*

*Bollard is not one for buying a round of drinks, or much
else for that matter. He claims to have never bought
a golf ball in his life, and his current set of clubs came
as a result of haggling with a widow of a member at
one of the wakes we'll be mentioning later. He'd done a
"cracking deal" on a set of Callaways before the vol-au-
vents and crab paste sarnies had been scoffed.*

*To supplement his income in the 1970's Bollard worked
security on a few nightclubs in Sunderland, and whilst
he likes people to think that his rather misaligned nose
is the result of one too many fights, it was actually the
result of a Newcastle Brown Ale influenced collision
with a patio door at his sister-in-law's bungalow.*

We begin...

L es Hamill hated golf with a vengeance (which,
interestingly, was the working title for *'Caddyshack 2'*),
but he hated it nowhere near as much as he hated
life in general, or his sad old sow of a wife in particular. They
might have been sleeping in separate beds in separate rooms
for the past decade, but the woman of his nightmares still
shared a house with him, and the sooner he could get out of
their ex-council prefab every morning the better.

(A house by the way named *'Eagle's Nest'*, not though as a nod to a quaint dream home in the highlands. I'll leave that one out there, feel free to do your own research).

Anyway, a vicious March wind, coming in from the east and just waiting to rip through Hamill's *'Sports Direct'* golfing garb, only served to temper his enthusiasm a little. As he chucked his MotoCaddy battery (*"How fucking much Guy? I could have a week in fucking Spain for that, including my beer money."*) into the back of his car he couldn't help but reflect on the fact that the Good Lord had not yet invented the kind of weather that would make staying at home with the woman of his nightmares a sensible decision.

Divorce wasn't an option. Not only was *"the money grabbing old bitch"* not getting half of his British Gas pension, but Hamill knew he was a miserable bastard and therefore he saw no reason to give her what few years she had left without having to endure his company.

Just a few miles to the south, Reg Bollard was also experiencing the worst of what the March weather could throw at him, but unlike Hamill, who he would be meeting at the Russet Grange car park in the next twenty minutes, there was no matrimonial misery to contend with, for Bollard had murdered his wife just 25 years earlier.

Luckily for Bollard, there was no way a murder charge was going to stick due to his well-documented mental health problems, so manslaughter it was, 20 years sentenced, out in 15. *"The food inside was better than at home, same amount of sex and I've still got the shovel I killed her with".*

And thus it was that Hamill and Bollard, fine examples of matrimonial bliss in their own ways, parked next to each other to greet the day and stroll to the course. With just an hour until daylight they were confident that there would be no more than half a dozen equally sad bastards queuing to beat the first tee time (we have those now), and the fact that neither of them could feel their fingers was of little concern.

"Ten pee a hole Les and fifty pee for the front and back nine?" The question was pointless. The two of them had been playing for such vast sums since ten pence was ten new pence, but the value was in the glory of winning, and taking money off of someone that each considered to be their role model of how true misery in the 21st century should manifest itself.

Hamill and Bollard were in no doubt that any fellow golfers would not invite them to make up a fourball and, as the two of them hoped, the half dozen golfers in front of teamed up into two threeballs. *"Perfect…"* thought Bollard. *"…they'll fuck off over the horizon in no time"*.

The two men of misery enjoyed the morning light casting itself over the first fairway, safe in the knowledge that just two people, eighteen holes, and a game they could stretch to five hours, would be enough to delay and annoy at least twenty to thirty fellow members on that chilly but fully-booked Wednesday morning.

And so it was. Two hours and thirty minutes to play the front nine, two hours and forty minutes to make the journey home. Sure they held people up, sure they could have played quicker, sure they could have called players through, but it was not in the nature of these two self-evident *'Grinches of the Greens'* to make anyone else's game more pleasant. They'd paid their fees, and they would play at their pace. *"What's the fucking rush?"* Bollard asked himself as gestures from the following group caught his eye. There was money at stake, pride as well, and whilst the two of them might have conceded the occasional four-inch putt to speed things up a little it wasn't in their nature, certainly not when there were quicker groups behind them.

The match was halved, frozen hands were shaken, misery had been shared and enjoyed. *"Same time next week Reg?"* enquired Hamill, knowing that the answer would be as it had been for the past decade following Bollard's spell in HMP Parkhurst. *"Sure, unless they discover the mother in law's body under the shed. Did her with the very same shovel. She'd have wanted it that way"*.

#Clubhouse closed for a #wedding tomorrow, apologies to all members and visitors for the inconvenience.

(There's not really a wedding, we just can't be arsed to staff the place).

A Tale of Tea and Other Herbs

Chapter	Par	Length	Joke Index
12	5	2,183 Words	29

Introducing four new people:

Phil 'Jesus' Cross (51)

Barman
Nationality: Cornish

Phil Cross

*O*ur part-time barman, full time God-botherer is a peaceful soul, and he's been tending the club's bar since he turned 18. Cross isn't what you'd call ambitious, he's just happy with his lot and knows that Jesus is keeping an eye on him. When asked what Jesus was doing when a pissed-up Cross put his Berlingo into a ditch resulting in his best mate being in a coma for six months, he gives one of his "Holier than Thou" smiles and claims it's "Part of His Big Plan".

As is often the case, a strict religious upbringing taught Phil Cross the ways of the church, and for many years he refused to work on The Sabbath until Jesus told him in a dream that it was OK to do it for time and a half.

Our barman receives full membership as part of his pay package, and whilst he can knock a ball around well enough, he's a lazy bastard. Indeed the only time he has been known to indulge in unpaid physical effort was when he got caught wanking in cubicle three because the lock was broken.

Phil Cross takes certain parts of the Bible quite literally, but we shan't go into them here because during my second edit I decided that I'd tone down the stuff that might offend someone and just use the word "fuck" a lot more. Bible things which don't bother him though are theft and adultery. We know this because he polished off a bottle of Baileys, property of the golf club, whilst smashing Katy Pleaser's back doors in over an important and expensive Konica photocopier.

With:
Edna Troggle (79)
Unsocial Member
Nationality: English

Edna Troggle

est mates with and also arch enemy of Joan Painter, Troggle is yet another odious old bag who can't stand young people, the middle-aged, fellow geriatrics or almost anyone else. She's a social member, but if there were an "unsocial member" category she would not only be in it, but she'd have been an honourary appointee on the day the category was announced.

Racist to the core, Troggle sees nothing wrong with referring to black people with more than the occasional racial slur and when Howard started appearing in adverts for the Halifax, she moved her mortgage in protest. Like Cross she's not keen on homosexuals either, and refers to a local club as being "for woolly woofters" because a gay man was recently appointed chairman.

Troggle made the national press in April 2014 when she ran over a Bangladeshi lollipop man twice with her mobility scooter, breaking his ankle in the first collision and then his collar bone when reversing into him when trying to turn round. The incident took place as she was riding home after an afternoon on the cheap sherry at the local bingo hall.

Plus:
Joan Painter (83)
Social Member
Nationality: *"Whatever Arthur says, he makes the decisions."*

Joan Painter

*T*welve years older than her "toy boy" husband Arthur, Joan Painter is a thrill-seeking, rip-roaring bundle of energy and excitement compared to the 'King of Tedium' she married in 1988.

A straight-talking Lancastrian, she travelled extensively in North West England, visiting towns as diverse as Burnley, Preston, and Rochdale. "I once went to Greggs in two different towns on the same day" she recalls: "I think one was in Wigan, and they'd both sold out of sausage rolls by mid-afternoon. I mean what are the chances of that?".

Painter was previously married to Brian, her childhood sweetheart, but things didn't work out so well when the discovery of a suitcase of women's clothes led to an admission that Brian preferred to be "Brianny" and spend much of his free time in bars where he could "be herself". Back in '98 he dropped five grand on getting himself some tits and a cock-tuck, money that Painter had earmarked for a new kitchen.

Not really one for golf, Joan Painter is just a social member. Despite her claim that she likes to support the club, her average bar spend really isn't much greater than that spent by Troggle (or that spent by some formerly alive members with still alive bar cards that those in the know sometimes make use of). She did once order a side of chips with a cheese panini though.

And:
Mikey 'Weed' Flowers (32)
Full Member
Nationality: English

Mikey Flowers

Another one who is into his herbs, Flowers was a very promising young golfer, but who ended up preferring the grass grown in his loft to that which adorned the hallowed fairways of any of Cambridgeshire's finest golf courses, near and far.

At 14 years of age he was chosen to play in England Golf's youth squad, but a rough upbringing in the slums of Gerrard's Cross eventually took its toll, and when selected for the squad four years later he turned up off his tits, never hit a ball and got sent straight home.

Still a brilliant golfer at 32 though, more than capable of shooting a 65 and once broke 70 in a 'three clubs and a putter' competition. This feat was even more remarkable given that he threw his driver into the pond on the eighth.

These days Flowers works at B&Q, spending much of his day mixing paint and dreaming of what might have been and it's good to note that he's cut down significantly on herbal remedies. Decent lad though, popular member, especially with one or two of the ladies who also like to enjoy an extremely relaxed round on a Wednesday afternoon.

We begin...

Phil Cross is a peaceful soul, a patient one too, traits that are important for any barman, but for a barman at a golf club the ability to not get flustered by the behaviour exhibited and the bullshit spouted by any number of members remains essential. (Visitors on the other hand are always a delight though, as anyone who has ever worked at a golf club will know).

Cross was proud of his temperament, as he would to tell anyone who would listen, and if not he'd just bang on about it to himself. An inner peace and tolerance of his fellow man, as we have already mentioned, were because he believed in one true Lord, and he followed His teachings. Having said that, whilst it is true that his faith was important to him, it was more than likely that a few sly spliffs (great name for a reggae band) during the day helped him maintain his persona of being such a happy and relaxed human.

Take Edna Troggle for example, many refused to have anything to do with her but Phil Cross tolerated the old bag, thinking it was the right thing to do, and also because he thought he might cop for a few quid one day. (The *"inheritance game"* seems to be quite the recurring theme in this book doesn't it?).

She really wasn't a kindly soul though, indeed she had been warned about her particular brand of bile on more than one occasion, most notably when, in a raised voice, she asked her good friend and arch enemy Joan Painter: *"Who was that* [foreign gentleman] *I saw in the office just now?"* Well as it turned out said foreign gentleman was fixing the computer system following a particularly nasty virus, which was the result of a certain member of staff visiting *'www.milfswithcocks.com'*. What followed was the least well-intentioned letter of apology ever written, but it saved her near-octogenarian saggy arse. Just.

Troggle was also a regular abuser of Phil Cross's good nature, often wandering up to the clubhouse bar to order three fifths of fuck all. *"Could I have a couple of mugs please Phil, I've brought my own hot water and tea bags. Just for me and Joan."* She knew only too well that this little act wouldn't rub with anyone else, and she'd have been charged £3.98 regardless, but Cross was, as we know, a soft touch, especially when a quick *"God loves you Phil"* was used as a well-considered equivalent of actual payment.

She wasn't a one-trick pony either. Troggle had another weapon in her financial assault arsenal, and a quick scan of the day's cakes usually revealed a *'runt slice'* that surely couldn't be sold. *"I see there's a spare bit of Lemon Drizzle Cake, shame for it to be wasted when there are people starving in the word. Shall I take it off your hands Phil?"*

Cross fell for it every time, and though for a fleeting moment he considered putting tea for two and a bit of cake onto Troggle's account, he let it go. He hated conflict and Troggle was one of the few members who knew about the sordid episode that we mentioned in Cross's bio. We can only speculate about what the copier might have copied on that fateful day had an arse cheek brushed the green button, but a quite innocent service engineer, wrote on the repair form: *"Some kind of 'goo' on the A3 paper tray and coffee liquer seepage into the yellow toner."*

Anyway, I think it's time to strike another chord with the golf club aficionados reading this, because to be frank it's a very weak chapter, so here we go…

Those with access to membership account details, (and like every golf club ever, at Russet Grange this was at least eighty more people than should have had them), might well have been interested to note that Edna Troggle had spent precisely the amount that her social membership bar levy dictated every year for the past decade. Not a penny more. Troggle would say that she was careful with money *"You had to be during the war, unless you were prepared to do unspeakable things with the Americans like Painter probably did"*, but the simple reality is that she hates spending her own money.

Needless to say that when the hot water from her Thermos flask ran out, and the last dregs had been coaxed from the brace of Tetley's finest that she'd brought along that day, it was Joan Painter's turn to pay, and thus a proper slice of Lemon Drizzle, which would be paid for in her preferred way (by someone else) was eagerly awaited.

Watching these events unfold was Mikey *'Weed'* Flowers. Not a religious man but having said that, his love of herbal pleasures endeared him to Phil Cross. In that respect they were kindred spirits, a relationship that Cross was keen to maintain with someone who he considered to be as good a friend as Jesus and an essential supplier.

Mikey Flowers however did not share Cross's patience, far from it. He was paying full whack for his golf membership and full whack for tea and cake. Also, the *'Hunt the Runt'* trick would never have occurred to him and having just paid full whack for four pints of San Miguel and a bowl of cheesy chips, he was like a pissed straw waiting to break the back of a camel with osteoporosis. He had just lost his knockout match he was about to lose his temper.

"Excuse me, it's Edna isn't it, Edna Troggle?"

"Yes my love, is there something I can help you with"

"I just want to know why the fuck you think that the club should give you free cake, free heating, free service, free hot water, free tables and chairs, and free use of plates and mugs. You pay fuck all for membership, you abuse the good nature of my friend Phil, and tight-arsed old sows like you are the reason that this clubhouse doesn't make a profit. How about you pay for your drinks, and you pay for your cake, like everyone else does?"

Troggle's *'Tena Lady'* began working overtime. She'd never been spoken to like this, never expected to be, and had absolutely no idea what to say in the face of the cold, hard truth that had just been drunkenly spewed right at its intended septuagenarian target. (She's 79, I checked).

She looked at Joan Painter, she looked at Phil Cross, she looked at Mikey Flowers and then decided to turn on the tears and play the sympathy card in a game that had very, very quickly become one she would surely lose.

"I'm so sorry, my husband died last week, he used to deal with all of the money. It's all so confusing for me now".

Flowers gave her a look, a look that hinted at sympathy, but he wasn't too sure what to make of this unlikely revelation. Painter however knew better, and had she been a samurai master, with a sharpened blade to hand, she could not have done a better job of sticking the knife in.

"Edna, Brian left you thirty years ago. We had a party here at which he said he was 'pleased to be rid of the tight-arsed cow'.

So how about you hop over to the bar, pay for the tea and cakes, buy a pint for Mikey, a large G&T for me, and say sorry to Phil for taking advantage of his good nature. I believe he only drinks Holy water, but I'm sure Mikey here can sell you a little home-grown gift that he'll enjoy this evening whilst he's watching Songs of Praise".

Troggle did as she was encouraged to do, and thus ends another chapter, the Joke Index of 29 fully justified. Fear not though, the one about a wake and a wedding is coming up soon, that really has got the lot.

Just had 20,000 score cards printed for next season, the fucking printers have put: "Russet Garnge" on the front.

Twats.

The greenkeepers have been trialling one of those new-fangled 'robot mowers' today.

Two robots dead, another one who'll need help opening jars in future.

A Tale of an Alcoholic and an Australian

Chapter	Par	Length	Joke Index
13	3	1,642 Words	24

Introducing:

Debbie 'Bambi' Watts (48)

Full Member and
Ladies' Vice-Captain
Nationality: Scottish

Debbie Watts

*D*ebbie "Bambi" Watts, the girl with the innocent face and the doe eyes. Reason enough for her to be nicknamed 'Bambi', but not so fast. Her cartoon namesake was also famous for trying to stand up and falling all over the place, legs akimbo, which is exactly what Watts did on a ladies' away day in 2007.

Two bottles of Prosecco on the bus, a "Cheeky G&T" on the way to the first hole, and then flat on her back trying to push a tee into the ground. As she tumbled backwards, ending in a most unladylike pose, the words "Oh fuck me I'm pissed" trickled from her mouth in a soft Dundee accent in a scene that would never, ever, have appeared in 'Gregory's Girl'.

Watts lasted the front nine, but then took the walk of shame to the clubhouse bogs and spent the rest of the day asleep, apart from the occasional waking moment to throw up again.

Our heroine is a hairdresser by trade, and being a bit of a feminist she all-too-predictably named her salon "Curl Power". She tried to get one of the Spice Girls to open it, but wasn't prepared to pay the perfectly reasonable fee, so instead she called on a friend who once had a bit part as a corpse in Holby City.

Watts' bubbly personality makes her a popular (but sadly useless) golfer and she isn't much better at choosing husbands. She married Clifford 'Sawn Off' Small in 1998 and just a year later he got 25 years for armed robbery. In fairness, the clues were all there.

Plus:

Mandy Hobson (44)
Full Member, Ladies' Treasurer
Nationality: English

Mandy Hobson

*"**M**andy Hobson, oh yes, she's the one who's about as interesting as Homebase magnolia". Words famously spoken by Steve Simpson at the club Christmas party, whilst behind him in the queue was the lady in question. In fairness, he's right, if Hobson were in a hostage situation she'd be released before the old people or traded for food.*

You might think that perhaps she becomes a little more interesting after a few drinks. Nope, not a bit of it. The only way you'd know she's been drinking at all is that she slurs her speech a little when talking about cheese or Eastenders and goes for a piss a bit more often.

Hobson plays golf most days, and in truth she gets on with everyone because there's nothing to dislike about her, and she's not actually too bad a player. She's been a club member for over 20 years, so you'd think she would have a few golfing stories to share with her playing partners. You'd be wrong, the only story she ever tells is how she once got two Picnic bars from a Pro-shop vending machine. "I don't know whether they were loaded wrong, or it just kept spinning. Talk about lucky." she regales to anyone still awake.

And:

Brian 'Cobber' Cooper (45)
Full Member
Nationality: Aussie

Despite growing up within a stone's throw of Bondi Beach, and spending most of his adult life down under, Brian Cooper is the least Australian person you are ever likely to meet.

Brian Cooper

He's got a complexion that is best described as
"milky", he's teetotal, he's a veggie, he hates sports,
he's never lived in Earl's Court and he's as gay as
a the 'Queers, Queens and Quiche' food hall at the
Brighton Flower Festival.

Cooper came to the UK for a holiday in 2016, he met
his partner Vince in a Brighton nightclub and they
married two years later. The two of them are regulars
at club events, though some of the older lady members
don't quite understand why two such eligible men
never bring a lady friend with them.

His dislike of sports doesn't extend to golf though,
but in keeping with his anti-antipodean persona he's
useless. Insisting on wearing one of those hats with
corks hanging from it doesn't help much, but he likes
a laugh as much as he dislikes the sunshine.

We begin...

Mandy Hobson loved Debbie Watts more than she loved telling her tale about the free Picnic Bar, and when fate threw the two of them together on the first tee on a late August morning it was probably the happiest day of her life.

She loved Bambi's clothes, her accent, her perfume, her haircut, her sense of humour and her ability to chuck Prosecco down her neck like a Pelican gorging on a hot tub full of Mackerel. (That's another story, we'll read about it later - update, we won't, I just checked.).

Hobson had previously sunk to the depths of harsh reality at the aforementioned Christmas Party, but now here she was, looking at the fat end of four hours of golfing Nirvana, with the woman who she just knew would have been her lover had she been a) lesbian, b) interesting and c) attractive. This of course also relied on Watts being *'Friends with Dorothy'* and as many at Russet Grange knew only too well, Watts is about as straight as a piece of B&Q skirting board isn't.

Here, as should always be the case, the sexuality of those in question mattered not one jot. (See what I did there? That will be good for another few thousand sales from millennials). What did matter though was that both had been let down by their regular playing partners. This was something that Hobson put down to fate, and Watts put down to the fact that a certain golfing buddy was currently getting a highly personal service from the bloke who was supposed to be building a porch at her house.

Pleasantries were exchanged, drives were struck, and both managed to avoid the pig farm with some ease. Always a positive start. Watts managed three shots before reaching for the hip flask and it took until the walk from the first to the second before Hobson regaled her playing partner with the story about the Picnic bar.

"Have you ever heard about what happened with the vending machine in the Pro-shop….?" Watts was as polite as she was honest. *"I have actually, you lucky girl"*, desperately hoping that her words would stop this line of conversation in its well-trodden tracks. Far from it. In truth she felt

a little sorry for Hobson, and her one-trick Picnic tale, but conversely she was not particularly proud of most of her past exploits, exploits that would have made an instant trashy novel had she simply printed her Facebook timeline. However, it took until the fourth hole for tales of free choccy to subside, by which point Watts was close to emptying her flask three holes earlier than normal. This was worrying, but in the back of her mind she knew that Andy Biggs was on duty, and therefore a Deliveroo-like Buggy delivering a bottle of Bacardi was an option.

Play was slow-ish, as ever, due to senior golfers trying to increase their odds dying on the course, and it was not long until Brian Cooper, everyone's favourite/least favourite gay Aussie caught up with the girls. Watts kept her thoughts to herself (*"Thank fuck for that, someone who is more interesting than a Brillo pad"*). Hobson did the same, barely hiding her relief that the person likely to make up a three ball was no threat to her naughty little daydreams.

From beneath his self-effacing cork-strewn hat, Cooper greeted the pair, pleased to receive the invitation he had hoped for to make up a threeball. (I don't know what *'self-effacing'* means, but this isn't the kind of book where such things matter).

Tenth hole, Hobson bends over to place her ball on the tee and drops an enormous fart. Hoping that neither of her playing partners have heard this little transgression she stands up slowly and prepares to drive. Watts and Cooper are smirking, she's busted, but worse is to come. *"Couldn't you drop your guts after I've putted love?"* Kevin Pudgett (remember him, he's got a dodgy ticker) is not amused. He's lipped out on 16 and he's lost his match. On the plus side, Hobson had a new tale to tell, and a good one at that.

Brian *'Cobber'* Cooper is a nice guy, well groomed, well educated, and fortunate enough to have been upwind when what will become known as *'fartgate'* took place. The least Australian person who ever lived steps up, and despite there being absolutely nothing at stake, Hobson hopes that fartgate has not put him off of his stride. Her hopes were dashed when the nearby hedge claims another ball. Cooper smiles *"Few birds shitting themselves in there as well"* he jested. Hobson wants one of two things, either the ground to swallow her or Bambi Watts to hug her, neither happens.

As it turned out the addition of Brian Cooper, and the breaking of the wind, simply added to the joy of the game. Cooper carried on being useless but did not care one jot. Watts found half a bottle of cooking Vodka in one of the less-often-used pockets of her golf bag and was thus able to continue. Hobson was thrilled as she had doubled the number of stories that she had to tell, safe in the knowledge that if Marge Simpson ever spoke about her in earshot again, she could look him in the eye and say, *"I might not be Mike Parris, but when did he ever almost shit himself and cost Pudgett a match?"*

And just to round off the round, the air ambulance had to fly in to assist a senior who had gone into cardiac arrest. The CPR was sadly administered too late though, and a six-hour round, played by an octogenarian with a pacemaker ended just how he'd have wished…

Unfortunately we've just circulated last month's Board minutes and forgot to change "wankers" to "members" in the final version. I believe the word is "Oops".

We'll get them back onside with the usual "Double up for a pound" bribe.

We're launching our "Get Out of Golf" programme in 2024. Most members seem so miserable it feels like the right thing to do.

To begin you drop to four day membership at 1/2 price. After six weeks it's two days and no fee. Finally, after three months, you leave the place forever.

A Tale of a New Membership

Chapter	Par	Length	Joke Index
14	3	1,502 Words	31

Introducing:

Simon 'Elton' Babbage (74)

Full Member
Nationality: Free Spirit and
Citizen of Mother Earth

Simon Babbage

*B*abbage was once an ageing hippy, now he's just an old hippie, but he's a good bloke and still partial to a bit of free love when his "I was a rock star" approach to a lady pays off. Truth is he did have a chart career, but it spanned just two weeks in 1978 when his debut single "A Special Kind of Candy" reached number 61. Reason enough for his friends to forever call him "Elton".

Real Ale is Babbage's tipple of choice, though when out on the course he's yet another one who tends to enjoy something a little more "herbal", becoming more and more relaxed as the round goes on. Indeed, when teamed up with an equally enlightened guest at a Pro-Am, he actually fell asleep in the queue to play the short par three after the turn.

He wasn't always a hippie though. Following academic success at school and college, topped off with an engineering degree from Loughborough University he took a job at British Aerospace. However, the 1960's were calling and Babbage quit the rat race before the rats even got under starter's orders.

Woeful golfer, he doesn't care though, and there's nobody at the club who wouldn't happily join him for a round, or at least as many holes as he can stay awake for.

Plus:

Tanya 'TK' Maxwell (32)
Admin Staff
Nationality: English

Tanya Maxwell

*E*veryone needs a goal in their life, and Tanya Maxwell's goal is to make sure she clocks on for exactly 16 hours each week to qualify for her benefits. Benefits that amount to almost two thousand quid of taxpayer's money every month, to cover the cost of keeping five children in replica football shirts, Playstation games and KFC bargain buckets.*

Maxwell's official job title is 'admin assistant' and between fag breaks, coffee breaks, loo breaks, lunch breaks and keeping her Facebook status updated, she does occasionally answer the phone, as quite clearly specified in the a job description that she has never read.

(A job description which a casual observer might also assume includes the requirement to dress like a cross between a five quid whore and Jet from Gladiators).

Some quite reasonably question how Maxwell remains on the Russet Grange payroll, but the truth is nobody has ever had the balls to sack her.

Also introducing:
Carol Brittan (62)
Full Member
Nationality: English

Carol Brittan

*T*he Ladies' Captain. Loved by the Gents but not so popular with the ladies to be honest, but with a section numbering just 90 souls, 70 of whom are heavily reliant on Tena pads to get them through the day, Brittan ended up being the number one choice of the three people who would take the job on.

(Of the other two candidates, one continues to bring stray kittens to the clubhouse and the third went before a disciplinary committee in 2015 having called the club captain a "Pencil-dicked Nazi").

Brittan's time at the club has not been without controversy though, including an incident with a Callaway driver at one year's Christmas party and being found as pissed as she was naked in the disabled bogs at a particularly raucous Charity Golf Day.

Brittan drives the obligatory white Range Rover Evoque, which her ex-husband, affectionately known as 'The Bastard' bought her as an anniversary present four days before she got caught banging a young stud at a local health club.

We begin…

S imon Babbage cannot recall why, two years ago, he was somehow drawn to the game of golf, though chances are it happened whilst he was off his tits listening to the subliminal messages of The Beatles' *'White Album'*. (I prefer *'Abbey Road'*, but it's not all about me).

He knew little of the game itself, though he was aware of his local club and its proximity to the pig farm. Indeed, he had been one of those who protested against the construction of said farm by joining some fellow bacon-dodgers. As protests go it was as laughable as it was ineffective, because the chief rebel had confused a tube of *'No More Nails'* with a tube of bathroom sealant, leaving a dozen hippies in a highly waterproof but pathetically weak bond to a fleet of excavators.

After twelve hours they gave up and wandered to the pub in search of warm soapy water for the first time in weeks.

Anyway, we are getting way off track (unintended excavator reference there). Babbage had been summoned to golf by what we might now refer to as the *'Fab Fore!'* (that's awful, even by my standards), and having done a little bit of research decided that a sport which involved wandering in the long grass and consuming large amounts of slightly discounted real ale couldn't be all bad, so the game of golf it was going to be.

Babbage arrived at RGGC, experiencing the range of emotions that I crafted in the introduction. A surprisingly well-placed sign read: *'All visitors please report to reception'*. He couldn't find reception (nor could the members to be honest) but he did find the Pro-shop. His joy was short lived though as both Potton and Harris were currently giving lessons, Potton to Carol Brittan on the driving range and Harris to a girl he met on Tinder in the store room of the local branch of Londis.

Third time lucky, Babbage found the club office. *'Lucky'* is perhaps not the right word though, because with Steve Simpson away for the morning, Tanya Maxwell was in sole charge of all things administrative and she really didn't have the time to deal with something as unwelcome as a new membership enquiry.

"Good morning, could you help me please?" Babbage's opening gambit was perfectly polite, *"I'd like to ask about becoming a member of Russet Grange"*.

Maxwell found time to glance up from her phone, but her disdain was palpable. *"Can't you see I'm on my break? Go into the Pro-shop, they probably do the memberships."*

No eye contact and a vague wave in the direction of Potton's confectionery shop was, she hoped, the only effort required to deal with this rather tiresome situation. Her attention returned to important matters on Facebook, in this instance a picture of a desperate looking Cocker Spaniel wearing a sombrero, embarrassingly festooned with heart icons and a comedy Cuban cigar.

"Um, well I tried but the door was locked". Babbage remained relaxed, he had known no other way since 1968.

"Oh for fuck's sake". Maxwell really couldn't be doing with this kind of interruption, especially whilst she was in charge, and even more especially when she knew that at least one of the two people whose job this was most likely having considerably more fun than she was. *"Go into the clubhouse, ask them to give Potton a shout, new people are his problem"*.

Babbage asked himself *"WWLD?"* (Lennon in case you were wondering) and, still relaxed, went in search of the clubhouse. It was not difficult to find, and his faith in humanity was swiftly restored by the smiling face of Andy Biggs and a fine pint of Toad Warbler, the current guest ale. (£4.25, but £4.35 to members as Hanley had fucked up the till buttons again).

"I was told you could call Guy Potton for me, would that be OK, I want to join the club?"

Biggs smiled. *"No need, he's just come in. That's him in the corner chatting with the ladies' captain, go and introduce yourself, they don't bite"*.

Babbage walked to the other end of the clubhouse, oblivious to the fact that his moccasins were adhering to the carpet far more securely than his hands ever did to a JCB when he was last in the vicinity.

"Hi, I'm Simon Babbage. I'd like to play golf and the lady in the office said you could help me with membership."

"She must have taken a shine to you love." Brittan knew (as did Potton) that Maxwell lived by the mantra that minimum wage meant minimal work. *"She usually just ignores people and hopes they go away."*

"Why does she work here then?" Babbage had a lot to learn.

Brittan glanced at a Potton, both had grins on their faces, the grins of schoolchildren in on a joke. Brittan then proceeded to do that thing with her tongue pushing against her cheek, right hand moving back and forth in a rhythmic motion. Yes, we both know what I'm getting at.

She stopped gesturing and chuckled. *"Let's just say she gets on extremely well with the Chairman."*

"Ah, fair enough." Babbage might have been a hippie, but he was a worldy-wise hippy. He suspected he had enjoyed similar encounters in the Summer of Love, but as his memory wasn't what it used to be, he couldn't be sure.

"Anyway, membership's not a problem and if you've never played before we can book you in for some lessons." Potton gave yet another cheeky schoolboy look to Brittan, *"And if you're really lucky, Carol might let you join her in one of her 'Welcome to the Club' group sessions, you'll learn about more than just golf. Fancy another pint of Toad Warbler?"*

"We just thought it would be available".

The response from eight members of the ladies' golf committee who just turned up two minutes ago and assumed that the Aguero Suite wouldn't be in use.

FFS.

Conversation between our Club President and our Bar Manager:

"Disgusting Brian. Whoever looks after those greens should be sacked. Too slow, pins in the wrong place, surface water, snails, thatch, bumps, crudge weed all over the aprons, course was an absolute disgrace."

"Did you win?"

"Did I fuck."

A Tale of a Wake and a Wedding			
Chapter	Par	Length	Joke Index
15	5	2,903 Words	3

Introducing:
Doris 'Large Gin' Lynn (94)
Honourary Member
Nationality: English

Doris Lynn

*S*ome would describe Doris as "Colourful, a little eccentric, but a sweet old dear who can be a bit forgetful". Others would describe her as a cheat; someone who blames her age when she doesn't quite count every shot she takes.

A stalwart at the club since 1964, when women were first allowed to join, she has seen it all, been involved in much of it, and been the cause of some of it. She was ladies' captain in 1974, the first year that there was a ladies' section and again in 2014 in honour of her 50th year at the club.

Her legendary lack of numeracy on the course is only matched by her equally astonishing frugality. Once she's completed her fourball she's straight into the clubhouse ordering tea for two, and a couple of extra mugs, followed by "Oooh, I'll have a large gin" when her playing partners take their turns at the bar.

Doris married Alf, her wartime sweetheart in 1950. Alf died in 1966, shortly after England's World Cup win. He fell off a step ladder when trying to trim a hedge into the shape of the Jules Rimet trophy. "He'd only got one handle left to do, and I still use those same shears. He'd have wanted that."

And also:
Sarah Shaw (60)
Full Member
Nationality: English

Sarah Shaw

The epitome of the lady other ladies love to hate but want to be. Shaw is 60 years of age, looks 50 at most, acts like she's 40, and as Guy Potton subtly speculates "probably shags like she's 30". She's the person the white Range Rover was invented for and she runs a pilates class at the club, which unsurprisingly is very well attended. (Andy 'Pikachu' Abbot once turned up at one of theses classes sporting a fake wooden leg, a parrot and an eye patch. Not one of the other eighteen people in the room got the joke, you probably didn't either).

In the 1980s she worked as a model and actress, the highlights of her career being an appearance in the Sun newspaper's 'Deidres' Photo Casebook' where she spent five days of pictorial loveliness, dressed in her undies, worried that her flatmate was turning her bisexual. (She earned an additional £100 when she sold the knickers she wore to Tony Royce)

She also had a bit part in the James Bond film 'A View to a Kill', appearing as a rather saucy looking stable lass.

Shaw divorced her first husband when he got spotted pulling out of the childminder's drive just ten minutes after pulling out of the childminder. Later in life she widowed when her second husband, a French millionaire businessman, was shot by a piss-poor assassin who was aiming for his boules partner.

She does love her golf though, but really can't stand playing with the other ladies, most of whom she describes as "pre or post menopausal moaners". The gents welcome her with open arms of course.

We begin...

Golf clubs are a commonly-chosen venue for wedding receptions, offering such niceties as free parking, disabled toilets, Chicken Supreme for under fifty quid a head, and members who simply love giving over their clubhouse on a Saturday afternoon in the middle of July.

(High heels on the practice green are very welcome too).

Note too that unless clubs are particularly high-end venues (exactly like Russet Grange isn't), they tend to attract weddings between those of a slightly more senior persuasion. The sort of people who've been through it all before and have either experienced the joys of the divorce court or, less commonly, the sadness of a loved (or at least tolerated) one popping his or her clogs early doors.

That's golf club weddings in a nutshell so let us get to the matrimonial meat on this particular bone.

Sarah Shaw has, as you'll have just read, experience of both scenarios and it will come as no surprise that her son Richard (known as *'Rick'* because it's that kind of book), has also been hit with the garden spade of a broken marriage. Luckily though, he's as good looking as his mum, and so it came to pass that Shaw junior's second wedding reception, at the tender age of 36, was booked into the Russet Grange clubhouse. A simple entry in the clubhouse diary (way too simple as it was going to turn out) read *"Shaw, 60 guests, 3pm"*. Brian Hanley had written it himself and he was most pleased when, just two weeks before the big day, the lovely lady in question popped in to check the arrangements.

"The wedding's at 1pm in the registry office, we'll be doing a few photos, bit of fizz, yada yada then here for three. Canapés on arrival, buffet three thirty". Hanley nodded, and did a quite superb job of maintaining eye contact with this vision of loveliness when all he really wanted to do was gaze at her chest. Shaw continued: *"Sixty people, I'll decorate the room on the Friday, new chef knows all about the food, stuff our faces then get pissed. Disco starts at eight. All very chilled, all in hand. Sound OK Brian?"*

"Yep fine. We've got plenty of good staff scheduled and the members know that they've only got the spikes bar that day." Hanley was being marginally economical with the truth, telling Shaw what he wanted her to hear, when in reality the

members hadn't been told. Why? Because, as he knew only too well, it was better to tell them the day before a closure like this as they'd be equally furious, but for less time.

Also, and this was an even bigger issue, he was struggling for staff. The eight available were on zero hours contracts, four of them were about as reliable as a flush toilet in Kabul, and the new chef was, to put it bluntly, a coke head. *"It will be fine."* he pondered, knowing deep down that like so many events at the mighty Russet Grange, it would probably all be fine, as long as there were no major cock-ups...

The thing about wakes is that, unless you've arranged a competent hitman, you don't really know when Fat Uncle Pete is going to finally lose his battle with whatever ailment is swinging the sword of Damocles above him. Thus they tend to be arranged at short notice. Luckily (if that's the right word), your local golf club can almost always accommodate a few grieving relatives, some mates who aren't averse to the abject delights of a free bar, and a widow (or the bloke equivalent) who will be somewhere between absolutely heartbroken and completely ecstatic.

Anyway, and this is important, should Russet Grange be your choice for a *'Celebration of Life'* (a phrase that some who knew Fat Uncle Pete well might regard as ill-chosen given the rumours), then chances are you'll encounter Tanya 'TK' Maxwell when making that initial inquiry.

And here readers is where the other half of this tale leaves its holding pattern and descends to the metaphorical runway.

Doris Lynn was sad to hear that her brother Eric had passed away, but equally it was not unexpected. The old buffer had been hanging on for weeks, and when she got the call her first thought was of how much cash she'd be getting. Eric had never married, so that was a plus, but there were nieces and nephews out there, and, as she had once drunkenly confided to Carol Brittan (in earshot of a packed clubhouse) *"He told me he was leaving it all to the lifeboats and donkeys so I'll probably end up with a grandfather clock, some Neil Sedaka albums and a fucking sandwich toaster"*.

Lynn, as Eric Shaw's closest relative (yes, the deceased's surname was *'Shaw'*, you knew that was coming didn't you?) felt it was her job to book a wake, and what better venue than her golf club, a place where her brother had never set foot, and certainly wasn't going to now.

"Thank you for calling Russet Grange, your call is important to us, please choose from one of the following options…. For the Pro-Shop press '1', for course conditions press '2', to ask about Sunday carveries press '3'… It's '4' to speak to the catering team, to be put through to the clubhouse it's '5' and for anything else please stay on the line….."

Doris Lynn duly stayed on the line, thinking, like anyone else who had ever phoned any golf club over the last three decades *"Why the fuck can't they make 'speak to the office' option one"*. (The more observant will ask themselves *"Bob Bridger left years ago, why is he still on the phone message?"*)

Tanya Maxwell (we met her recently, nice girl) was in no mood to answer the phone. Normally she would ignore it, let the caller leave a message, and then play her favourite game of *'message delete roulette'* after her fag break.

Right now though Steve Simpson was in the adjoining office and ignoring the phone wasn't really an option.

"Russet Grange Golf Club, how may I help you?" Maxwell had perfected the *'going through the motions but I really would rather be reading 'Hello' magazine or catching up on Love Island gossip'* voice, and despite her hope that someone had simply pressed option five by mistake, this was actually one of those annoying calls that she had to deal with.

"Hello, it's Doris Lynn here. I'm an honourary member. Sadly my brother died and I'd like to book a wake."

Maxwell couldn't believe her ears. Not only did she have to deal with a real enquiry, but it was from someone who didn't even pay a membership fee, otherwise known as *'her wages'*. So what she wanted to say was *"Oh for fuck's sake, isn't there a pub you could go to?"* but years of training came to the fore:

"And.....?"

"Well,..." (Lynn was fighting back crocodile tears, she knew she might need the practice). *"...he's being cremated Saturday at One O' Clock, would you be able to accommodate a Wake for sixty people?"* (Readers should know that for the purposes of this chapter the crematorium at whichever town is near RGGC opens for business on a Saturday because otherwise the conflicting wedding would be on a Friday and the members wouldn't care. Luckily, I can make up whatever I want so that we can have a vaguely amusing story. Right then, moving on)...

"You should have chosen option four or do you want to hold the thing in the office? Which you can't because it's shut on

Saturdays. I'll put you through this once, but remember for next time, although I suppose there won't be a next time in your case". Compassion was not Maxwell's forte (that should be the name of an instant coffee), but when nobody in the bar picked up the phone, she did find an ounce of the stuff. *"There's nobody answering, I suppose I could check the diary."*

Maxwell dragged her ass to the bar to check the club diary, and almost immediately her prayers were answered. Joy of joys, someone else had already booked the wake. She knew Hanley's handwriting when she saw it so everything had clearly been arranged. Tell the old bag it's sorted, and get back to reading about how some minor-celeb got back-scuttled backstage at a Westlife gig.

"Good news love, not only can we do it, someone's already booked it in." Maxwell's voice had an audible spring in its step. She liked to be paid, she didn't like having to do any actual work. Result.

"Oh, er, really…. Who booked it in?"

Maxwell's patience was running thin. *"I shouldn't tell you due to data protection"* (a gift from the Gods for office staff the world over) *"…but it was the clubhouse manager. 'Shaw, 60 people, Saturday'. Was there anything else I could do? I've got the Chairman and four other people on hold here"*.

Doris Lynn was mildly confused, she hadn't expected anyone else to book a wake for her dead brother but clearly someone had done so. *"Um, no…. Thanks for your help"*. She went back to reading Bella, in which, unlike Maxwell's magazine of choice, the only bedding tales involved flowers and the colourful choices of this month's featured guest writer, a former expert from *'The Antiques Roadshow'.*

We've gone a bit off track here but I wanted to do the bedding thing, so let us rejoin the action on the big day.

Sarah Shaw had done a decent job of decorating the clubhouse for Rick's big day. Nothing too flashy, a woodland theme reflecting the rather decent tastes of her son and soon-to-be daughter in law. With a buffet meal and therefore no need for place names or a table plan, the only real indication of a celebration was a balloon arch festooned with a simple message *'CONGRATULATIONS'* written below in the big letters you can buy from Clinton's Cards.

Thus, when sixty guests from Eric Shaw's wake turned up for arrival drinks, a few canapés and a slap up buffet to give their friend and/or relative a send off there was little suspicion that something was going to go a little bit wrong, very soon. Yes, the *'CONGRATULATIONS'* banner was a bit weird, but the deceased had been a bit of a joker and it was assumed that this was merely something he had himself requested as one last little bit of japery. The free bar was appreciated too, though Brian Hanley was a little surprised at the rather early arrival of the wedding guests. Clearly they weren't going to let this gift horse leave the stable.

Sixty people, a few tears, most genuine as they knew they were getting nothing in the will. Canapés going down very nicely and on this rather hot summer's day the Stella flowed as quickly as it could be pumped. Andy Biggs was helping out (obviously) because none of the *'Kabul Bog Squad'* had turned up for their shift, and only two of the supposedly reliable other four had made an appearance. After that eighth or ninth rendition of *"I need this, it was fucking hot in that place…. Still, could have been worse…."* Biggs was struggling to muster a smile, and like Hanley he was starting to get the faintest inkling that something wasn't quite right on this Saturday afternoon.

Doris Lynn nipped into the kitchen, and asked the chef (who she thought seemed rather excited about everything) if the buffet could go out at just before three. Apparently this wasn't a problem at all, one of the few positives about a chef off his tits on marching powder.

Another of Sarah Shaw's *'nice little touches'* was a brace of bottles of a cheeky little Pinot Grigio and an equally cheeky brace of a Merlot on each table. With only two bar staff available, one of whom was very much starting to put two and two together, the queue for booze was suitably bypassed and 24 bottles of Waitrose's finest lasted just 17 minutes, bringing us nicely to the point where the Bride and Groom rolled into the car park (not literally, they were in Kevin Pudgett's Aston which had thankfully started that day, along with their wedding guests).

3:04pm, the wake literally in full swing. The timing of the first fight could not have been more perfect. A haymaker thrown by an octogenarian missed its target, a septuagenarian with whom a fifty year old grudge had reached its head, by an arm's length. Half of the buffet had already been scoffed, and as our pugilistic protagonists (or it might be antagonists, I have no idea and I really don't care) fell across the table, the remains of the food offerings found their way to the floor.

This horrifying scene seemed to play out in slow motion, and even though the clubhouse carpet had been carefully selected to not show any stains, there was no getting away from the fact that the remaining chilli, a range of tasty dips, half a pint of balsamic dressing, a marie-rose sauce and a bowl of fresh fruit salad was going to leave its mark. Stains upon stains upon stains (ooh that's like *'In the Bleak Midwinter'*), which would surely form a comedy backbone for countless speeches from Club Presidents and Club Captains for many years to come.

Hanley was now in no doubt, but he called over Doris Lynn, who was, at that moment, mixing crocodile tears in front of a newly-discovered executor, and actual tears relating to the fact that some random wordsmith had rearranged the banner to read *'CONGA TOTS URINAL'*.

"Doris, I think perhaps there's been a bit of a mistake, could I ask what dear Eric's surname is?"

"Shaw."

"Oh fuck".

Handley put his head in his hands, Andy Biggs knew too. This was a Titanic-esque disaster, and as some members let their tempers get the better of them and joined in with the fighting. Drunken uncles fell to the floor as if performing Bolero in a show called *'Dancing on Trifle'*, and as the chef just assumed than none of this was actually happening, there was a moment of perfect crescendo as the best man waltzed into the mayhem, called for a moment of peace and announced:

"Ladies and Gentlemen, the Bride and Groom".

Some of our members object to Charles being King outside normal office hours, so they've blocked the car park entrance in protest.

Course closed due to overnight reign.

Club legend has it there's a dragon named "Fiery Brian" sleeping under the 16th fairway, apparently he's been there since before the club was opened in 1897.

That's got to be bollocks, he'd be dead by now.

R.I.P Brian

A Tale of Many Things			
Chapter	Par	Length	Joke Index
16	4	1,670 Words	17

Introducing:

Andy 'Pikachu' Abbott (34)

Full Member
Nationality: English, but would
be LGBTQ+ if it were a nationality.

Andy Abbott

*H*e's a jolly fellow is Andy Abbott, and with rather pointy ears and a susceptibility to jaundice, his nickname needs no explanation. Also a bit of a joker, Abbott once walked the length of the 18th hole with his flaccid cock out, in full view of a wedding party on the clubhouse terrace.

Abbott works as a Flight Attendant on a budget airline, spending his working hours serving snacks and beverages to Brian and June on their way to Malaga. And because we're not avoiding stereotypes, he's gay and in a long-term relationship with Tristan, a graphic designer from Newbury. Dad is in denial though, just hoping upon hope that one day his son will return home bearing a partner with a reproductive system.

Away from the golf course and the joys of international aviation, Abbott is a bit of a wizard in the kitchen.

He got through to the final of Junior Masterchef in 1996 and whilst dishes of: 'Artichoke Soup with Roasted Parsnip Croutons', and 'Rack of Wiltshire Lamb with Heritage Greens and a Pomegranate Jus' stood him in good stead for the main prize, a dessert of 'Gooseberry Trifle on the Floor' cost him dear.

Loved by all except Reg Bollard, who cannot hide his disapproval of Abbot's sexuality. "He's got a pink cover on his driver, God knows what he does in the showers".

Plus:

Amy 'Instagram' Ellis (23)

Non-paying yet playing
member for some reason
Nationality: English

Amy Ellis

You look at Amy and you think "Ooh hello". She won't be looking at you though because the last time she looked up from her phone she gave herself a neck injury. Indeed, she chose to take up golf because A: She fancies Harry Andrews and B: It's a sport she can do whilst keeping an eye on her social media accounts.

She's a looker for sure, An Alpha-female but with the mental capacity of a wardrobe. Back in 2017 Ellis had her fifteen minutes of fame when she nearly got chosen for that year's series of 'Love Island'. She wasn't too fussed though "I shagged four of the blokes from the auditions, made the papers, and the Daily Star paid me ten grand to get my tits out".

As is always the case with young fillies of this standing, Daddy has a few quid, but not as much as Mummy who copped for a seven figure sum when Daddy was caught balls-deep in the thirty-something graduate from the London music school who was employed to teach piano to our hero.

Overall though, the boys love Amy. She's good fun to be around and not too bad a golfer, but she's unlikely to be picking up a Nobel prize this side of Christmas.

And also:
Mike 'Plough Boy' Smockman (37)
Full Member
Nationality: Bristolian

Mike Smockman

*M**ike Smockman is a simpleton to the core. Had he grown up in a village he'd have been a shoe-in for the job of idiot, but he was born and raised in Bristol, so despite having the intellectual clout of a poorly-educated parsnip there was no employment by natural selection.*

Smockman managed to get himself expelled from school at 14 to embark on his dream career as a casual farm labourer, and 23 years later he is still living that agricultural dream.

He likes the ladies, but in general they don't like him, so any relationships with the fairer sex tend to involve cold hard cash. Luckily his chosen field of employment means he always has a few quid at hand to pay for such hobbies, though on more than one occasion he has fallen foul of His Majesty's Revenue & Customs and had to cough up hefty fines.

As you might expect, Smockman is not one for bank accounts, but he does have a credit card for some of life's essentials, mainly the Just Eat app, the Wetherspoons app and a monthly subscription to various 'special interest' websites.

Typically for someone who works on a farm, he has absolutely no time to play golf, yet manages to squeeze in at least five rounds every week.

We begin...

How the annual *'Two Blokes and a Bird'* Stableford got onto the Russet Grange calendar was anyone's guess, but there it was, in the club diary and proudly taking its place on the honours board.

Rumour had it that someone (most likely Gertrude Muller) had complained to the Golf Committee that the *'Husbands and Wives'* competition discriminated against those who had never married, and further rumour suggests that the committee Chairman's response of *"Well it discriminates against gays too and no fucker has complained about that."* was met with both tears of laugher and utter derision. The minutes of that meeting are probably in the loft somewhere, no doubt suitably redacted. (That means crossed out with a big black marker pen).

However, the existence of the competition being chronicled here implies some sort of compromise to appease spinsters, widowers, homosexuals, lesbians and the various swordsmen around the club who thought the only point of marriage was to provide a steady stream of other people's wives.

Amy Ellis put her name down for *'Two Blokes and a Bird'* as soon as the entry list was published, she added her friend Andy Abbott in the second slot, leaving a space for whoever fancied making up a threeball. That space was filled within the hour by Mike Smockman, someone who didn't so much follow Ellis on Instagram as stalk her. The team was complete and in truth it was just as well that golf was being played rather than some kind of quiz event, because the collective depth of intellect assembled rivalled that of a retarded *'CBeebies'* viewer.

Abbott, Smockman, Ellis. Game day, games faces. (Pretty, pretty ugly, pretty, in that order). Points to be played for, fun to be had, and photo opportunities for two of this spectacularly average trio. Ellis took selfies of Ellis. (Obviously, otherwise they would be called *'Someone Elsies'*). These photographs were important as she never wore the same golfing kit twice, raking in countless thousands as an *'influencer'* for a golfing brand. She played safe in the knowledge that a million *'likes'* would have been forthcoming before she left the first tee, and all too aware that more than a few teenagers would have had *'happy endings'* before she reached the second green).

Smockman also took photos of Ellis, shared with considerably fewer people. Captions as diverse as *"Look at that arse."* and *"Look at those tits."* demonstrated the limits of his literary prowess. Ellis took this in good spirits.

The first few holes passed, points were scored. Abbott sank a twenty foot putt on the third to rack up four valuable points. *"Get the fuck in you fucker."* shouted Smockman, to the dismay of the President, waiting to strike a mighty blow on the fourth tee.

Sixth hole, Abbott smacked two drives into the pig farm. Smockman went all *'Billy Big Bollocks'* and then did the same. Ellis took an eight. Nil points, competition probably gone, so our trio consoled themselves with a few cans of cider whilst waiting to play the par three seventh. (Can I just make the point again that for all I know the seventh is a par five in other chapters, no actual planning or forethought went into this drivel).

Suitably lubricated, the golf became worse and the banter became somewhat more *'illuminating'*. Ellis needed a trip to the portaloo when Abbott, faced with a short putt confirmed that he *"Once sunk an eight-incher in the bogs of an Airbus"*. Smockman, on his ninth gin could barely stand, the not-so-subtle innuendo ironically flying way over his head.

12th tee, Abbot's turn for a visit to the bogs, Smockman hatched a brilliant plan. As Ellis took her stance he whipped out his phone and grabbed what would surely be a legendary upskirt pic, one that he could derive some *'gentleman's enjoyment'* from later that day. (Editing update: I honestly can't believe I wrote this stuff, I really can't).

The 13th hole and talk turned to football, on the 14th it was religion. (Nothing highbrow you understand, with a shitfaced Smockman admitting he fancied Jack Grealish, and Amy Ellis wondering why Australians *"... did Christmas in summer"*).The 15th hole saw a heated discussion on which flavours of own brand Pot Noodles Waitrose should sell (Reindeer Chop Suey was a popular suggestion, Smockman suggested Vegan Lentils which Ellis, in a remarkable showing of intellect, pointed out were probably vegan anyway) and then on the 16th the subject of immigration reared its ugly head.

"My mate Dave's got a fucking good idea..." slurred Smockman *"...reckons he'll make millions"*. Ellis liked the idea of millions, it would buy many handbags. *"What's that then?"* she asked, genuinely keen to find out more.

"He's going to buy a boat, fuck off to France and bring in hundreds of illegals." Abbott, despite his general shitfacedness couldn't quite believe what he was hearing. *"He'll get caught by a British Navy the first time he tries"*.

"Ah, but that's the brilliant bit..." observed Smockman, *"... he's going to reverse from France and if he gets stopped he'll say he's taking them back"*. Abbot fell over, the combination of laughter and Thatcher's Haze. Ellis, blissfully unaware of the abject stupidity of the plan, thought it was a great idea. *"Daddy's got a boat, I'll see if you can borrow it"*.

Two more holes, and like Jemini in Eurovision 2003, nil points. Our intellectually-challenged heroes managed a mighty last place, and it wasn't even close.

Later that evening Smockman reflected on the joys of the day, and then, feeling a little frisky, he remembered his upskirt pic of the lovely Amy Ellis. Semi-flaccid todger in hand, and having not given much thought to the technical challenge of camera phones, he made history. By virtue of having selected the front camera on his phone, he became the first non-greenkeeper ever to pleasure himself whilst looking at nothing more than the tidily mown turf of the 12th tee at Russet Grange.

Course closed this weekend. We made so much money from yesterday's society that we don't need to open again until Monday.

The members can fuck off, they're more trouble than they're worth at the best of times..

A Tale of Dubious Entrepreneurship

Chapter	Par	Length	Joke Index
17	4	2,047 Words	21

Introducing:

Arthur 'Emulsion' Painter (68)
Full Member and Board Member
Nationality: Lancastrian

Arthur Painter

*I*n a world of dullards, and indeed a golf club of dullards, Arthur 'Emulsion' Painter takes the word down to a whole new level. Imagine watching the Dallas Cowboys' Cheerleaders ride superbikes naked through a chocolate fountain, that's exactly as exciting as Painter isn't.

You would think that a man who has dragged his sorry ass through 14 years of education without being noticed, followed by 40 years working as an actuary (something to do with insurance but more boring) might have at least one tale to tell, but far from it. Indeed, when questioned about the stories he must surely have collected on his way to taking his pension, he recalls nothing more than getting a puncture on the A303 "Just after Stonehenge, what are the chances...?" and that he used to live next to someone who knew a bloke who appeared on '3-2-1' with Ted Rodgers.

A life free of stress, excitement or indeed anything or note has left him in rude health, and a complexion reminiscent of an 'own-brand' Rich Tea biscuit suggests that leaving his house isn't something he's too keen on. As we will discover in Chapter 22 he's a dirty old bugger, and we'll assume he's a reasonable golfer, but nobody ever remembers playing with him, not even his wife, who we met about 50 pages back.

Painter served on the Russet Grange Board of Directors having been forwarded and seconded as a joke. He was however elected and remains there to this day as, in his words: "I like the free sandwiches, especially the cheese and ham ones, plus the excitement of it all".

Plus:
Jenny 'Vasquez' McCulloch (45)
Full Member/Killing Machine
Nationality: Currently Danish

Jenny McCulloch

*O**bviously every golf club has a body-building marshal arts specialist lesbian vegan, but few can boast one who spent a decade teaching close combat skills to the men of the South African Special Forces. Vasquez is basically a killing machine and because we do so love stereotypes in these pages, many at the club assume she can open a* *bottle of San Miguel in a very special way. None has ever dared asked if this is the case.*

McCulloch chose her own nickname after watching the token Hispanic in 'Aliens' go full hard-ass before being ripped to shreds, but don't be fooled, she's about as Spanish as Dolph Lundgren eating Haggis in an igloo whilst wearing a Stormtrooper costume.

She's not been playing golf long, in fact she only took it up when taking on a new identity back in 2018, a move that was probably a wise one. Mercenary work is risky at the best of times, but when you are personally responsible for the deaths of at least five of Kosovo's most notorious crime syndicate it's probably wise to become someone else, at least until you've got your handicap down a bit.

And also:

Billy 'Whizz' Holsworth (42)

Full Member

Nationality: Norfolkian

Hollsworth is 42 years of age, but having spent all of the late 1990's off his tits he looks nearer 60. He is a likeable chap though, and whilst he's proud to be a Norfolkian, he does tend to

Billy Holsworth

drift into speaking Manchester when he's having one of his more 'excitable' moments. At such times he also tends to walk a bit like Liam Gallagher.

Holsworth has lived with his Mum all of his life, other than a few years working on the trawlers out of Lowestoft, and a few brief weeks at the turn of the century in rehab. His mum does not believe for one moment that her son is a smackhead, but then his mum also believes that fairies put the water in taps at night and that the SAS killed Princess Di.

He's a very good golfer though, all the more impressive when you consider a complete inability to stand still, and despite his rough and ready persona, and a taste for chemical stimulation, he's got a heart of gold.

We begin...

As we've just learned, Billy Holsworth does indeed have a heart of gold, but he also has the brains of a tree sparrow, and when a bloke down his local approached him with an offer that he really, really should have turned down he really, really didn't. The bloke in question was someone that Holsworth knew dabbled in a bit of *'warm'* merchandise (stuff stolen from some who had themselves stolen it), but they had never spoken until one fateful evening in mid-August.

"Alright mate?..." The Stockport accent immediately struck a chord, and he was all ears. *"...Yer a bit of a golfer aren't ya"?* asked said bloke. Going *"full Madchester"* in the blink of an eye, Holsworth nodded with unbridled enthusiasm.

"Yeah, I play a bit pal, why yer askin'?" Instantly he knew he was dealing with one of the sons of his adopted city. *"Come out back, there's some gear I need to move on".*

Holsworth gave a twitchy look around the bar, wary that he might be about to get dragged into the heist of a master criminal, but the drinking population consisted of three old blokes playing cribbage, one who had clearly pissed himself, and a woman more engrossed with *'Candy Crush Saga'* and her *'Double up for £1'* gin than anything going on nearby.

"Out back" consisted of a small car park, scattered with various items of catering waste, an Iron Maiden *'Slaughter your Daughter'* pinball machine that had been smashed to pieces, empty beer barrels, a cement mixer and a transit van which, as it turns out, contained the proceeds of last week's robbery at Wigan's *'Mega Golf Megastore'.*

"Excess stock mate, our kid works at Argos and they doubled up on an order, it's not dodgy or nuthin', five hundred quid the lot, will sell for ten grand all day long".

Holsworth knew an offer when he saw one, and having been reassured of the legality of the merchandise on show he wasn't going to turn down this opportunity, one for which he had been personally selected. Ten minutes later he had been to the cashpoint, collected his car, handed over the money and was on his way to Russet Grange to look for gullible saps. He knew the members well, this would be an easy bit of profit and in no way likely to upset the Club's professionals.

Tuesdays were, as Billy Holsworth was only too aware, Guy Potton's day off (well his day off from the Pro-shop, he was know doubt working his magic somewhere) and with Guy Harris (Chapter 19, I wouldn't rush) running the show he had no hesitation in setting up *'shop'* near the driving range.

Not for one moment did Whizz consider that the 30 sets of high-end golf clubs in his possession were the spoils of a well-planned heist, and even if he had worked out that they were, it still would not have occurred to him that selling stolen golf equipment from the back of a seven-owner Nissan Qashqai diesel at a once-prestigious golf club was illegal, immoral, and a gross undermining of Guy Potton's legitimate business. (There's some poetic licence here, as correctly pointed out by my son. You can't fit 30 sets of golf club in the back of a Nissan Qashqai, but let's not get hung up on facts).

It had also not occurred to him that Potton himself might like a piece of the action, given that the price he paid to a dodgy bloke in a dodgy pub was almost certainly going to be massively lower than Potton would normally pay via the conventional/legal trade price route.

Jenny McCulloch (who I feel is going to have a bigger and better part to play in the second book) drove into the car park. She checked that she hadn't been tailed, and then went to open her boot. She was not someone you fucked about with if you wanted to retain an even number of limbs, yet Whizz was undeterred.

"Hello my lover, need any new golf clubs?". Holsworth had reverted to his native Cornish tongue and McCulloch couldn't quite believe why someone she assumed was the local idiot was asking such a question, but her response was polite.

"Well not reality, my clubs are fine I think, and why are you selling these anyway? Does the Professional know?"

Billy Hollworth wasn't keen on the line of questioning for which he had no good answer (or any answer at all to be honest, so he changed tack). *"Love your accent, is it German?"* At a different place and time she might well have killed him where he stood, but today he had a chance of escaping with his life. *"No, I am from Denmark, it is a Danish accent"*. Sensing a chance of a sale he was quick to retort. *"Well I fucking love ABBA, I love your pastries too, and these clubs were made at the steel plant which Volvo use"*. (Readers might be imagining that Holsworth is perhaps a Cornish/Mancunian *'Del Boy'*, this wasn't planned but I think he is too).

"Just a hundred quid for a full set, you'd normally pay that for one just one club of this quality". McCulloch smiled, *"Oh OK. I will buy some clubs"*. (I nailed the Danish accent there). With a few hundred thousand in the bank from a tricky little job involving a South American drugs cartel McCulloch didn't mind a bargain, and what better way to stay fully undercover than buying a hookey set of Callaway's finest from a stupid Cornishman with the worst Geordie accent she had ever heard. *"I assume you have a left-handed set…"*

"Ah fuck it" thought Holsworth, but he was not too distraught, he had very nearly clinched a sale and heading his way was everyone's favourite old pervert, Arthur Painter. (As I said, we'll meet him later, he a big fan of *'acquired taste'* videos). Holsworth knew that Painter was a Board Member, but he had never really worked out the whole *'Board'* thing.

Why? Well whenever someone said *"Board Member"* he heard *"bored member"*. (Yes, it's a poor joke at best but it's a useful device to help me finish this truly average chapter).

"Alright Arthur, still bored? Well I've got something a bit exciting for you today." Painter was a bit confused, he was anything but bored. Boring, but not bored.

"How are you doing for golf clubs at the moment?" asked Holsworth with the boundless enthusiasm of a trainee estate agent. He smiled at Painter and did a bit of a *'game show reveal'*, reminiscent of a speedboat being shown to a bloke from Bromsgrove on *'Bullseye'*. *"Hundred quid for a full set, Potton would charge a grand. Cash only, and if you're left-handed I'll need to order them in"*.

Painter was rather taken aback, this was a lot of excitement in one go, but given that he appeared to be dealing with a fellow Lancastrian (Hollworth had slipped back to Madchester-mode) he was prepared to take the biggest financial gamble of his life. He was not naive enough to think there was a genuine bargain to be had, but this appeared to be a bargain nonetheless.

"Well I've got some clubs, but they're a few years old now, how did you end up with all these?"

"Met a bloke in a pub, his brother works in the trade, excess Argos stock or something like that".

This was good enough for Painter, and satisfied that just £100 for some high-end golf clubs which were selling for ten times that price just eighty yards away was a legitimate deal, he handed over the cash to a delighted Holsworth.

"Cheers Arthur, sorted. (full Gallagher), Glad you're not left handed like that German bird over there, talk about awkward".

"Well I do like a bargain..." smiled Painter, *"...I'm sure you'll sell a few sets but keep things a bit quiet, Potton won't be best chuffed when he finds out, but having said that there's probably a deal to be done, he'll be paying five hundred quid wholesale".*

Painter winked at Holsworth, *"...but keep it quiet that you sold a set to a Board Member, that really wouldn't go down well with the Chairman".*

"Don't worry, your secret's safe with me mate, and I do hope you find something to interest you soon".

We have new options when calling the club:

*Press **"1"** For the Pro-shop because you couldn't be bothered to look up their number.*

*It's **"2"** To remind us we're a members' club.*

***"3"** To have a natter with Tanya in the office.*

*and **"4 "**To order cheap fags from Spanish Terry.*

Course open over 18 holes. Trolleys, buggies, Zimmerframes allowed, whatever. Play in stilettos for all we care.

Visitors only today though, green fees waived, as part of our program to show the members who's boss. (Clue: It isn't them).

"But Friday is always Quiz Night".

Not this Friday Maureen, we've got a golf society of 90 blokes from Wales, they've put three grand behind the bar and they reckon they'll have to top up.

The eight of you will have to find another venue where you can smuggle in your own Cinzano.

A Tale of Ladies Fighting at the Summer Party			
Chapter	Par	Length	Joke Index
18	4	1,662 Words	33

Introducing:

Dawn 'Karen' Hailwood (22)

Full Fat Member
Nationality: Chubster

Dawn Hailwood

*T*he second best day of Dawn Hailwood's life was the day she discovered Facebook. The best day of her life was when a so-called "Social Media Influencer" clicked the 'like' button under a photograph she posted of her post-op tits.

Known at the golf club as 'Karen' (for obvious reasons), she took up the game so that she could dump her two little shits, Kyle and Kylie, onto their grandmother for a few hours on a Sunday morning. Granny is just 37 years of age and knows that a large bag of fizzy cola bottles and a DVD of 'Frozen' are all that any child needs while "mummy is at church".

Hailwood once set fire to her kitchen because late night chips and half a bottle of Pernod don't make for a safe environment, and in fairness she had the good sense to call 999 the moment she had finished posting photos of the raging inferno online.

On the positive side she's quite a lot of fun and would actually do anything for anyone as long as they don't mind her telling the world about it. Weighing in at just under 15 stone, she manages to knock a golf ball 200 yards, straight and true, with little effort.

Also introducing:
Julie Boseman (50)
Full member and Board Member
Nationality: European State
of Bullshitonia

Julie Boseman

*Y*ou name it, she's done it and if she hasn't done it she's going to do it. Boseman claims she was picked for the British Ski Team for the 1994 Olympics in Lillehammer, but pulled out because she was offered a role as an extra in Jurassic Park. Her scene got dropped but she did get Jeff Goldblum's autograph. Another corker is that her Dad worked for MI5 for most of the 1980s and that his second hand car dealership, located in a lesser part of Mayfair (Lewisham), was just part of his cover.*

The bullshit continues with tales about her uncle owning a ranch just outside of Las Vegas, where she spent her childhood summers. The truth is that her uncle wears an ankle tag and cleans the toilets at Strensham Services, though he did once spend some time in the 'Viva Las Vegas' amusement arcade at Pontin's Camber Sands.

Boseman is good fun though, as evidenced by an accidentally shared WhatsApp video of her getting some plastering done by local builder Mikey Price. She sounded like she was enjoying the work though and Boots did quite the trade on wet wipes that day.

A poor golfer by any standards, but that's because she used to play left handed before she broke her arm whilst test driving for Aston Martin's racing division.

Plus:

Ron 'Tank' McAndrew (90)

Full member and Golf Committee member
Nationality: Scottish Hardman

I ronically nicknamed 'Tank' because of his seven stone frame and sparrow-like legs, McAndrew is the short Scotsman with an even shorter temper.

Ron McAndrew

He once threw his entire set of clubs into the pond on the 7th, followed by a hasty rescue when he realised his car keys were in the top pocket.

McAndrew was Club Captain in 1970 and Club President in 1980. He was also a club representative in court in 1990 when he took a 7-iron to every panel on a fellow member's shiny new car following a dispute over a £20k debt. Understandable behaviour perhaps, but also rather awkward when the indebted member arrived in an almost identical vehicle whilst said 7-iron was being wielded in anger.

To rub salt into the wound it was noted that McAndrew missed the drivers side headlight twice before connecting, and that's how an air shot at Russet Grange became known as a 'McAndrew'.

He's calmed down a bit these days, partly due to old age taking its toll, but also because a daily dose of valium and a half bottle of Tequila from the 24 hour service station on the way home still works wonders.

We begin...

Whoever made the table plan for the Russet Grange Summer Party had really not given any consideration into which members did not get on with each other, and that same person had certainly not taken into account the festering *'relationship'* between Julie Boseman and Dawn Hailwood.

Said *'relationship'* had all begun with a badly-considered and yet utterly avoidable *'reply all'* sent when Hailwood was serving on the social committee. Over a couple of years the mutual despisement had slowly grown, waiting to erupt in a way not seen since John Hurt encountered a bit of a tummy ache in the 1979 gut-busting classic '*Alien*'.

"*Two-faced dumpster who is on first name terms with her colon*" The words should never have reached a certain member of the Board of Directors, but reach her they did. In truth, Hailwood should have been aware that copying in a bloke who had been regularly '*noshed*' by Boseman over the previous few months was asking for trouble, but equally she had a history of embracing trouble in the way a randy Doberman embraces the leg of an unexpecting, but not always unpleasantly surprised, Amazon delivery driver. The description, in fairness, was not wholly inaccurate. Boseman had risen to her position on the Board by treading on people who could be trodden upon and abusing the good nature of those who had a good nature waiting to be abused.

Ticket sales had gone surprisingly well, unusual for an event at Russet Grange, but the price of just five quid for all you could eat and drink was too good to resist. A price by the way which had been negotiated between Rob Farnham-Blink and the Managing Director of a local drinks company, someone who really didn't want his sexual exploits at last year's Pro-Am exposed, exploits which the Chairman might have dropped into the discussion...

"*I've heard there are photographs John, quite graphic, astonishing even, showing the sort of debauchery that doesn't befit a respected local businessman*". Enough said, deal done.

Ten people fit around a six foot diameter table, twelve at best. Thus the fourteen men and women squeezed around table seven at the club's summer party were rather cramped.

(Table overcrowding is a problem that crops up later in the book, at least I think it does. At 50 hours into a 20 hour rewrite I'm past caring). Worst of all was that Ron McAndrew's skinny frame did little to alleviate the spatial and psychological pressure between him, the *'Curvy and proud of it, all woman'* Hailwood and Julie Boseman, *'pre-loaded'* with the best part of a bottle of low-rent *'Baileys-a-Like'* on board. A creamy beverage locked and loaded, ready in her gullet to see the light of day again very soon.

Starters were served at 7pm, and by 7:05pm the first verbal salvos had been fired. *"What the fuck are you looking alco-flops?"* Ill-advised words at best, but as far as Hailwood was concerned it was game on. Boseman had only been searching for condiments, but a single glance to the poster-child for type two diabetes just two places to her left really had lit a very short fuse.

"I'm looking at a 'Flabbage Patch Doll' love. Getting a bit hungry are we? Has your chip flask run out again?" (I quite like the idea of a chip flask. Who says flasks have to be reserved for liquids? - The Russet Grange Chip Flask was just conceived and will be available to buy when the profiteering merchandise site sprouts wings).

Moving on though…

Ouch. Brilliant, highly inflammatory, and bang on the money. McAndrew had been on the sauce since midday, and the verbal jousting did little to sober him up, but everything to bring out his inner-Scotsman. *"Dinnae take any shit from her love"*. The instinct of a man with a short temper and a long history of *'getting involved'* took over in a split second.

A TALE OF LADIES FIGHTING AT THE SUMMER PARTY

Neither female antagonist (yes, I know, let's just move on shall we) knew or cared who McAndrew's comment was aimed at, but both felt the call to arms by the ageing Scotsman, a man who was now far more interested in the confrontation unfolding in front of him than he was in his surprisingly adequate ham hock terrine.

Seats flew, food flew, drinks were left sensibly alone, as two ladies who, in a wonderfully near-instantaneous fit of rage, found themselves wrestling on the clubhouse carpet. Around table seven reactions were mixed, with a few looking on in horror and others assuming that this was some kind of flashmob as part of a cabaret. Pete Whittington was loving the show, nursing his first erection since the ladies' pole-vault final of the Los Angeles Olympics.

Punches remained unthrown, but hair was pulled, slaps delivered, and underwear unworthy of the 1988 Freeman's catalogue embarrassingly exposed. (Whittingdon was unable to ignore what was going on *'down below'* and decided that as attention was focused on the impromptu sex show taking place he could probably get away with *'rubbing one out'* under the table).

Another salvo of insults swiftly followed , readers can imagine these for themselves, but they basically involved accusations about sexual acts with the Chairman and hanging around Asda until the yellow stickers went on the out of date pastries. You get the idea, and although it was messy, there is a certain thankfulness to be had that the actual mess would, ironically, have been greater still had it taken place during the dessert course of Eton Mess.

Alcohol, the heat of summer, and two women who hated each other were always going to be a potent mix, and at the Russet Grange summer party of 2014 that potent mix turned into what, at other golf clubs, might have been a shameful happening to taint a wondrous history.

But we are Russet Grange Golf Club, we are proud, and the reality is that what the members came to refer to as *'The Battle of the Bulge"* merely took its place amongst many other fabled happenings, stories to be regaled to future generations at this particularly wonderful and impressively notorious sporting establishment.

Right, that's the third worst chapter out of the way, but 'A Tale of Cocks and Clocks' is next, rightfully at Joke Index 33. It plumbs new depths but it's mercifully short.

> *Already looking at a sequel to "Tales from Russet Grange".*
>
> *Opening line: "It was the worst of times, it was the worst of times".*
>
> *(Don't bother looking this up if you don't get the joke, you're not my target audience anyway).*

Introducing:

Hugo 'British Bomber' Harris (30)

Assistant Pro

Nationality: Duh

*H*arris was born with a silver spoon in his mouth and a shotgun in his chubby little hands. A blue-blooded stallion who makes Jacob Rees-Mogg look like an east-end barrow boy.

Hugo Harris

He's a charmer, he's a cad, he's a good old-fashioned old Harrovian who would bring back National Service, Victorian workhouses and public hangings in an instant. For for now though he's slumming it as an assistant golf pro because his old man (Lord Harris, who he describes as "King of Western Europe or some other bollocks") told him to: "...go and get a fucking job you fucking lazy odious little shit".

Nicknamed 'Bomber', not because he's related to the bloke who dropped vast amounts of bombs on Dresden (which he is), but because he once polished off a rack of Jaegerbombs with a golfer's breakfast and dropped the lot on the practice green before shooting a 64.

Harris lost his firearms licence for a year when the drunken husband of a recent conquest turned up at a grouse shoot and challenged him to a duel. What he imagined was nothing more than a jolly jape turned out to be all too real, when, at fifty paces, he ended up with a right thigh full of lead shot. By all accounts he was lucky to escape with his cock and a testicle still attached to his body. As Harris says "She was an absolute pig, I though I was doing the bloke a favour".

Plus:

Karen 'Margot' Young (62)
Full Member
and Board Member
Nationality: English

Karen Young

*A*h, Karen "Margot" Young, exactly the person you think she'll be. Young is desperate to be a Margot, as the tragically excessive lettering down the side of her golf bag makes clear, and when "Karen" became a thing she cried for 30 hours straight. It will be no surprise to learn that she is so far up her own arse she can watch her digestive system in action.

Nobody at RGGC is more desperate to be thought of as wealthy, but the fact is she's up to her neck in store card debt and if she doesn't manage to scrape together the next payment on her car she'll be greeting the bailiff-driven 'Repo Transporter of Shame'.

Not that she doesn't have any kind of income, far from it, but alcoholism doesn't come cheap when you won't stoop lower than Waitrose. Night after night the booze sends her off to sleep, and morning after morning a 'cheeky one' helps her face the day.

With the alcohol levels set just right Young can be quite fun, but there is nothing sadder than watching her down one too many glasses of House Red during a ladies' section match and trying to humiliate the waiting staff whilst simultaneously referring to the spikes bar as "Cattle Class".

We begin...

They say that you should never meet your idols, but Karen Young had been drooling over Russet Grange's Assistant Pro, Hugo *'Bomber'* Harris ever since his arrival at the club some eight years earlier. At the time he was 22, she was 54, old enough to be his grandmother but still young enough to want to ride him like a stolen Deliveroo moped.

Harris was out of reach though, or at least she thought as much. Her looks had long since departed on a one-way ticket to a distant place and time, and there were countless younger and better looking fillies circling this particular piece of British beef. From visiting golf reps and the *"cheeky little piece"* who delivered Mars Bars and lesser confectionery, to a number of her fellow members, who would either like to experience *"a bit of Bomber"*, or experience *"a bit of Bomber again"*. Yes, there were many well ahead of her when it came to the metaphorical queue for Russet Grange's apex predator.

Young had to accept that despite her name, she was anything but, and that the best she could do was reach for a buzzy little *'bedtime friend'* and dream about her dreamboat on the nights when Dr Smirnoff or Captain Bacardi hadn't paid her far too long a visit. At least that's what she thought…

Anyway, you never know what hand fate is going to deal, and on this particular Monday morning in very late March, Hugo Harris had arrived for work positively *'tooled up'*. One fucking big shotgun, one fucking big knife, and a crossbow gratefully inherited from Uncle Bertie, a relative lovingly known to Harris as *'Posh Rambo'*. This was not a day to be a pheasant on the hallowed fairways, or a rabbit, or a squirrel. Even being a senior who fancied and early nine and needed a piss on the fourth tee was risky, as Martyn Sykes could testify, having got buckshot in his left bollock in similar circumstances a few years earlier. Harris intended to go a huntin'.

As it happens that same hand of fate had also dealt a card to Karen Young, a card that saw her in the land of nod by early Sunday evening, and in no fit state to turn the clocks forward to herald the start of British Summer time. By 5:00am she'd had her ten hours of kip. A quick glance at her knock-off Rolex *'Oyter'* (you couldn't make it up) acquired from a swarthy north African chap trading as *'Timepieces from Torremolinos'* was showing 6:00am.

"Perfect." thought Young. An hour, or so she believed, until her tee time. (I think we've established a bit earlier that you can't book tee times quite this early at Russet Grange, but we're long since past the point of caring).

My dear reader, you know where this is going, I know where this is going, so I think we shall go there together.

Young was used to seeing a fairly empty car park, but on this particular early morning it was surprisingly devoid of vehicles. One of her few pleasures these days, apart from the sound of ice dropping into a large medicinal one before watching her box set of 'The Good Life', was an admiring glance or two when she drove past a club member in her admittedly tidy (though as we know, financed to the hilt) Mercedes convertible. A pleasure which she increased the chances of experiencing, by taking an excessively long route to her preferred parking space. Not this time though, which was weird, but she thought no more of it as she loaded her infamous *'bag with someone else's name on it'* onto her trolley.

As Young rounded the corner to the Pro-shop, clubs in tow, she was stopped dead in her tracks. Standing just yards before her was Hugo Harris, shotgun over his shoulder, heat being packed. He was in the Killzone, ready to ruin the day of any* wild animal that crossed his path, before transitioning to his hateful day job of selling choccy bars to a motley selection of gutbuckets, drunks and dullards.

Sidenote: It wasn't the selling that was hateful, and here we shall quote Harris himself: *"Every time, every fucking time, they have to tell you about the putt that paid for their fucking Kit Kat…. and every one they missed as well, every fucking one… 'if I hadn't lipped out on fifteen I'd have been buying two Kit Kats today'. Wankers, the fucking lot of 'em"*. Fine words spoken to Mike Parris, sadly overheard by the Chairman, still on speakerphone.

Anyway, I digress, and we must explain that previous asterisk. *'Any'* should read *'almost any'*, because right here, right now, a certain member of the Board of Directors felt a wildness inside her. (Yes, I thought of writing what you're thinking, but we're better than that).

Arm extended, hand cupped, Young felt young again. Unable to control herself she instinctively grasped what she knew would be a fine pair of testicles, partly driven by a strange post-menopausal instinct, partly by the slowly fading influence of last night's bottle of Stolichnaya. (That's about as Jilly Cooper as it goes in this book, if you want raunchier then you'll need to visit your local Oxfam shop and grab a well-thumbed copy of *'Riders'* for 50p).

Harris was, to say the least, a bit shocked, but experience had taught him that not only could a good tune be played on an old fiddle, but that a 62-year-old woman holding his most precious jewels wasn't likely to be after a mere discount on a Snickers bar.

"We've got almost twenty minutes until I tee off, and my dear boy, I've got you by the balls". Karen Young had no idea why she seemed to be quoting from the aforementioned novel,

but she liked what she heard herself say, and so it seemed did Harris. (Insert your own rude bit here, this isn't soft porn, we're saving that for the TV series).

Anyway the Assistant Pro had, at this most remarkable moment, concluded that there almost certainly was a tune to be played on this particular old fiddle, and he wasn't about to let her British Summer Time faux-pas go to waste.

"Actually love it's quarter to six, not quarter to seven…" smiled Harris as he looked down at this most unexpected grasp on his plums *"…come into the back of the shop, the first lesson is always free and it looks like we've got an hour to do something about that grip"*.

(That, right there, is why this chapter got the *'34'* joke index. I tried to end it with better, but it just wasn't happening. Use discount code 'KAREN' for 10% off the sequel by way of an apology).

No Sunday Carvery at Russet Grange today, we do ours on a Monday. We could call it a "Monday Carvery" of course but then we wouldn't have the sadistic pleasure of people turning up on a Sunday for it.

*Russet Grange Golf Club –
Cambridgeshire's "Hidden Gem" thanks to our
fucking awful #MarketingTeam.*

*The book is out before Christmas,
where you can read about how said Marketing
Team accidentally posted donkey porn on the
club's Facebook account.*

*There are some people out there who
wouldn't know what to do if a wash basin
knocked on their door.*

Let that sink in.

A Tale of Comedy Night Planning

Chapter	Par	Length	Joke Index
20	3	1,537 Words	22

Introducing:
Eric 'The Razor' Wibble (72)
Full Member
Nationality: Hard Bastard Wannabee

*T*here's being a hard man, and there's wanting people to think you're a hard man. These are almost the lyrics from 'Love Action' by 'The Human League' of course, but here we are referring to Eric 'The Razor' Wibble. A man who really, really wishes he'd been part of a crew in 1960's London.

Eric Wibble

Wibble will tell his nickname to anyone who'll listen, dropping a hint of Danny Dyer into his Wiltshire accent in the vain hope they'll assume that he is indeed connected to some of Britain's most wanted. The real reason he's called 'The Razor' though is that he was once asked how his late wife Gill died and his stammered reply was :"G, g, g Gillette herself to death". (Yep, that nickname just for that joke). It's true, his late wife died of obesity just a few days short of her 40th birthday, and a few pounds short of 30 stone.

Wibble claims he "did a twenty stretch" for armed robbery. What he actually did was six weeks for selling dodgy meat from a Ford Transit in Camden market. Some of those who bought the meat spent longer on the toilet that he spent inside.

He's got a few quid too, courtesy of a tasty little compensation payout. You'll read about that over the page and it's all because I wanted to get in the name I thought of for an ambulance-chasing firm of solicitors.

As to golf, well it's all tales of dodgy capers, shooters, bent coppers and the Trowbridge underworld for 18 holes, but Wibble is good company. Just don't ask if he knows Ross Kemp.

And:

Charlotte 'Charlie' Sheen (32)

Full member
Nationality: Anglo/Greek/
Stupid

Charlotte Sheen

Charlotte Sheen is a bit of a livewire. She is currently working as a PA at a law firm but in truth this young lady was employed for her looks rather than having any kind of intellectual abilities. The fact that her "uncle" runs the firm helped more than a little bit. Let us just say that "favours were exchanged".

A TALE OF COMEDY NIGHT PLANNING

Sheen's first job was as a holiday rep in Ibiza, but a love of the booze and an atrocious driving record that included writing two tour operator's minibuses tells its own story. The second of the minibus write-offs made the papers when she reversed off of a sea wall, whilst trying to reverse into a parking space outside a mud-wrestling venue into 30 feet of water, with a number of drunken Brits on board. Each and every one of them survived though a couple of instances of mild brain damage and paralysis ensured little change from a seven-figure compensation payout. (Hmmm, another compensation payout chapter, I really ought to be more imaginative, but on other hand, Harry Potter is just castles, wizards and air hockey).

Upon returning to the UK Sheen moved back in with her parents, and behaved herself for all of six weeks before being caught with a few grammes of cocaine when the police pulled her over for speeding. With her track record she pays more to insure her VW Polo than it cost Volkswagen to design it.

In an attempt to bring some calmer pursuits into her life, Sheen's exasperated father introduced her to golf, and of course, Russet Grange. Against all odds she discovered both a talent and a love for the game. The chances of her and Guy Potton not getting it together at some point are zero, and indeed, our Pro-Shop hero already has a 'nudey pic' she sent him safely stored in his Samsung Galaxy's 'Wank Bank'.

We begin...

Amore unlikely friendship between that of Eric Wibble and Charlotte Sheen would be harder to imagine, but for some unknown reason these two had always hit it off. Sheen admired Wibble for his down to earth honesty, his cockncy banter and, because she was such so gullible, his tales of when he worked as a technical consultant on series six of *'The Bill'*. Wibble on the other hand admired Sheen because she, and I'm quoting him here *"...has a cracking pair"*. (Look up *'lowbrow'* in the dictionary in a few years, you'll find this book listed in the *'literary examples'* sub-section.)

Anyway, the pair often found themselves in the clubhouse or on the course together, partly because both genuinely enjoyed the game, but mainly because neither of them had lives that were in any way tainted by a need to work. Daddy subsidised Sheen and a missing finger from an incident in the bogs at Romford Asda, combined with a firm of ambulance-chasing 'no-win, no-fee' lawyers run by three spotty youths, *'Injury and the Blackheads'*, subsidised Wibble.

Sheen liked a drink, Wibble liked a drink, and during a swift one that lasted four hours following the Betty Minogue (no relation) Mixed Doubles Open, talk turned to the abject failure of the current social committee.

"Fackin' useless, the fackin' lot of 'em". Wibble's carefully considered analysis was certainly worthy of a man who had never, ever, lifted one of his remaining fingers to do anything for the club, and it struck a chord (and a major one

at that) with the young filly sitting opposite, still hoping to find out what Sun Hill police station was really like. (The fact that it didn't actually exist was not something that Sheen considered relevant, or indeed considered at all).

"You're right Reg, that committee hasn't got a clue, who the fuck wants to go to a 1920s night?" remarked a gradually inebriating Sheen, *"The music was crap and there was a war on".* Wibble corrected the historical error but agreed about the music. *"Elvis fackin' Presley and a bit of Bernard Manning, that's what people like. How about you and me organise a bit of a do, show those fackin' twats on the committee how to do the job they're not paid to do?"*

Sheen hadn't heard of Bernard Manning, but she was well aware of *'The King'*, having spent many of her formative years being forced to watch *'Roustabout'*, *'Jailhouse Rock'* and *'The [insert year] Comeback Special'*, whilst her rather eccentric old man tarted around in a sequinned white jumpsuit. She was so well informed in fact that it was her turn to correct Wibble. *"Whatever you say Eric, I'm not doing anything else this year, sounds ideal. One thing though, we can't get Elvis because he's dead."*

Wibble did one of those *'facepalm'* things, but he quickly returned to his default position of staring at Sheen's chest, with the occasional eye contact to maintain a veil of politeness. (Sheen's arse was epic too, and unlike her breasts which couldn't politely be subjected to a constant gaze, it could be enjoyed at will during a round of golf by merely remaining a few paces back).

"Manning's dead too, popped his clogs years ago but there's plenty like him on the circuit. Dick Frenzy is a good mate, still doing the clubs for the fackin' northern monkeys. Then there's Mike 'Honky' Best, I did a five stretch with him in Parkhurst nick, he's funny as fuck". (It should be noted that Wibble's *'five stretch'*, like the *'twenty stretch'* I made up in his bio, was quite the exaggeration too. It ran to five days, but it might as well have been five unicorns as far as Sheen was concerned, she didn't have a clue about the language of the criminal underworld bullshitter).

And so it seemed that two bottles of a very average Pinot Grigio, and six pints of something liquid that barely met the legal definition of lager, had brought about a comedy night consensus between the most unlikely pairing since the *'Megadeath'* mash-up of: *'Bright Eyes'* and *'The Birdie Song'*. Sheen realised that she was in the presence of a man not only connected to the highest levels of disorganised crime, but who was well acquainted with some comedy turns, one of whom would surely be more than happy to bring an assumedly inoffensive act to the Russet Grange clubhouse.

"Let's do this" bounced (literally) Sheen. (Had I thought about it I could have given her a few months in the army cadets and now referred to here as *'General Pinotsheen'*). Pissed but happy she was certain that not only was their planned undermining of the social committee a very fine idea, but that her adopted arch-criminal/father figure was the man who could make it happen.

Wibble stole another loving glance at Sheen's *'Double-Delights'* (Daily Star, March 1987), and then semi-reluctantly allowed his gaze to drift upwards to the bubbly young lady who was clearly very keen to be part of this rebellious pairing, all too eager to deliver a club event that people would actually be prepared to attend, despite the guaranteed absence of both Manning and Presley.

"Go on then darlin', should be a laugh. I'll get in touch with Dick Frenzy, you go and wiggle your bits in front of Hanley, he'll agree to anything that fills the place".

Later that same day, fate intervened. Eight tickets (four of them complimentary) had been sold for the 20's night in the same number of weeks. A terrible result, even by the standards of a social committee of morons. Event cancelled, a Friday night in summer became available, and Dick Frenzy confirmed his availability.

What could possibly go wrong? Well fear not, we shall find out later…

Been doing a bit of Salsa dancing this afternoon. Great fun but now my socks are covered in tomato.

Special birthday celebrations happening at Russet Grange tomorrow.

One of the clubhouse televisions will be 30 years of age.

We've banned conversations about Air Fryers in the clubhouse.

There are only so many times Andy Biggs should have to listen to: "Oh we weren't sure about buying one, everyone says how good they are, but well... will it get used or gather dust like the spiraliser we bought from Argos...?"

Just fuck off.

A Tale of a Seniors' Match

Chapter	Par	Length	Joke Index
21	5	3,434 Words	10

Introducing:

Pete 'Dick' Whittington (60)

Club Handyman
Nationality "Sarf Lanndaannn"

Pete Whittington

*D*ick by name, dick by nature. Pete 'Dick' Whittington is one of those people you know is a twat even before he opens his gob and goes full cockney, desperate to sound like 'Harold Shand' from 'The Long Good Friday'. (Remarkably similar to Eric Wibble from the previous chapter, but you're probably past caring by now).*

Whittington is a West Ham fan, and if he spots you in the shower he'll show you his "Hammers Legends" tattoos, followed by pointing at his anus and proclaiming "Staaaammmford Faaaaacking Bridge".

He claims he was part of football's notorious 'Inter City Firm'. (He wasn't but it doesn't matter). Anyway, as Whittington says: "...back in the glory days, I'd take 'Stan' along for the ride (If you don't know I'm not explaining, Google it if you must), and either beat the fuck out of someone or get the fuck beaten out of me. It was all harmless stuff mind. Panorama, Ten O'Clock News, Elland Road CCTV, I was on the fackin' lot".

Whittington is employed as the club's handyman, and whilst he's not a huge golf fan, playing only five or six times per week, he is currently Seniors' Captain.

He once had to write a letter of apology to a member of staff having asked for "A pint of wifebeater love and one for yourself" before being told that the poor young thing was currently under police protection.

When Jenny McCulloch heard about the wifebeater incident she pinned Whittington to the clubhouse wall with a particularly tight clench of his bollocks, and told him of the joys he could look forward to if such a thing ever happened again. Rumour has it that said bollocks swelled to the size of oranges and it was certainly a number of weeks before he was seen in the showers again.

And also:
Don 'The Don' Cavani (68)
Full Member
Nationality: English/Italian

Don Cavani

Not only did Don Cavani go to Venice once, he drives a shitty little Fiat Punto and does a third rate impression of Joe Pesci. You don't get more Italian than that without running a money laundering operation from a chip shop in Putney (more on that opposite).

*Cavani's Pesci impression is so bad he has to tell
everyone who he's doing in advance, but that didn't
stop him scaring the shit out of Carl Doller at a
particularly drunken comedy night (not the one that
was planned in the previous chapter, obviously).
'The Don' actually brought along a replica pistol
for a performance of that most famous scene from
'Goodfellas'. Doller genuinely shat himself. What are
the chances that this could happen again very soon…?*

*Cavani lives in a trailer park. He's not trash, far
from it, but when you spend every day at a golf
club you really only need somewhere to sleep and
a place to watch 'wildlife' videos. Indeed, Cavani
is actually very wealthy, partly because he sold the
family printing business for around five million quid,
but also because he used to run a money laundering
operation from a chip shop in Putney. Customers
who wanted a little something extra asked for "Cod
and Chips and five grand in used tenners". The
Metropolitan police never worked out the code.*

*As you may have assumed, Cavani is great company,
on the course, in the pub, or in court as a witness for the
defence. He's a poor golfer though, with his only notable
golfing achievement happening at Pontin's Brean Sands
in 1974. 32 shots round the 'Pirate Adventure' golf
including an ace on The Windmill hole.*

*Whatever you do though, don't tell him you think he's
a funny guy. Ever.*

We begin...

Pete Whittington was proud, very proud, to have been elected as Seniors Captain for whatever year this book is set in, and the fact that eight other people were asked and refused point blank to take on this most prestigious of roles did nothing to dampen that pride. Reasons for turning down the role ranged from *"No fucking way"* to *"I'd rather walk down Oxford Street with my knob in a frozen turkey."*

His acceptance speech at the Seniors' AGM one year earlier was certainly a thing to behold, including as it did the phrase *"Any old fackers coming onto our manor looking for a war will facking get one"*. Fine words perhaps in the pubs of Newham in what Whittington describes as *"The good old days."* of the 1980s, but perhaps a little confrontational when most of the *"old fackers"* he was referring to couldn't manage a brace of holes without needing a piss, let alone be involved in any sort of physical combat.

His year as captain was going well, most matches won via a combination of cheating and intimidation, with Don *'The Don'* Cavani as his Vice-Captain sidekick. An obvious choice for Whittington as he had always assumed that his good friend was, shall we say, *"well connected to one or two local firms"*, though in reality nothing could be further from the truth. A fact evidenced by Cavani's horrified expression when, at the same AGM, Whittington announced his right hand man as someone who would *"have your cock pickled if you concede a putt"*.

Anyway, let us leave all the talk of violence behind and move to the present day, where some octogenarian rivals from Leylandii Park Golf Club (known locally as *'LPG'*, ironically as it turns out given the gas explosion of '98) were arriving for a match against our heroes, the Russet Grange Seniors. A team of twelve people turning up in eleven cars. Why two people were car sharing we will never know, but we can assume that someone from their number was serving a driving ban following a typical *'five and drive'* attitude prevalent among a certain demographic.

The previous year's match at LPG had resulted in a 4-2 win for the hosts, and a few of today's visiting team, especially those a little unsteady on their feet, were rather shaken by Whittington's rallying call to his foot soldiers, a call deliberately in hearing aid range of today's opponents: *"NOTHING, we give away NOTHING. We make them putt EVERYTHING, we NEVER look for their ball, no weakness, no regrets, no losers, NO FACKING SURRENDER!"*

Scary words for a visiting team to hear, and even Rob Farnham-Blink, a man made of reasonably stern stuff, felt a little bit of wee appear at a speech that erred on the side of terror rather than serving to inspire his troops.

Cavani, who was considerably more placid, greeting his opposite number with humility:

"Don Cavani, we met last year, looking forward to another good game today and then a few drinks afterwards, chef's done a beef curry with rice, any dietary requirements among your chaps?"

"Hello again. David Mullinder-Best, and yes we did meet at our place, lovely to be back though your captain seems to be rather over enthusiastic".

"He's harmless enough," smiled Cavani, *"...all talk, and between you and me, a bloody awful golfer. Put your best pairing out first with me and him and that's a point in the bag."*

The visiting Vice-Captain smiled, he remembered Cavani, and that he'd put him down as a good guy right away *"And no dietary requirements, we're pensioners, not attention seekers. We eat what's put in front of us, just like your lot I'm sure".* The Don smiled, in a world going progressively insane, where green-haired nutters covered themselves in paint and identified as ironing boards or fridges, he knew his age group were the last of a breed who would say such things.

With no need for pandering confirmed, he gave a thumbs up to the current chef, another chap from an agency, but this time someone who knew which end of a ladle goes into the big pan. The chef gave a *"thank fuck for that"* smile, relieved that he wouldn't have to find a few courgettes and carrots to feed yet another soul whose particular life choices made his job harder than it needed to be.

Anyway, there's a golf match to be played and I honestly can't be bothered to look back over the previous pages of this nonsense to decide who else made up the RGGC Seniors' team that Thursday afternoon. Feel free to do your own research and make your own assumptions, you won't be far wrong, as I think there are only about twelve old duffers among my fictional brethren, and by the time you're reading this half of them would have taken that final one-way coach trip anyway.

You've paid your money for a golf book, so you do deserve the occasional bit of golfing action, so we'll concentrate on a few holes of the first match out. Cavani and Whittington versus two generic golfers from the club where the trees give a skin rash. Let's call them *'Bob Trestle'* and *'Whitlock McNeil'*, a pair who can not only play a bit, but when they think they can get away with it, cheat a bit too. (I already don't like them and I only invented them a minute ago).

"Pig farm stinks as much as it always did then?" A rhetorical and rather untimely question from Bob Trestle, delivered just after he split the fairway with his three wood. His playing partner did the same. Game on.

Whittington turned to Cavani as they strolled down the first hole. *"Any chance you get, wind these bastards up, any time you can bring the foot wedge into play, do it. No facking mercy, none, we win this or their cocks get the pickle treatment."*

Cavani wasn't really one for the foot wedge, or any other kind of gamesmanship, but equally he didn't like to lose and this was his Captain giving instructions. Foot wedge and other foul play it would be.

All square after five holes, though God knows how. Despite assurances to David Mulliner-Best, a coughing fit on the third green from Whittington had helped him halve the hole, and how Cavani didn't get spotted improving his lie by around three feet, having found the rough on the fourth, was anyone's guess.

McNeil wasn't averse to a bit of *'creative'* golfing either. Indeed, he was one of the tragically common type whose motto was *"It's not cheating if you don't get caught"*. The slightly-improved lie, the subtle six inches gained via *'ball marker management'* when putting, or the opening of a fizzy beverage during an opponent's downstroke (golf downstroke, this isn't a smutty chapter). He had the lot in his armoury and he was a master.

Cavani needed a piss. No idea why I mention this, perhaps all the talk of cheating has got a bit tedious, but having paid a visit to the hedge urinal it was clear that he could have used another shake or two, or that he should have worn darker trousers, or both.

"Hope you haven't shat yourself as well." quipped Trestle, taking a cheeky rear view with the sole aim of putting one of his opponents off of his game whilst hitting his tee shot on the seventh. It worked well, eight iron into the pond to the disgust of Whittington.

"For fuck's sake Don, don't let these wankers get to you". Words best spoken with restraint, and in hushed tones out of earshot of opposing golfers, but Whittington didn't do restraint. The atmosphere immediately became quite a bit more tense, and the match swung two holes to the good for the visiting wankers…

I think we can safely assume at this point that the Cavani/ Whittington combo was in a bit of golfing difficulty, and I honestly can't be bothered to describe in detail the ins and outs of the back nine, suffice to say the home team's lead pairing got out-cheated by quite some degree. They had come up against masters of gamesmanship and came up very, very short.

The only positive to be taken from their match, as had been the case over countless years, was that there was no need to play the eighteenth, losing 4&3 well in advance of what the marketing team had described, in the language of bullshit, as *"An iconic conclusion to your round at Russet Grange"*.

Begrudging handshakes were exchanged whilst Whittington *'stared down'* Whitlock McNeil for no apparent reason. There's not much point in trying to psyche out your opponent after you've been soundly beaten, but he did it anyway.

Anyway, you get the idea, the Captain/Vice Captain combo had been outplayed and out-cheated though it has to be said that the other five matches plodded along in a much more cordial manner. (By which I mean *'friendly'*, they weren't drinking squash the whole way round).

Right, let's move to the free wine, fighting talk, actual fights, a curry hotter than the sun and, thankfully, the general consensus when things had settled down from the excessive booze that a 3-3 draw was the right result…

Two tables of six, or one table of twelve? If you've ever run any kind of event where twelve people sit down for dinner this is a question you will have asked yourself. I have done so on many occasions, it's a ballache. Tex Hanley went for the two table option, it meant lots of room for people to be able to get up for a piss every few minutes. Having to wash two tablecloths stained with mango chutney and merlot instead of one was hardly an issue, Cleaver was working the day after, and she'd probably be able to squeeze in the second one in amongst her own piles of ironing that she would surely bring to work.

Talking of wine, Brian Hanley remained extremely proud of the deal he had negotiated with the Seniors' Chairman

(I have no idea who that is, feel free to make up your own *'Wing Commander with chronic eczema'* or whatever). The Seniors would bring their own wine to matches, they would pay £1 corkage per bottle, Hanley wouldn't have to order supplies and the Chairman got points on his Tesco Clubcard.

Had the Club's Financial Director known about this arrangement he might have questioned the wisdom of throwing away ten quid profit per bottle, but as it was he just assumed that the thirty five quid bar take at a typical Seniors match merely reflected the thriftiness of this particular demographic, despite their near universally enjoyed gold-plated final salary pensions and income from a few rental properties to boot.

As the generic plonk flowed freely the tense post-match atmosphere abated somewhat. Talk turned to typical topics such as how difficult is was to find a decent gardener to work for minimum wage, why racism in cricket should be seen as *"just a bit of fun"* and how if young people gave up avocado on toast they could afford a £300,000 mortgage on an ex-Council flat with dry rot.

"Time to be seated Y'all". Hanley had donned his cowboy hat to announce dinner. It was a little moment that he looked forward to during every seniors match. The home players shook their heads in embarrassment and the visitors gave *"What the actual fuck?"* looks to each other as they spent almost ten minutes deciding who would sit where. You might think that given the use of circular tables such things wouldn't matter, but premium spots offering close proximity to the toilets and fire exits were always in high demand.

Seating people at Russet Grange Seniors matches under Whittington's tenure was as complex as it had always been, as he had long since given up making the case for a home table and an away table. He knew he was in a minority of one when it came to regarding an opposing team in a friendly golf match as mortal enemies.

Beef Curry and Basmati Rice with Popadum and Mango Chutney, followed by Jam Roly Poly and Custard. What could possibly go wrong?

"Holy fucking fuck". The first to dig in was a visiting golfer, not normally one to swear, but the Beef Madras hit him like a train on one of the rare days when the drivers weren't on strike. Simultaneous mouthfuls provoked similar reactions, with only Whittington bucking the chilli-led trend. *"Tasty, good kick to it"* he commented, fighting pack the tears of intense digestive pain. (Tummy, not the biscuits).

The budget Merlot did little to quell the fires burning within this room of ageing gentlemen, and for almost all just one mouthful proved to be more than they could possibly cope with. Cavani summoned the agency chef, keen to find out why he had delivered such a gastric challenge to those least up to the task.

Since it seemed that nobody was going into cardiac arrest (just as well as the defibrillator was stolen months ago), he decided that his Joe Pesci party piece was in order, and as he rose to his feet he gave a brief knowing smile to eleven other diners, diners who had witnessed this very same act at LPG a year ago to the day. Straight face at the ready,

Italian accent primed, Cavani, all five feet five inches of him, looked into the eyes of a chef towering above:

"Is this a joke? Do you think this is funny? You think this is how to feed my friends do you? These people are my family, is this how you treat family? Is it?"

The chef was somewhat confused. Why a short bloke with mango chutney on his tie was speaking in a Jamaican accent, and in such an aggressive way, made no sense.

Whittington however wanted a piece of the limelight, bringing an appalling gangster pastiche, a *'Nowhere-De-Nearo'* if you will, to the performance. (That's terrible, it really is. I am so very sorry).

"My friend asked you a facking question, don't you facking mug him off. What's the faaacking idea....?" (I continue to avoid the *'C-bomb'*, it's a horrible word and has no place here, but feel free to imagine it for authenticity. I'm fairly sure that's what Whittington would have said).

Smirks were being hidden around the room, the chef was now even more confused, Cavani wasn't letting up:

"My friend asked you a question, don't you fuck with him, or I'll bust your balls right here. Curry, who the fuck serves a bum-burner curry to friends who struggle with parsnip soup?"

"Well he asked me to". The chef, with a near total lack of comprehension at this farcical scene, pointed at Pete Whittington. *"Looks it's on WhatsApp, here you go: 'Beef Madras, no veggie crap, make it faaaaacking hot' Cheers, Pete".*

Cavani could keep up the act no longer, bursting into laughter along with almost everyone else in the room, everyone except Whittington who was, by his own admission, *"Bang to rights, done up like a facking kipper"*.

But dinner progressed, the rice and sundries, along with complimentary crisps and a few lukewarm, yet somehow overcooked pasties satisfied the collective hunger, and the Jam Roly Poly went down a treat.

Two dozen empty wine bottles were testament to what turned out to be a jolly evening, and Handley was more than pleased with the £24 quid corkage handed over, accompanied by an extra quid for his trouble.

All in all it had been a pleasant day of sport given the pre-match tension that Whittington was in no small part responsible for, and with over a gallon of blisteringly hot Beef Madras sat festering in the kitchen, tomorrow's daily special, much to the chef's abject joy, was ready to go.

The amount of hilarious tweets I delete because someone somewhere might be offended is astonishing. It wasn't like this back in '87.

Mind you, they didn't have Twitter then.

We've got World Cup specials starting next week, pie and a pint for a fiver during England games.

If the national team get through to the quarter finals then the deal gets better. Pie and a pint and a Ferrari for a fiver.

Reports coming in of a Hedge Porn find next to the 16th tee.

It's days like these that our Greenkeepers live for.

A Tale of Cake and the Ladies' AGM

Chapter	Par	Length	Joke Index
22	4	1,783 words	32

Introducing:
Mary Pewter (51)
Full Member
Nationality: English

Mary Pewter

*T*he typical convent school girl turned bad, though she was never really very good. Pewter wasted most of her years in education being completely wasted, with a peak performance on her 16th birthday resulting in a need to have her stomach pumped. Some say Mary Pewter was drinking before she could walk. (Yes, another pisshead, sorry).*

Pewter is a functioning alcoholic and also an astonishingly good golfer for someone who regards vodka as a food group. She needs to play before 11:00am though or standing up becomes a problem. This became all too clear at the 2014 ladies club championship where a morning round of 63 shots was followed by a lunch of another half dozen. She managed to complete the first five holes of the afternoon round before falling semi-conscious into a ditch.

Pewter doesn't drive because she's hardly ever below the legal limit, and the brand new car that she treated herself to for her 40th birthday has barely moved from her garage. This is why a tee shot that achieves no real distance is known locally as a 'Pewter's Mini'.

Also introducing:
Polly Palmer (80)
Full Member
Nationality: English

Polly Palmer

*P*olly Palmer is one of those odious old bags who thinks that if she chucks enough make-up on she will look Demi Moore. The reality is that she just ends up looking like a sad old woman covered in too much make-up trying to look like what Demi Moore won't look like when she turns 80.*

You might think that with her advancing years she would have one of those typical "happy go lucky" attitudes that many pensioners possess because every day is a bonus. Far from it, she sees every day as one nearer the big box in the ground (or the 'toasty' alternative) and she makes sure that everyone knows it.

When she's pissed up, often by mid-morning, she lightens up a notch, though still remaining many fathoms from anything resembling happiness. Sadly though, and in a bitter twist of reality, the alcohol makes her think she's attractive to men with a series of all-too-embarrassing flirtations being the all-too-predictable result of eight too many gins.

Thom Hankey, in a rare moment of mirth, said "she's probably got a fanny like an Ethiopean's rucksack".

On the course she's dreadful company, with her playing partners having to endure a mixture of racial slurs and sexual innuendo from the first tee to the 18th green.

Palmer drives a Subaru Legacy estate that smells of wet Labradors and piss. Said vehicle is just coming up to reaching 30 years of age and to complete the 'big birthday' thing, the engine oil is about to turn 20.

We begin...

Let the record show that this was the last chapter I wrote for *'Tales from Russet Grange'*, but it was never my intention for it to conclude the book. I doubt it will be a barrel of laughs (and to be honest I haven't set the bar very high) so you're probably reading this one buried in the middle of the book. (Stop Press - you are).

Also, when it comes to Ladies' AGMs, my experience (none, but it doesn't matter) is that the truth is often stranger than fiction, but we'll give it a go and see what we come up with. I'll work on the assumptions of cake and a complete inability to make any kind of decisions, that should put me in good stead…

It had fallen to Ellie Carter to prepare the clubhouse for today's big meeting, and she had really gone to town. Jugs of water (some matching) had been put out, the least-stained tablecloths carefully selected and laid, name badges made for the top-table dignitaries and coffee cups neatly arranged, each with a solitary *'Elizabeth Shaw'* mint nestling daintily in its saucer. (Carter had been told, on pain of death, not to leave out the box of mints, because some of the ladies, we'll say those who are not too familiar with Park Run, would take advantage of bonus confectionery like a buzzard would take advantage of a dead or dying sheep).

The ladies' section numbers around 90, all of whom were invited to the most prestigious of events, and had it not coincided with the final of *'Strictly'*, more than fifteen might have attended. In fairness, eighteen had turned up but Carter was stupid enough to welcome each and every one of them with *"... not watching the Strictly final then?"*, resulting in three sneaking away on the basis of the newly acquired televisual knowledge, hoping they hadn't been spotted. (It would have been four, but Debbie Watts felt she should stay, given that she was about to be elected as the new Ladies' Captain).

I mentioned cakes, and yes, there were lots of cakes. Had these ladies spent as much time practising golf as they did making cakes there would be a few single figure handicappers and at least one County Champion among them. Never in the field of baking had so much Tupperware been brought by so many to feed so few.

Right, I've done the bit about cakes (I promised the wife I would). Karen Young, representing the Russet Grange Golf Club Board of Directors and the local branch of the AA, (not the breakdown people or the airline), opened what were to be fairly short proceedings.

"I'd like to welcome you all to the Ladies' AGM, it's good to see so many of you here tonight, and to conduct the important business of electing our new Ladies' Captain, signing off on the work of fiction that is our accounts…" (Hobson was initially horrified but she quickly realised that Young was totally bollocksed) *"…and then dealing with any other business, such as who the fuck thought it was a good idea to do this tonight, of all nights."*

Polly Palmer rose briskly to her feet (quite an impressive accomplishment for someone of her age considering the weight of make-up she was wearing), to formally enquire about Karen Young's state of lubrication:

"Given the low attendance this evening, could I ask our guest from the Board of Directors if, when she said 'so many of you here tonight' she was being ironic, or whether she's been enjoying a tipple or two this afternoon and is therefore seeing around 45 people?"

"Yeah, sorry Pollyfiller" (ouch), *"I'm a bit pissed, well fucking spotted. Don't worry though, I've done my bit".* Young wobbled like a drunk trifle, tried to grab one of three jugs of water (two virtual, one genuine), missed by a foot or more and then did a pretty hefty belch. *"Over to you Mandy, tell us how much money we've got, then we'll vote in Bambi as Captain, eat all of the cake, have a few drinks and we can all fuck off home to catch the results".*

Hobson responded, with alarming clarity. *"You should have all seen the figures, we've got just under a thousand pounds in our bank account, a little bit less than last year. Our biggest expense was moving and relabelling the portaloos, and then moving them again and making more new signs"*. (We'll read about this later. I can't be bothered to move that chapter to before this one. Jeffrey Archer would have done, but he's a proper author, I'm crap at this). *"Also, we had to pay for quite a lot of carpet cleaning in our changing rooms after the Christmas party"*. Nobody really gave a toss about the finances, other than Hobson, who had waited all year for her big moment. *"Are there any questions?"*

Mary Pewter decided to have her say. (I have to confess at this moment that I hadn't realised just how many of these characters were total pissheads, but hey, no great story, or indeed any story, ever started with a vegan Sausage Roll).

"I'm not one for swearing" (she is) *"But who the fuck thought it was a good idea to do that stupid unisex thing with the toilets?"* Some bloke who thinks he knows about golf clubs will probably write a book about the subject one day and include that shameful incident. (See what I did there? Possibly my cleverest moment, that's Wetherspoons' Prosecco for you).

Margot Young felt the need to respond, but standing up made her feel all wobbly so she sat down again. Then she fell onto the floor, quite a feat from a perfectly stable chair, but that's the ladies' AGM in a nutshell.

Captain-elect Watts had felt it was time that she had her say: *"I don't want to name names but it was Rose Lubworth who did the thing with the bog names, she's not here tonight. Funny that".* Her comment raised more than a little bit of laughter, it has to be said.

Carol Brittan, having been Ladies' Captain for three years, because, as she admitted to Andy Biggs in yet another shoulder-crying incident: *"The only ones who could do the job refuse to do it, and those who would do the job couldn't find something cock-shaped in a dildo shop"*, addressed the meeting:

"I'll make this quick before she changes her mind, Debbie Watts was proposed to be my Vice Captain at last year's AGM, she's a great girl, a total piece of ass, I'd do her and I'm not even a lesbeen. If you lot don't vote her in as the new Ladies Captain I'm going to set light to the building". Brittan was serious. *"Ladies, a show of hands please, all of those in favour…"*

You might assume at this point that the assembled ladies would have given unanimous support to Debbie Watts, the natural successor to Brittan, but don't be so hasty. Despite vegan Battenbergs, vegetarian Swiss rolls and gluten-free Victoria sponges being rejected, (*"woke crap"* as Polly Palmer put it), you can't raise your hand when engaged in a real-world and cake-based game of *'Hungry Hippos'*.

Post-cake Debbie Watts was however elected to serve as Ladies' Captain for the coming year (potentially for the next decade judging on the current state of play) but only by three votes to none. She wasn't allowed to vote for herself, but Brittan, Young and Hobson had given their endorsement and that was good enough.

"Any other business?" asked Carol Brittan, but her words fell on deaf ears. Eighteen ladies had turned up, fifteen had stayed, the business of the evening was done (as was a pile of cake the size of a small family car) and, to polite applause, she was finally relieved of her duty.

"Time for a coffee…" she smiled as the pressure of office was finally lifted, *"and then we'll get that one with the big tits to tell us where she hid all of the mints."*

> *It was on this day in 1964 that we bought our fake Christmas tree.*
>
> *In those early years Ron "Twinkle' Pebbles would decorate it under the guidance of the ladies' committee, followed by a nice glass of sherry.*
>
> *Simpler times that ended in '68 when Ron got done for armed robbery.*

Introducing:
Carl 'Piss' Doller (22)
Intermediate Member
Nationality: Lad

Carl Doller

*Y*ou know when
some twat drives
a tricked-up
*Vauxhall Corsa up and
down the local High Street
for no reason other than to
annoy people? That's Carl
'Piss' Doller driving, or someone like him.*

*He's the lad with the lifetime subscription to 'Max
Power' magazine and a bedroom wall adorned with
a 'Cannonball Run' poster, complete with a fake Burt
Reynolds signature and suspicious stains around the
'Farah Fawcett-Majors in silk jump suit' section.*

*Doller once took a week off from his job as a
bricklayer's mate to clean his car and then take it to the
Nurburgring. The cleaning went well, the trip ended
within two miles of his home when he rear-ended a
Jewsons lorry at a mini-roundabout.*

*He earned his charming nickname "Piss" because he has
a bladder the size of a BabyBel cheese, rarely managing
to play more than three holes without needing to empty
it. God knows how this plays out when he's a senior.*

Despite his car obsession and urinary tract issues, he's not a bad lad, and he's certainly a good golfer when he's not in a nearby hedge with his cock innocently in hand.

Doller was Club Champion in 2014, narrowly missing the course record with a second round 64. It might have been a 62 but a touch of 'disco dribble' on the 8th and a piss-break on the tricky 17th, both of which interrupted his concentration and cost him two shots.

And also:

Adam 'The Hat' Bobble (42)
Full Member
Nationality: Geordie

Adam Bobble

*D*espite his nickname, the only time that Adam "The Hat" Bobble wears any kind of headgear is when he's working on a building site, and as a Geordie he's not particularly keen on wearing long trousers either. Or shirts for that matter.

'The Hat' is a third generation bricklayer and it was this trade that brought him down south to find his fortune. Work had dried up on Tyneside, partly because of a downturn in construction but mainly because his Dad was involved in organised crime. Known as

A TALE OF A SOCIAL MEDIA "FAUX PAS"

'The Hodfather', Bobble Senior made a lot of enemies, and Bobble Junior had no desire to become part of the A186 flyover.

Bobble likes the ladies, but he also likes the blokes too. He's openly bisexual, which nobody has a problem with, though Doris Lynn remains blissfully confused about.

Golf-wise, our boy is a solid single-figure player, and he's great company out on the course, possessing the Geordie wit that others (you know who) can only dream about. He's a prankster too, achieving legendary status by sneaking a live conger eel into Liam Flange's golf bag at the club 2016 championships.

We begin...

Firstly, I'm not expecting this bilge to appeal to the *'Wuthering Heights'*, crowd, so you might need to know that *'Faux Pas'* is French for *'Fuck Up'*.

Steve Simpson was far too busy to have anything to do with social media, but even if he had found himself with hours to spare, the last way he would have filled those hours would have been by telling people he would never meet, but knew he hated, that the *'Pie of the Day'* was Chicken and Vegetable or to post photos from one of those tragic *'it's all about me"* gender reveal things that some low-rent member had sent in just minutes ago.

However, his fellow office *'worker'* Tanya Maxwell was anything but busy. (I think we've already established that she regards her salary as nothing more than an attendance fee), so she spent most days honing her social media skills.

To the casual observer she would therefore have been the obvious choice to take on the responsibilities of Tweeting, Facebooking and Instagramming, but Simpson knew that asking her to be responsible for this particular marketing task would have resulted in either:

a: refusal as it wasn't in her job description,
b: grudging agreement if the work involved substantial salary hike or,
c: agreement followed by the instant dropping of one of the other regular tasks that she didn't do, such as answering the phone.

None of these options appealed to Simpson. He did however recognise that every time one of his members popped their clogs (hopefully with a few hundred quid still on their bar account), a new one was required, and that meant marketing the shithole that was Russet Grange Golf Club by modern methods.

Thus, in the late Autumn of 2018, almost two years since Russet Grange had launched its woefully inadequate website (something for the sequel), an item was added to the agenda for the upcoming board meeting. *"Social Media Guru Urgently Needed"*.

Simpson always attended Board meetings, he recognised that his £50k salary for running the place came with a modicum (look it up) of responsibility, and he knew that by timing his arrival to perfection he wouldn't need to buy a drink all evening.

"Item four, Social Media". Farnham-Blink spoke, but couldn't have been less interested. As far as he was

concerned new members were, as he had once mentioned rather too loudly to Haydn Duke, *"...a pain in the fucking arse"*. Blink's opinion was that the club should be desirable enough that people should have to apply to join, then be interviewed and subsequently black-balled if they didn't meet certain standards. (Public school education, 25 years as an officer in the armed services or another role of equal stature, plus absolutely shit loads of cash). Furthermore he was of the opinion that *"chucking another few hundred on fees"* would not only *"keep out the wrong sorts"*, but cover the financial losses that those *"wrong sorts"* would otherwise have alleviated.

"I think Alan Bobble does this kind of thing for a living..." Arthur Painter, who at least got half of the lad's name correct, couldn't have been more mistaken, *"...let's give him the job for a few pints and a parking space"*.

The assembled minds all agreed, none of them really gave a toss, and thus Simpson agreed to summon the *'bricklayer-come-social-media-guru-in-waiting'* to his office.

As luck would have it, Bobble had a knockout match scheduled for the next morning against Carl Doller. The two happened to be friends, both being in the building trade, and the match promised to be a good tempered affair. It was indeed, and as hands were shaken on the 16th green, with Bobble winning 3&2, a text message from the club office was greeted with amusement.

"Marge Simpson thinks I'm a Facebook expert, now what that's about?" enquired Bobble. *"Not a clue, maybe Arthur Painter mentioned your name given the stuff you send him"* replied

TALES FROM RUSSET GRANGE

Doller with a well-practiced vacant expression. (We met Painter a few chapters/visits to the toilet ago. You probably remember he's a dirty old bastard). As it turns out, Doller was bang on. Despite Painter's age, and his reputation for being as boring as his wife, he maintained a keen interest in the kind of videos that Bobble shared with him in return for crate after crate of contraband Slovakian vodka. In his eyes, Doller was a technical genius worthy of recommendation.

Bobble duly answered his summoning to the office, and almost put his big Geordie foot in it straight away: *"How can I help Mar…. Steve?"* asked Bobble in pure Geordie, flanked by his playing partner and supporting witness.

"I heard you know about this social media bollocks, can you do a bit for the club in return for a good few quid behind the bar?" Simpson didn't play his entire hand in one go.

"Well, I'm kinda busy like…" replied Bobble (hopefully you're doing a *'Boys from the Blackstuff'* accent here, or for you youngsters, Sarah Millican or maybe Cheryl from *'Girls Aloud'*), *"…but I might be able to spare a bit of time. I cannae' promise anything though"*. Bobble knew he had the upper hand and Doller raised the stakes. *"He's fucking brilliant at it, got my sister loads of new clients on Facebook and my mate Dave can't keep up with demand."* Doller conveniently forgot to admit that his sister was, to put it politely, selling services of a personal nature, and that his mate Dave, to put it equally politely, was selling Class A drugs whilst doing his shift at the local tip (I won't glorify it by calling it a *'recycling centre'* because it really is a tip).

~ 208 ~

"We'll give you a parking space with your name on it too". Simpson's sweetener was surely going to close the deal. *"Next to Farnham-Blink?"* haggled Bobble. *"Yep"* Simpson nodded. *"Deal"* smiled Bobble.

"Deal indeed." Simpson was just looking forward to getting the two wasters out of his office. *"If Doller says you know what you're doing that's good enough for me, very pleased to do business with you"*. Simpson managed to contain his irony far better than Doller contained his need for yet another urination break, and thus highly secure login information to the club's various accounts was shared. (username: *'russet'* password: *'grange'*).

Bobble and Doller wandered to the bar, a celebration was due given that what amounted to no more than ten minutes work each week was resulting in a whole load of bar credit and a parking space alongside the elite of the club.

A pint became two, and two became three, and three became four. (Inverse *'Spice Girls'* right there). As midday approached neither of our two *'salts of the earth'* felt like there was any point in going back to work that day. Yet again we know what's about to happen, but we shall tell it anyway…

Bobble's phone gave a tell-tale *'ping'*, a notification from his favourite vodka-toting senior, with a message that read: *"Got anything new for me mate?"*. Painter was as predictable as he was insatiable, and Bobble showed his phone to his friend. *"Dirty old bugger, his Mrs must have gone shopping"*. Doller smiled *"Send him that video with the donkey, the nosebag of carrots, the two fat birds and the traffic cone, he'll fucking love that"*.

Oops. It only took one little accidental tap, one little share with one thousand people, rather than one little message to a perverted octogenarian, but right at that moment, a 30 second clip of an act that many would consider physically impossible found its way to half of the members at Russet Grange. It also reached approximately thirty professional golfers, three food suppliers, fifty potential members, a couple of national sporting associations and finally, to little old Arthur Painter who, it has to be said, instantly realised that he was not the only recipient of this particular piece of *'specialist'* entertainment.

It does not take a great deal of imagination to have a reasonable idea of the fallout from *'Donkeygate'*. Bobble was left looking for a new golf club, there was to be no parking space for him at Russet Grange.

Doller resigned as he felt partly to blame and Steve Simpson was lucky to keep his job. The only real winner was from this sorry tale of misplaced trust and technical incompetence was Tanya Maxwell, who was given a salary bump of a couple of thousand quid to chuck an ill-worded content onto the club's social media account. Her maiden post on Facebook, on behalf of RGGC said it all:

'Membreship's now availabel, call the Russett Grang Pro-shop for fuhrer infromation.'

A Tale of Sky Sports

Chapter	Par	Length	Joke Index
24	4	1,923 Words	13

Introducing:
Thom 'Silent W' Hankey (40)
Full Member
Nationality: Cockney

Thom Hankey

*H*ankey is the sort
of person who
people take one
look at, think "twat", and
are spot on. Despite being
born in Lincolnshire, and
just like Pete Whittington,
and Eric Wibble, he talks
like he grew up within the
sound of Walthamstow dog track. When he shakes hands
with people he does it "biker style" which often confuses
anyone he happens to be playing golf with, and when
those people happen to be senior golfers they invariably
assume there's something wrong with him.

Hankey sees himself as a bit of a 'ladies' man', though
the ladies see him as a bit of a prick. It's possible that
back in '86 the fillies he encountered whilst mending
washing machines might have responded favourably to
an "Awight' darlin" and a tattoo of a Cherokee warrior,
but these days not so much. Pam Cleaver once pointed
out that "The "h" in his first name is silent, just like the
"W" in his surname.

When he's not ripping off people for spare parts that Zanussi's finest don't need he loves ragging his Impreza down his local High Street, to the sounds of Acid House, leaving shoppers in no doubt about that silent 'W'.

In addition to his culturally inappropriate tattoo, Hankey also sports one on his left calf of a 'Fast and Furious' logo, accompanied by the words: "Dan Walker - RIP". Since this particular bit of ink came to adorn said leg, Hankey has been made aware that Dan Walker is a TV sports presenter, and that it was in fact Paul Walker who starred in the highbrow movie franchise. Blame for this hilarious error is laid squarely at the feet of a Spanish tattooist who wrote precisely what he was asked to by our pseudo-cockney moron.

And also:
Jacqui Fletcher (65)
Full Member
Nationality: English

Jacqui Fletcher

*F*letcher fancies herself a sports guru because she spent two summers teaching netball as a foreign sport in Japan, and then when back in the UK she dated a guy who claimed he was an F1 driver. Turned out he drove for 'F1 Trucking' of Hartlepool and she has frankly never *lived it down. Some of the less kind club members have a cheeky nickname for her, no need to repeat it here, though one of the words is 'trucker'.*

She's a bloody good club member though, always the first to volunteer when help is needed and following a very generous donation to club funds from a family inheritance, the spikes bar became the 'Fletcher Suite'.

Fletcher is not the sharpest tool in the box it has to be said, and she became one of the few people in history to score just three points on Ken Bruce's "Popmaster" quiz. She is however an animal-loving vegetarian, an environmentalist, and a lifelong member of Greenpeace. She rather tore up the textbook image though when she treated herself to a brand new Jaguar and ate sperm whale steak in a Reykjavik cocktail bar.

Now that Jacqui Fletcher has entered the latter stages of her life she's decided that she's a lesbian.

We begin...

There are only two schools of thought when it comes down to the *'prickly'* subject of paying for sports to be legitimately shown on a big TV in any golf club you care to mention. School of thought one is: *"Why the fuck should I pay for other people to watch Sky Sports, nine fucking grand, fuck off, that could be spent on the course"*. School two takes the contrary position: *"Money well spent, get a few in to watch the footy and golf and it pays for itself in bar sales"*.

Jacqui (not *Jacky* because *"I'm not from a Council estate"* or *Jakki* because *"I'm not a porn star"*) Fletcher was a pupil at school two and she really loved to position herself as the authority on all things of a sporting nature. So when Steve Simpson categorically ruled out a subscription to Sky Sports and BT Sports (and the various competitors who might be able to offer ladies' darts on a Tuesday night and horse racing from Lithuania), Fletcher was not a happy bunny.

Indeed, at her next visit to Russet Grange she made a point of wearing a suitably revealing top, a pair of those *"trying too hard"* shiny trousers, and casually popping in to see Simpson. The ensuing conversation was disappointingly short-lived.

"Steve my love, is there no really way we can have Sky Sports? It doesn't cost much in the great scheme of things, plus loads of people would watch footy and spend money at the bar."

"Jacqui, it's nine fucking grand and that doesn't even include any of the golf. The clubhouse roof leaks, our newest mower is thirty years old, the deep fat fryer is fucked and I've just spent a shit load of money on agency chefs because the last bloke left two members shitting themselves whilst simultaneously puking to an Olympic standard. Of all the things I could spend nine grand on, money that we haven't got by the way, Sky Sports is bottom of a fucking long list".

Fletcher knew that she had lost this little piece of verbal jousting, but was not prepared to give up. She had a plan, and she knew a man (who you'll have already read about just a couple of pages back, and who we all agree is a bit of a twat), but that particular personality trait was no barrier to what she had in mind.

Thom Hankey's phone pinged. (Well I say *'pinged'*, but he had actually set his notification sound to be a recording of a particularly enthusiastic bimbette in the throes of as much joy as is possible in the back of a Ford Focus in a KFC car park). A message from Jacqui Fletcher no less. (They had played in a mixed-knockout competition a decade ago and had shared phone numbers. Fletcher because she might need a playing partner again one day, and Hankey because he knew that one day he'd be pissed up enough to want to shag her).

"When are u at club nxt". Hankey was mildly intrigued and replied, leaving streaks of fat from last night's doner kebab all over his brand new iPhone, a device that was surely headed for *'Cash Converters'* as soon as a newer and shinier version was launched.

"Ths aftnoon"

"See u there"

"Hmmm.." thought Hankey, *"...what the fuck does she want?"*

And thus a liaison took place in the Russet Grange clubhouse just a few hours later. A liaison that a decade ago might have resulted in Hankey chucking five pints down his tattooed gullet and trying his luck, but these days Fletcher was not only showing her age, but having decided that she was a *'donut bumper'*, really wasn't his type.

"Thom..." (and she pronounced the 'th' as she was stupid), *"the Board don't want to pay for Sky Sports. I hear you might be able to sort something that is perhaps a little less legal and massively more affordable".* Fletcher hadn't minced her words.

She was convinced that bar sales would boom if a clubhouse with very little else to offer could show sports from around the globe on a twenty year old plasma TV which weighed over 300 pounds and sucked vast amounts of power from the national grid. *"Yeah, forty quid for a stick that's got the lot. Footy, golf, latest movies, filth. You name it, it's on there".*

Fletcher was chuffed, an opportunity had arisen to not only allow for her to letch over some women's golf, but she'd be able to prove Simpson wrong and win her little battle.

Cash changed hands and that following Wednesday Hankey delivered the merchandise in question to Fletcher. One dodgy device and ten minutes later, Wednesday Night Football was up and running on the big telly, with almost six people in the clubhouse giving it near-zero attention.

The following Saturday however was a different matter, and when the Gusset Rangers dragged themselves into the clubhouse, four at a time, all as pissed as we had come to expect, they were very excited to be able to watch some scantily clad young ladies as Penn State took on Michigan at beach volleyball. (During said showing both *'Cock Out Dave'* and *'Dildo Baggins'* could barely contain their arousal, having both chosen to wear shorts to prove their manhood/ idiocy during a particularly cold October day).

Beer flowed, more beer flowed, more sports appeared and when the women's cage fighting came on *'Pasty Fucker'* simply couldn't contain himself *"She's grabbing her tits! She's grabbing her tits!... she's grabbing her fanny as well! This is fucking brilliant!"*

It really turned into quite the evening of sport and drinking. Hankey was not present but he heard from Jacqui Fletcher soon enough. *"Good job mate, forty quid well spent, clubhouse was packed, Simpson won't be able to say no once he sees the bar sales".*

And thus it came to pass, that on the following Wednesday morning, Jacqui Fletcher put on her smug face and waltzed into Steve Simpson's office. She was primed and ready to put her case, backed by the sales figures from Saturday evening which, she assumed, would have been more than double the normal amount when the Gusset Rangers were playing.

"Jacqui, I'm glad you're here. Take a look at this letter I received yesterday. It's from the trading standards office. As I understand things, and do correct me if you feel the need to do so, you and Mr Hankey have conspired to drop the club, how shall I put it…? Right in the fucking shit. Did you honestly think that when Sky want nine grand for their sports package it would be OK to give Hankey forty quid cash and hope they didn't find out about that prick and his magic fucking box?"

Fletcher's fake bemusement lasted around five seconds as Simpson continued his accusations. Sadly for her those accusations were based on cold hard evidence in the form of the club's CCTV and what he described as *"technical but presumably fucking accurate details about the precise location of Hankey's dodgy device, what it was used for and when."* Fletcher had to agree that the information presented to Simpson on Sky TV headed notepaper was pretty damning.

"In short Jacqui, the minimum fine for your little caper is ten thousand fucking pounds, and you know what, that means we can't mend the roof, lease a new mower, or replace the fucking deep fat fryer. What the actual fuck were you thinking of?"

Fletcher's darkest day was upon her, and in her heart of hearts she knew that she'd have to cough up at least some of the fine, a fine which, she hoped, would be partly funded by a refund from Hankey. She pulled out her phone and fired-up What's App.

Twenty miles away Hankey was parked up outside a builders' merchants, waiting to meet up with a bloke who had a few impressive looking but ultimately lethal Chinese *'CutGood Treematic'* chainsaws for sale.

A message from Jacqui Fletcher popped up on his phone, accompanied by the groaning sounds of finger-lickin' joy from the back of Ford's finest. *"We need to talk…"* Hankey smiled, he knew the score, his manly charm had obviously had an effect on a lady who, on reflection, was perhaps not too old for him, or as gay as she thought, and anyway it was about time he had a new ringtone…

> *Our new vegan menu launches*
> *at Russet Grange tomorrow.*
>
> *Aboard an Ariane 5 rocket.*

A Tale of Mowers and Moaners

Chapter	Par	Length	Joke Index
25	3	1,448 Words	23

Introducing:
Freddie West (33)
Greenkeeper
Nationality: English

Freddie West

*D*on't confuse Greenkeeper Freddie West with the mass murderer of the same name. Our hero has never killed anyone, though that's not to say that, rather worryingly, he hasn't given it some thought..

"If that had been me I'd have buried them under the 7th fairway, hardly anyone ever goes there" he quips with a half smile whilst caressing his favourite chainsaw. People do wonder though, and whilst his vacant stare is more likely to be a product of leaving school at 11 years of age, he does have the look of a many who is just two or three pints of rough cider away from a killing spree.

Despite spending almost all of his working life outdoors, West has the complexion of pancake mix. This, coupled with the fact he looks eternally knackered, gives him the appearance of a middle-aged teenager who has spent ten years sat in his room wanking between games of 'Call of Duty' whilst being sustained by Deliveroo.

West has a girlfriend named Freya. She loves him to bits "He's not like that other one" she says with a slight hint of doubt in her voice. At 22 stones there are some who suspect Freddie "likes them big". Whatever you do though, don't tell Freddie that members refer to her as "Deep Fat Freya". (Yep, all those words for that 'joke').

And:
Alex 'The Taxi' Barnes (50)
Greenkeeper
Nationality: Jersey, just like
the potatoes

Alex Barnes

"An empty taxi turned up and Alex Barnes got out". A twist on an old adage applied to various dullards throughout the years and Barnes is as dull as they come. Once he's told you that "he cuts fairways as well as greens", and "you wouldn't believe how much these mowers cost" you have heard his entire conversational repertoire.

Because he is about as interesting as skirting board, making up stories about him has become somewhat of a game at Russet Grange, with "John Barnes is his half brother" and "He bought his Citroen Saxo from Bonnie Tyler's next door neighbour" being popular falsehoods.

Early mornings mean early to bed, so Barnes isn't one for pubs and clubbing, though he does play darts on a Thursday as he gets Fridays off. Like all dart players he once took on Eric 'The Crafty Cockney' Bristow in an exhibition match, but unlike most, he won a leg as Bristow fell asleep.

When Barnes is doing his job he listens to language courses on his mobile phone, a useful skill which allows him to tell the natives of Spain, Germany and Devon that he cuts fairways as well as greens...

Barnes has been married twice. His first wife drowned in a Basildon lido, his second wife continues to try and drown herself in boxes of Cabernet Sauvignon.

We begin...

"*Look after your Greenkeepers and your Greenkeepers will look after you*". This is probably an expression that someone once said at a golf club in a fit of pseudo-intellectuality, maybe trying to impress a club Chairman during an interview for the role of '*Temporary Part Time Assistant Marketing Team Leader*'. Whether it has ever been said I have no idea, but what I do know is that it's complete and utter bollocks.

Looking after Greenkeepers is simple. Pay them a fuck load of money for what is effectively mowing a big lawn, mowing a few smaller lawns a bit more, and then giving an understanding nod when they want another £50k in their budget "*to deal with plugworm carcasses*" or a "*serious infestation of Bavarian crudge weed*".

You don't question Greenkeepers, you just let them get on with it, and when they go for lunch at 7:00am because they got up the day before yesterday, so that you can play six temporary greens due to over two millimetres of rain last month you will be grateful.

John 'Conrad (we met him earlier) knew this, but yet with a few cans on board (because it was his birthday), he took the metaphorical path of most resistance along the seventeenth fairway, slurring a perfectly polite but ultimately ill-advised enquiry to Alex Barnes, an enquiry that despite being a bit *'Stella wobbly'* he regretted the instant he made it.

"Is it ever the right amount of rain mate?" Those who have seen *'Casino'* could perhaps visualise the *"Is this your pen?"* scene. That didn't end well either. *"Last week we were on sixteen temps because the course was too dry, this week you've closed the front nine because the fairways are waterlogged from a shower that lasted no more than twenty minutes".*

"Typical fucking member." uttered Barnes under his *'Thai Curry Pot Noodle'* breath, who, given that it was almost 10:00am, was mentally and actually at the end of his working day. He'd had enough of perfectly reasonable questions from those who thought that paying his inflated salary gave them some God-given right to ask them.

"You do your job and I'll do mine, you'll soon be moaning when all you've got left is the practice nets and one of those putting machines from Argos." Not exactly a well-reasoned stance I am sure you'll agree, but Barnes cared not one jot about upsetting members, safe in the knowledge that finding

greenkeepers is a harder job than finding prime rib of beef being cooked on the vegan edition of *'Masterchef Mumbai'*.

"Fucking members, think they know the fucking lot. I doubt any of them has ever used a lawnmower or had to deal with rainfall slightly below average for the time of year". Freddie West (no not him, let's make this perfectly clear) sided with his fellow professional. *"Just a thousand quid a year and they…" "…plus bar levy and golf union fees."* interjected Barnes with what we must assume is one of those Greenkeeper *'in jokes'*. West laughed, *"Yeah, that as well mate… thousand quid a year and every fucking one of them knows how to mow a bit of grass."* Much nodding of heads ensued, with Barnes chipping in again: *"Or use a hole-making tool* (it's probably got a special name, I can't be arsed to look it up) *to make a hole and use the bit you just cut out to fill the previous one. Twats."*

Barnes and West (No, not him FFS) gave each other a look of mutual respect, and then moved the conversation on to how an outbreak of the newly-invented *'hobble bugs'* could be used to close the 18th hole during the following Saturday's Ted Bovis Stableford. Why? Because most members (the vast majority in all honesty) annoyed them. In fact the only ones who didn't were the *"slightly less ugly ones"* (Trevor Bishop's words, and there were six at most) who were willing to give a cheeky little smile or additional arse wiggle before hitting a shot, in exchange for half a rainforest of logs that would heat their holiday homes for the next four years.

We've drifted off track, sorry. Please cast your mind back a couple of paragraphs. John Conrad, having taken both barrels during one of those *"You do know I can hear you."*

conversations should probably have felt suitably admonished. but he was fairly pissed. A condition which meant he couldn't really pull off being admonished, so he decided to have another little dig at the horticultural heavyweights still within his thinking range.

"How come Witheridge Park is on eighteen main greens then, they're only four miles away?"

West shook his head and gave Conrad the kind of look that plumbers have perfected. *"Different eco-system mate, not that you'd understand. They're on 90% clay soil, our is 88% at most. You could always go and join there I suppose, but I hear they've got a long waiting list"*. Barnes had played his trump card, West gave him another nod of approval. His mowing buddy had, so he thought, verbally taken down yet another member who simply wanted to enjoy a fully open course without fear of being bitten by a newly-invented insect or attacked by a non-existent mutant triffid.

"Of course they've got a waiting list…" slurred Conrad with a cunning mix of beer bravado and perfect logic *"…their fucking course is open most of the time"*.

Barnes and West looked at each other. Conrad wasn't wrong but they were in no mood to concede ground in the face of a perfectly fair comment, even though it came from someone whose state of inebriation meant his golf trolley was doubling up as a walking frame.

"Just get on with your golf mate or we'll open the eighteenth hole and then you'll have a five hundred yard walk back to the clubhouse. Hadn't thought of that had you Capability Black."

A Tale of Bingo Night

Chapter	Par	Length	Joke Index
26	5	2,942 Words	6

Introducing:
Sidney 'The Miracle' Waters (74)
Full Member
Nationality: English with organs of many nations

*T*here are medical miracles, there are Jesuses coming back from the dead, and then there's Sidney 'The Miracle' Waters. A man who should have been dead when hit by polio as a child, and then dead when hit by a Volkswagen Polo on his 60th birthday. A man who,

Sidney Waters

let's be honest, is no stranger to the operating table or countless medical professionals.

Luck seems to play a funny old hand when it comes to Sidney. This is a man who gave a kidney to his brother, then his remaining kidney failed, then his brother died, so he had his kidney back. Just one of any number of medical tales which he has acquired over an extraordinary 74 years of life.

Waters spent his working days in the army, doing paperwork. He had hoped for a role which, in his own words, meant "shooting foreigners on a regular basis", but the lack of a spleen, gall bladder and half of his full complement of lungs did rather compromise his usefulness at the dangerous end of military operations.

This is a man who had a quadruple bypass operation for his 50th birthday and about whom it has been said "The only bit left that he was born with is his head, or at least some of it".

But none of this matters, people love Sidney Waters. He's grateful for every day and when he dies many will benefit from third-hand organs as he carries what he lovingly calls his 'Sidney Donor Card.'

Plus:

Gertrude Muller (81)

Full Member
Nationality: White Supremacist

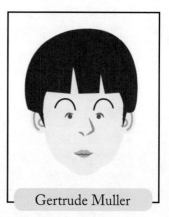

Gertrude Muller

*T**he most odious, two-faced old bag you are ever likely to meet** and the classic 1970s racist. Muller thinks that right here in 2021 it's OK to be a racist. It's not OK and it never was. (another literary bullet dodged there on the sound advice of my dear wife).*

Muller's rather Germanic surname does certainly hint at someone who might be second-generation third-Reich, and a completely unfounded rumour has it that

*her grandmother was an Obergruppenführer in the
SS. To allow for another awful joke, we'll give her a
daughter named Bethany. Whilst not being as extreme
as her mother, she has been known to make more than
the occasional racial slur. Obviously she's nicknamed
'Muller Light'.*

*Muller is teetotal most days, recognising that once she's
had a sherbert or two there's a danger that some 'not
out loud words' will make an appearance, at which
point she'll be up in front of a club Chairman (again)
and kicked out a golf club (again) with not a chance of
any subs being refunded (again).*

*Her grandson is doing 20 years for a string of
convictions spanning the many laws of the land.*

And also:
Paula 'Vampire' Nelson (41)
Social Committee Chairperson
Nationality: Welsh

*P*aula Nelson describes
her shape as "cuddly"
or "curvy" and
*indeed some of her clothes
contain as many X symbols
as the winning line on a
bingo card. She's obese, she's
going to die young, and she
knows it. This makes her sad
so she cheers herself with doughnuts and topic bars.*

Paula Nelson

And why is she nicknamed 'Vampire'? Because she's a Buffet Slayer. (Honestly, in a book with some terrible puns, that one really does dredge the depths).

Nelson joined the club as a social member "because it gets me out of the house", but what she actually means is "because they have cake", and as you may have gathered, she's not one for physical exercise. On some days her most calorifically intense tasks involve scratchcards.

When it comes to employment, she's officially a carer for her mother, who is twice her age and half her girth. She receives a cool two hundred quid a week a rent-free Council flat for doing nothing more than occasionally replacing the batteries in the Sky remote and picking up her blood pressure pills from Boots the Chemist (conveniently next to Greggs).

Welsh by birth, grossly overweight by life choices, that's Paula 'Vampire' Nelson.

We begin...

Ellie Carter was having a decent enough day, her preferred shift of eleven to three meant a few of the old boys would be finishing their rounds whilst she was on duty, and some of this year's crop of octogenarians would soon be heading for that great driving range in the sky.

A place where there were never buggy bans, no holes that needed a fifty yard carry from the tee to cross a ditch, or young people wanting to rush round in under five hours.

Taking a one-way trip to that place meant there were also wills to be read (Oops, I did it again), and as Carter knew

only too well, there's nothing so easily influenced as a
bloke who needs five pisses at night when confronted with
a young floosie wiggling her tits in a dance of rhythmic
delight and the seductive caressing of a beer pump. (Carter
rarely went *'Full Monty'*, which is the act of a slight twisting
of the hand on the down stroke, or the eye contact / lip
licking combo - she had no wish to witness another former
Captain having a cardiac arrest).

But yes, on more than a few occasions, she had steered
conversations to such matters, and heard those most
wonderful six words that a girl can hear from someone she's
never had to slept with *"There's a little something for you"*.

Sidney Waters had begun his game at six in the morning,
just two hours before sunrise. A pairs match with Gertrude
Muller making up his crack team of 38 handicappers.
Who they played against (and beat) is something I can't
be bothered to work out, and let us assume they fucked off
home having lost, but as Carter's shift began Sidney Waters
ordered his *"first of the day"*. Beer that would travel, in just
twenty minutes through a kidney with a story to tell and
reach a bladder that has once graced a Welsh lamb.

"Tough game today love." smiled Waters, *"I need this"*.

"Didn't play well? Never mind, there's always next time".
Cheery words delivered with purpose, and followed up
with the routine described above, *'Full Monty'* considered
but wisely avoided.

*"Played fine, won the match, just didn't expect to be playing with
the membership secretary of the Cambridgeshire Nazi Party"*.

"Oh Gertrude, I had heard she's a bit like that, haven't you played with her before then Sidney?"

"Couple of times, but apparently a homosexual couple has moved in three doors down. Let's just say they won't be asking for a cup of sugar again".

Muller appeared. She'd had a shower and having been on the winning side her attitude had lightened just a little. This, combined with the fact that she knew it was probably best to keep her more extreme opinions to herself in the clubhouse, meant that the conversation was somewhat more genial.

"What are you having Gertrude?" Waters was a gentleman, though he was slightly tinged with displeasure when Muller asked for a Gin & Tonic, he had hoped that her choice of tipple would involve a beer handle, but no such luck.

"Five eighty please Sid".

"Ooh these prices, they're robbing us pensioners blind, it's only three eighty down the Conservative Club and you can double up for a pound". Muller loved to have something to moan about. *"They should do more for the old folk up here, it's disgusting, we have Bingo twice a week at Boris's Bar and the fish supper is only a fiver".*

Waters smiled, he'd heard it all before, though pre-2004 it had been via his original left ear. These days 50% of his audio capacity was courtesy of a young black man who had sadly died, but not before bequeathing any useful body parts that doctors could put to good use. (You've got a mental picture here haven't you?) *"Well we pay the same fees as everyone else but plenty of us play four or five times a week, I don't think there's much to complain about"*. He was correct.

Carter handed over Muller's drink *"... and it's lovely to see you up here so much Sid, you're a long time dead as they say"*. She thought she had Waters on the metaphorical hook of inheritance discussion but instead he picked up on his playing partner's comment, moving his gaze away from its natural resting place turning to Gertrude Muller.

"Bingo you say … I used to go to the local Mecca every week back in the seventies. It's a branch of Lidl's now, and there's a branch of Screwfix next door, pretty sure that used to be a brothel." (None of our trio got the accidental joke, but you my dear reader may have raised a smile at a piece of humour I've been dying to drop in. Further note at final edit: *'Toolstation'* works here too).

Waters was suddenly struck by sentimentality - a cardiac arrest was some years away, his baboon's heart coped with ease at the sedentary lifestyle of an old duffer, evolved as it was to cope with swinging through trees and shagging on an hourly basis. *"There's a social committee meeting tonight, I'll see if they wouldn't mind me organising one"*.

The social committee was more than accommodating when Water's request was received. A social event that required not one jot of effort from their massively overburdened members, and given its nature, one that would reflect well on the committee. Perfect.

"Bingo Night - 20th July - Eyes Down 7pm. (Fish supper five quid - vegans can eat beforehand)". The posters were not

exactly inclusive but given the target audience, it was felt that culinary pandering was unnecessary, and indeed, might help to set the tone of the evening.

And so to Bingo Night. Sixty eight people bothered to attend, including Paula Nelson, the Chairman/Chairwoman/Chairperson/whatever of the social committee. She had found a gap in her hectic schedule of watching the *'Bake Off'* before cocoa and taking a hot bath. Her reasoning being that her presence would result in some Bingoists assuming that the evening was the spawn of the current crop of reluctant social committee members who, it has to be said, only did it for the free sandwiches.

The propensity (no, me neither) for those present to have brought their own dibbers showed that this was a serious occasion, and given that the collective IQs averaged that of a wheely bin, it was no surprise to hear more than a few snide comments along the lines of *"Troggles here, she's good. Once had four corners in five numbers"* and *"Vampire knows someone who lives next door to a bloke who won 'The National' once. She won't spend anything at the bar but you can bet she goes home with at least a tin of Quality Street"*.

High stakes, half-packed clubhouse, prizes ranging from a litre of cooking sherry (still with three months left on its *'best before'* date) to a sleeve of three Pro-V1s with one missing, and to a tub of *'Miniature Heroes'*. A fabulous bounty to a group of people who had known serious hardship just sixty years earlier, and for whom index-linked triple-lock pensions were scant consolation for the fact that some of their number wouldn't see another birthday.

"All the sixes, sixty… oh hang on, six and five, sixty five." The game was underway. Five cards before fish supper (or a chance to lecture some poor 14 year old clubhouse assistant on £3.50 per hour about the Cod stocks of the north seas) and four cards after. Sidney Watts's mistake on the first call was not unexpected, the Bingo balls had not seen the light of day for almost two decades, a time during which they had experienced the joys of bat shit, spider shit and whatever other shit you might find in a clubhouse loft.

"On its own, number nine". Waters was in his stride now, this was what he was born to do no question about it. Indeed, showing remarkable foresight he had brought a spare battery for the PA system's radio mic, a device which had worked properly no more five times in the eight years since it was purchased.

"Oh just three away". (How stupid are these people? I'm making it up as I go along but it's still annoying the crap out of me).

"Two and eight…….. ten…" Waters made a funny. The two people waiting for number twenty eight to complete a line who called *"Yep"* didn't find it funny. Everyone else thought it was hilarious, a giant Toblerone still up for grabs…

"Seven and Two, Seventy Two." *"Yep, over here."* Collective groans elsewhere as a four pack of Foster's Lager went to Trevor Bishop. Not only one of the youngest in the room, but as a member of staff there were mumblings.

"Doesn't even play Bingo, this is bent." complained Painter.

"Fucking ringer, you never see him in Mecca." spouted a gin-drizzled Doris Lyn.

"Language Doris, please". Sidney Waters sensed tension, and as custodian of the balls and the spinning machine (Argos 1998 vintage) he felt well within the scope of his self-proclaimed authority to restore order to the room.

Games came and went, and as might be expected given the demographic of the players, even the disabled crapper got full use, with many opting for a piss before they needed one lest they end up at the back of the queue for the food.

Talking of food, everyone had assumed that a fish supper meant something along the lines of Cod & Chips, and they were half right. The chips were a given, but as to the fish, well it was nearly white, nearly flaky and nearly tasted of something. The Chef (new bloke, we've long-since sacked Royce), when questioned about the quality of the offering, responded with a professional courtesy and gave a well-reasoned reply. *"If you wanted fucking Cod it would have been a tenner each, minimum. Call in the chippy on the way home if you don't like it"*.

Most ate the fish-like fodder and those who couldn't finish what they'd taken wrapped the remains in a serviette. On the face of it a fine example of thrift, but it was all for show. It would all be chucked in the hedge before leaving the car park for the Russet Grange rat population to gorge on in style.

Bingo resumed, Sidney Waters was growing beautifully into the role of caller. Corners completed, lines and full houses too. The Pro-V1s were eagerly grabbed by Les Hamill. Not his choice of golf ball though and, true to form, he had sold them for £2.50 each before he'd even got back to his table.

"That's my supper paid for." he proclaimed with more joy than he had expressed during the entire year.

"Four and Two, Forty Two, Five and Nine, The Brighton Line, Legs Eleven…" Waters was achieving a Zen-like command of the room. Then, for the first time that evening, the *'Devil's Number'* came into play:

"Two Fat Ladies, Sixty Six".

"What the fuck?" Paula Nelson couldn't believe what she had just heard. She stood up, chair still attached as her arse was jammed between the arms. *"Curvy ladies, it's curvy ladies nowadays. Some of the larger ladies in here might be offended by that. Betty's got Fibro Nigella and Maud is just big-boned aren't you love?"*

"Well if you weren't so curvy your chair wouldn't be stuck to your bum cheeks". Muller had enjoyed rather too many gins, but her line brought clubhouse-wide laughter.

"Ladies, ladies, please calm down, it's just a game of Bingo."

"That's easy for you to say Waters but there's a box of Milk Tray and some Asti Spumante miniatures to be won, we haven't all got huge pensions". Reg Bollard would never change, he was still reeling from his soul-mate's effectively free supper.

"Go woke or go broke" cried Nelson. She'd read the phrase on Facebook, appearing as it did underneath an image of one of the Megans (Fox, Markle, Trainor… take your pick). She had no idea what it meant but it sounded good.

"Sit down fatty…." *"She's already sat down…."* Both barrels from Carol Brittan and Ron McAndrew, an absolutely shitfaced pair, each needing one number for a full house.

The tension of Bingo night reached a peak, abuse hurled left, right and centre. Paula Nelson wobbled out of the clubhouse in floods of tears, chair still stuck to her arse, stopping only to grab a box of confectionery from the prize table, self-awarded compensation for the humiliation she had just endured. In the morning she would be resigning from the social committee but tonight she would fight back the tears with a few hundred Cadbury's calories. Heroes every one of them. (Sorry).

Waters, with the help of Andy Biggs, Ellie Carter and a few of the more sensible Bingo players gradually restored order.

The last card of the night was completed and most were more than pleased to see Alcoholic John win the sherry. Not that he had actually completed a card, far from it, but nobody could be arsed to check. Should they had done so they would have realised that not only were five of the numbers on his card uncalled, they would have remained uncalled had the game gone on all night. For stuck in the corners of the original box for the *'Argos Bingomatic'* were at least nine balls, including seventy two, *'Danny La Rue'*, which Lionel Darcy had eagerly waited for all night, and number eight, just the *'One Fat Lady'*. How lucky was that?

I just mistook someone in a Bigfoot outfit for #Chewbacca – A wookie mistake.

Introducing:

Ingrid Magnusson (37)
Full Member/Goddess
Nationality: Redacted (Icelandic, but keep it to yourself)

*D*espite being born in Iceland, and not having moved to the UK until 2016, Ingrid Magnusson speaks better English than at least 90% of the members. In fact she speaks it so well that Alcoholic John cannot understand her.

She's intellectual, interesting, impeccably well mannered,

Ingrid Magnusson

has a degree in botany and is an astonishingly talented cellist, being a regular with the Reykjavik symphony orchestra. Magnusson also has great set of tits plus and arse that Carl Doller once said was "so perfect she probably craps Ferrero Rochers".

There are rumours about her involvement in Black Ops with the national military, but given that the Icelandic army consists of 30 reservists who patrol a single airport and a small selection of state hot tubs, the rumours are probably untrue.

Magnusson is in many ways the perfect human female specimen, and given that her partner Christian is basically a cross between a WWF wrestler and Steven Hawking(and I don't mean a someone of low intelligence who uses a wheelchair), the two of them would be the ideal candidates to repopulate the planet should aliens invade and kidnap everyone else. As Doller himself once said "Their kids would be Gods, but if Thor is shooting blanks I'll give it a go".

Golf? She's brilliant. Obviously.

And also
Brynn 'Bo Peep' Morgan (70)
Full Member
Nationality: Unquestionably Welsh

*E*very golf club outside Wales has a token Welshman, and our man from the valleys is Brynn 'Bo Peep' Morgan. He never stops telling people how great Wales is "The home of rugby, coal mining and cheese on toast", but he personally has no problem with not living

Brynn Morgan

there. Brynn Morgan is nicknamed 'Bo Peep' because he once had a lorry full of prize sheep stolen right from under his nose whilst he was parked at Newport Pagnell services taking a break from driving.

Morgan likes a drink, usually a nice glass of Scotch, and when he won £10k in the postcode lottery he put it all on his bar card. It was gone in eight months, though he did manage to get £4.70 refunded, which had been mistakenly charged to his account. "There's no fucking way I bought a fucking vegan breakfast."

He's a decent golfer, Club Champion in 1992, and is damned good company on the course, though the joke of a playing partner emerging from bushes with a toy sheep and shouting "I've found one you haven't fucked Rog" is wearing a bit thin these days.

Morgan has never married, but a string of rather elegant lady friends in his company has left nobody in any doubt about his hobbies away from the club.

We begin

As a bit of a treat we've got another chapter that actually features some golf, and this time around we present a few holes of a mixed knockout competition. In the red corner we have a pairing made in heaven, Magnusson and Morgan, who you've just met. In the blue corner, a pairing made on a Saga coach trip to Camber Sands.

If you've done this book in the right order you'll have just read Gertrude Muller's and Sidney Waters' biographies in the previous chapter when things got more than a little out of hand at Bingo Night.

Brynn Morgan slid his Yonex *'Big Dog'* driver out of his golf bag (that will keep my brother happy as he's a self-appointed Yonex ambassador), did some of those silly limbering up exercises with an unwavering belief that such things could ever make a difference to his geriatric mobility, and then smacked one of those *'natural fades'* into the semi-rough that every golfer with a twenty-something handicap hits at least a dozen times each round.

"Have some of that Boyo… oh, oh, oh…. oh bollocks to it". This in-flight commentary was a feature of Morgan's game that all expected and some enjoyed. He really didn't take things too seriously, unlike his playing partner, who was certainly not about to provide a ball-by-ball account of her game.

It takes both self-confidence and talent to hit a two-iron *'stinger'* beneath a strong breeze on the first tee, in full view of the clubhouse, and Ingrid Magnusson knew she had both. The Icelandic Ice-Maiden split the fairway with her weapon of choice. No in-flight commentary for her, just a spin of the club, a smile to her playing partner and a chilling look that said *"You've already lost"* to her opponents.

Gertrude Muller kept her thoughts to herself, they weren't ones to be expressed out loud, but Waters couldn't resist a comment: *"Just missed the pig farm, nice shot love"*. To be honest Waters had already decided that two people watching Magnusson's tee shot was plenty, so he kept his gaze firmly on her bum.

'Team Muller' played unremarkable drives and as the four of them set off down the first tee, Waters and Morgan enjoyed a bit of banter, choosing to walk as far downwind as possible from today's particularly potent piggy aroma. Muller rode her little buggy ahead of everyone, aiming

to avoid any kind of conversation. (Incidentally, she had managed to swing a buggy permit on health grounds. Physically there was nothing wrong with her but she'd turned on the tears in front of Steve Simpson claiming *"I love my golf but it's only a matter of time before one of my knees gives way"*). Simpson would normally have shown no sympathy, but Muller accidentally dropped an envelope containing a fat wad of cash when rubbing her left leg and that did seem to nudge Simpson to take an unusually appeasing stance.

Second shots from the British contingent were sprayed all over the place, with Morgan's in-flight info restricted to *"Bollocks, caught it fat"*. An expression, like *"thinned the bastard"* or *"blocked it right"*, that every golfer has heard or said and not a single one knows what it means.

Magnusson gave a polite smile as she stuck her second to within six feet, hole conceded and Muller already thinking of hitting her emergency hip flask of Johnny Walker's least decent but most affordable tipple.

The next couple of holes were halved, with the frankly abysmal Muller scraping a bogey on the second, having suspiciously found her ball in the rough some thirty yards further than where it landed (and having mysteriously changed brand in the process), and with Magnusson missing a short putt on the third. *"Ooh bad luck, just lipped out"*. Muller tried and failed to contain a smile. *"You might be entitled to compensation."* quipped Waters in a rare moment of near-comedy.

Fourth tee, Morgan's drive ends up in a field. *"No sheep in there mate, just cows"*. Waters really was the *'King of Comedy'*, but when he did exactly the same thing, Magnusson's subtle *"mooooooo"* (in an Icelandic accent, please try to imagine it) brought laughter to the blokes and drove Muller to hitting the hip flask a little bit harder. *"That Norwegian bitch even does funny"*. A geographically inaccurate thought that she kept to herself at this point, but this self-restraint was not to last much longer as Magnusson creamed the most elegant of drives with wondrous precision. *"Great shot Inbred, sorry... Ingrid"*, spoken in a slurred voice just loud enough to be heard.

"If only I were forty years younger." commented Morgan to Waters as the two of them watched in awe of this Icelandic maiden. *"If only my bollocks weren't still in Port Stanley"* bullshitted Waters, hinting at being right in the mix back in '82, when in fact the nearest he got to the South Atlantic that year was eating a prawn baguette at his niece's wedding reception.

The lead, in what had become a grudge match between Muller and the other three, changed hands a couple of times over the next four holes. Waters played some decent golf, though he slightly embarrassed himself when a piss on the eighth, unfollowed by a suitable shake, left a tell-tale dark patch on his all-too-lightly-coloured shorts. Magnusson drained a thirty footer on the ninth, despite Muller breaking wind on her backstroke. *"Sorry Helga, it just slipped out, honest. Oops, there's another one"*.

All square at the turn, all to play for on the back nine. There was a bit of a wait on the tenth tee so Waters, with his shorts still damp and the odour of his partner's flatulence continuing to tickle his nasal passages, decided to move the conversation to something more cultural.

"So what's Iceland like love? Is it all volcanoes, smoked herring, naked mud baths and whale hunting?"

"Yes, mostly those things, but also long winters where we keep warm by having lots of sex. Often in large groups"

Morgan chuckled, he loved Magnusson's subtle humour and after a brief pause for a mental treat replied with the second thought that came into his head: *"Not much time for golf then really?"* Muller made an all too predictable reference to shopping for frozen chicken dippers.

The par three 10th (might be a par four elsewhere in the book) was one of the simpler holes at Russet Grange. Three tee shots found the green, but Waters couldn't shake a mental picture of Magnusson spending most of January *"keeping warm"*, pausing only for the occasional chomp of some whale steaks. This delightful image did rather affect his game. *"For fuck's sake Sid, concentrate on the golf and stop thinking about Princess Fucking Iceberg"* slurred Muller as they left the 10th green one down.

Sadly, trying not to think of a stonkingly attractive Icelandic Goddess enjoying the pleasures of the flesh, on what Waters imagined would be a vast rug made from polar bear fur placed in front of a roaring fire, was simply too much to ask. His game had gone and it wasn't coming back, much like his ability to maintain an erection some thirty years earlier. Muller pretty much carried her partner over the next four holes (metaphorically speaking, there was barely enough room on her buggy for just one of her arse cheeks, let alone two cheeks and a skinny old man entertaining sexual fantasies of a highly entertaining but improper nature).

Morgan and Magnusson soon found themselves three holes to the good. It's amazing what a bit of decent golf combined with a massive psychological advantage can do. Also Muller had long since emptied her hip flask and was having to choose the middle of three balls when playing a stroke. In truth the match was over by the fourteenth. (Which is just as well, this chapter is rank average, hence the Joke Index of 28, and it needs to end).

The inevitable was delayed a little when Water's wayward tee shot on fifteen made the best use of a tree since Magnusson's ancestors had fashioned them into battleships, with a huge slice of luck leaving a two footer for a gratefully received birdie. Muller was most complimentary to her playing partner: *"You jammy fucker, now we've got to play another fucking hole. You twat"*.

Magnusson also made birdie, on a hole where she too was receiving a stroke, and Morgan's comment *"Shot Sid, you're still in the game"* was both well-meaning and a quite simply huge exaggeration.

It had been an eventful match. Sidney Waters had fallen in what would always be unrequited love (though like many readers he didn't know what *'unrequited'* meant),

Brynn Morgan had played in the company of greatness. Ingrid Magnusson had discovered the joy of being able to deliver the unexpected one-liner and Gertrude Muller had something to celebrate too.

In her own words *"I got drunk as fuck, pissed before the back nine, only had to play fifteen holes, and as far as Hagrid Fucking Magnesium is concerned, well she can fuck off to Antarticaland and spend the summer getting fucked as well"*.

The greenkeepers are very excited. Their "Chicks with Chainsaws" calendar just arrived.

I must say that whilst I applaud the use of safety glasses, I have doubts that a bikini offers much protection from a 48" trunk destroyer.

Miss August looks like a good sport.

In town just now I saw a bloke listening to what I thought was a pork chop.

Turned out to be a ham radio.

We've got a #GolfSociety of Mathematicians visiting Russet Grange today.

The Chef has embraced this with a special offer of "Chicken Pi" for £3.14 and "Avogadro on Toast" for £6.02.

The Pro isn't so keen though, with his message board simply reading: "10:00am – Nerds"

A Tale of the Gusset Rangers and the Whelk Wheel (Part Two)

Chapter	Par	Length	Joke Index
28	4	2,057 Words	11

Introducing:

Harry 'Prince' Andrews (26)

Intermediate Member

Nationality: British Thoroughbred

*S*olid British beefcake *from well-heeled stock, Harry Andrews is the privately-educated (Harrow) son of a Harley Street neurosurgeon, who is quite simply the person everyone at the club would choose to be. There's not a lady at the club who wouldn't do him, and at least one of the supposedly heterosexual male members has said he "Wouldn't mind a go".*

Harry Andrews

Andrews completed his *'DofE Gold'* by working at an Orang-Utan orphanage in Borneo (obviously) and upon returning to the UK took up golf, playing at a rather famous club in Surrey where his dad sat on the Board of Directors. He joined Russet Grange when he moved to the area with his girlfriend, a humble young lady whose father owns most of Lincolnshire and all of Kent.

And
Curly 'Pubes' White (49)
Full Member
Nationality: Ginger

Curly White

*P*ossibly the most ginger man ever to have lived, worsened by the fact that his natural hairstyle would look more appropriate in the bollocks region, but even with this particular life-hurdle he is unbelievably successful with women. There's rarely a visit to the club without a new doe-eyed bimbo in tow, and despite White's 49 years of age, each 'plat du jour' tends to be of the twenty-something age group, with a lack of any mental capacity another common and unsurprising trait.

White works as a mechanic at the local Audi dealership, so it is only a mild exaggeration when he tells another potential conquest that he races cars for a living. Many a local lass thinks that she's slept with the ginger Lewis Hamilton, later to discover that the bloke who serviced her car yesterday is the same one who serviced her lady garden last weekend.

He is an average golfer, being far more interested in the social aspect of the game. At the 2014 club championships he put a buggy in a ditch when a well-shaken can of Thatcher's Haze exploded in his face.

A TALE OF THE GUSSET RANGERS (PART TWO)

We begin...

arlier on in this very book you'll have read the first chapter featuring the Gusset Rangers, or at least you should have unless: a) I fucked up, or b) you started at the wrong end of the book, in which case you are an idiot.

Anyway, here we are about to head onto the course, to play for the *'Whelk Wheel'*, a coveted trophy, an artefact if you will, that means more to The Rangers than the Club Championship (not unreasonably, most of our heroes are shit at golf and are never going to win it anyway).

We've already mentioned the likes of *'Stain Devil'*, *'Anal Andy'*, *'Tapeworm'*, *'Officer Dribble'*, *'Cock-Out Dave'*, and the Gusset Rangers President, Pete *'Balcony'* McTorry. Also making up today's group are players (who we shall never meet in this book, but maybe next time if someone gives me a publishing deal) nicknamed *'Flabdul'*, *'Captain Twat'*, *'Dairy Milk'* and *'Sonic the Hedgebog'*, a man named because he'd rather take a crap in a hedge than in the clubhouse.

There are others playing too, around forty souls in total, and as any of you golfers know, it takes about ninety minutes to get that many out playing. Allow an hour for a bit of beer, breakfast and more beer, three hours on the piss afterwards, and you can say goodbye to an entire day, which is why many of the Rangers had previously said goodbye to an entire marriage.

First tee then, and our newly-introduced characters are paired with Rob Farnham-Blink (GR nickname *'Biggles'*), which really, really cheered them up. In fairness though, he's unlikely to mention that he used to be a pilot.

"What do you lads do for a living then?" asked Blink. He'd rarely played with the Rangers and didn't know White or Prince at all well.

"Two hours a week on Youtube" smiled Andrews, *"I think it pays the bills, Dad's accountant would tell me if it didn't".*

Pubes answered too: *"I work at Audi in town, pretty boring stuff but I get to drive some decent motors, ragged the tits off an R8 last week".* In truth, Pubes *"ragged the tits"* off of anything he got to drive at work. *"I'll probably grow up one day, but it won't be this day."*

Blink had hit the jackpot. *"Sort of a car test-pilot then?"* he commented. *"Talking of which, that's like what I used to do, thirty years at British Airways, when it really was the 'World's favourite airline'. That's why they call me Biggles."*

Andrews hadn't heard of *'Biggles'*, but he knew only too well that British Airways employed people in many roles.

"Who was Biggles then? Was he a baggage handler?"

"A Spitfire Pilot" replied Blink, shaking his head in an *"oh for fuck's sake"* kind of way.

"You flew Spitfires for British Airways? Sorry mate but that's bollocks. Anyway, good luck, let's win this fucking wheel".

Our crack team put two out of three drives into the pig farm, a measly two points scored on the first hole. (Don't worry, there won't be too much golf here, but we need a bit every now and then otherwise I might just as well have written about a pub staffed by barmaids waiting for wealthy customers to die).

Up ahead, *'Officer Dribble'* had just made eagle on the third. (I assume it's not a par three, I still can't be arsed to check and there was no way I was making a scorecard for a course that doesn't exist). *'Tapeworm'* gave him a kiss, right on the gob. Normal behaviour for the Rangers, *"Always show love for your fellow man"* as *'Cock-Out Dave'* liked to say.

Over on the fourth, *'Sonic the Hedgebog'* was taking a dump. He'd held out all morning (*"Stoff berühren"* as they say in Munich), and he had a favourite spot behind the tee where he wasn't overlooked by more than a dozen golfers. You have to admire a man who has a toilet roll holder attached to his trolley. *"I'd give that ten minutes lads"* he joked to team-mates who knew him only too well. Good golfer, just make sure he's washed his hands in a pond before exchanging pleasantries on the 18th green.

The trio of White/Pubes/Biggles had not fared any better on the second hole, at least not in golfing terms, but Pubes had got the herbal remedy out, so he and Andrews had gone from keen to win the Whelk Wheel to not giving a flying fuck about anything in the space of two hundred yards. Nicely done boys, nicely done.

"You fancy a smoke Biggles?" Pubes assumed not, but it was polite to ask and having just heard the story about sticking a tree through his conservatory, he decided that Biggles was an OK sort for his age.

Traditionally the Rangers liked to have a little more on-course entertainment than that which was naturally provided by *"Cambridgeshire's Finest Semi-Woodland Par 68 Championship Course"*. (The one-man marketing team really went to town with that bollocks back in '85, based as it was on it being one of the four courses chosen as possible hosts for one of the Seniors' County Championship qualifying rounds that very year). So today the par three 15th (just assume it's a par three, I've spent enough time writing this crap, if I sell more than six copies I promise I'll go and check for inconsistencies), hosted a very special competition.

"Nearest the pin gets to set light to 'Captain Twat's old golf bag". Who doesn't love a bit of pyrotechnics? *'Twat'* had won a brand new bag *"Valued at £299"* (trade price £70 at most), following four hours of decent golf at a local open, and four years of protecting his handicap for this very purpose. Why put the old one on eBay when you can cover it in lighter fluid and reproduce the best scene from *'The Wicker Man'* as dusk draws in on Whelk Wheel Saturday?

On the fifth fairway *'Flabdul'*, *'Dairy Milk'* and *'Stain Devil'* thought they were going well, but sadly none of the trio had understood the format (though in fairness very few did), and they were playing an almost unheard of threeball scramble. Not that they cared much, they were three quarters of the way through a bottle of *'Lamb's Navy Rum'*, a situation that might have been a bit troublesome but for the ever-helpful Andy Biggs who was on his way, via one of the club's least-fucked buggies, with emergency rations.

Progressing up the third fairway, Curly Pubes and Harry Andrews were throwing the usual questions at Farnham-Blink, a man they were now referring to as *'Biggles the*

Baggage Handler'. *"Ever shag an air hostess when flying your jumbo jet?"* asked White, predictably. *"How many times have you been hijacked?"* enquired Andrews followed by *"Can you really fly upside down like Denzel Washington did in that film where he was pissed all time?"*

Blink smiled *"No, never, and no. To be honest it was all pretty tame stuff, though me and a mate stole an Airbus once, picked up a couple of female hitch-hikers, ex-Hooters waitresses and went for a joyride round the Med".*

Andrews, (who I have now decided is a bit thicker than I had him down for) was impressed. *"Really? Wow, that's cool, bet you got a right bollocking."* White wasn't anywhere near as susceptible to bullshit as his golfing buddy. *"Of course he didn't steal a fucking plane you knob, let's get on with the golf".*

Anyway, I think I've written enough on-course action, so let's just summarise the rest of the golf in a few lines. The boys on the rum never made it past the 12th, deciding instead to get back into the clubhouse to beat the rush and *'Genital Ben'* (haven't met him, never will) threw his driver into a pond, followed by his three-wood and his putter.

In our chosen group Farnham-Blink continued to make up bollocks of an aviation nature, such as the story of how he once successfully landed a F-15 that had only one wing remaining, much to the semi-bemusement of Andrews and the complete-amusement of Curly White.

'Officer Dribble' got attacked by a pheasant but he saw it off with a few well-aimed blows from his three iron. *"First time I've used that bastard since Potton sold it to me ten years ago."*

'Dairy Milk' ate a bar of *'Dairy Milk'*. (Well what did you expect, he was hardly going to be chomping away on the *'Fruit & Nut'* was he?).

We haven't yet mentioned the trio of *'Crash Test Brummie'* (Bloke from Dudley with a circular birthmark on his temple), *'Mensa Pete'* (failed his eleven plus aged 18) and *'Boring Adrian'* (because he's boring and his name is Adrian). They were scoring well and having a very fine time until *'Boring Adrian'* decided that what the day needed was a martial arts demonstration. Thus he attempted a *'roundhouse'* kick at a long-since abandoned wasps' nest and broke his ankle. A buggy/ambulance recovered him from the 8th fairway and his playing partners continued their game.

And thus, the golfing competition came to an end, and the getting on the piss began in earnest. The lads who played the scramble format were mocked and disqualified, *'Hedgehog'* was presented with some toilet roll and anti-bacterial handwash, much to the amusement of all, and *'Captain Twat'* was subjected to a song whose lyrics involved nothing more than a repetition of the words, *"Captain Twat, he's a twat"* whenever he left his comfy chair.

It wasn't all singing and shot glasses though. Over in a quiet corner, the half-Lithuanian Alan *'Vicarov'* Dibley was taking mock confession from any of the Rangers who, in the previous week, had done something (or someone) they shouldn't have. I know I've got my religions all mixed up here, but the fact he was using Smoky Bacon Pringles as communion wafers in some bizarre forgiveness ceremony tells you how serious things were being taken by his flock.

Nearest the pin on the 15th was won by *'Dildo Baggins'*, who took great delight in dousing *'Captain Twat's'* golf bag in lighter fluid before setting it ablaze. Many of the Rangers danced around the resulting inferno, creating the *'Wicker Man'* scene which I promised earlier. (The film, not the ride at Alton Towers).

The winners? Oh I don't know, but let's give it to White, Prince and Farnham-Blink, the new custodians of the Whelk Wheel, that most cherished of trophies. Popular winners, and as Harry Andrews was led to believe, appropriate ones too. *"What a bloke, a fucking legend"* he slurred to *'Stain Devil'* who was seated calmly at the bar. *"Did you know, my new best mate Biggles the Baggage Handler once drove Concorde into a ditch at Heathrow and wrote the fucker off, fifty grand of damage and they let him keep the joystick.... what a fucking legend."*

Love this time of year. Around 50 members will sit in the clubhouse and try to stream the #USMasters. Then they'll complain that our #broadband isn't fast enough.

We're in the middle of fucking Cambridgeshire, we only got flush toilets in '86.

To celebrate the World Cup we've got the same bollocks on the menu that we always have but the chef has used a font that looks a bit middle-eastern.

In fairness his title of "Clubhouse Qataring" is quite amusing. (He didn't really think of that, I did, we don't have a chef or golf club.)

Our "Nine Months for the Price of Twelve" works brilliantly. Every April we pull in about 50 gullible fools.

It's the best thing our #MarketingTeam has done in years, though in fairness the second 'best' thing was when they spent £5k on drone photos of the wrong course.

A Tale of Drinking Titans			
Chapter	Par	Length	Joke Index
29	3	1,383 Words	15

Introducing:
Alcoholic John (59)
Full Member
Nationality: Unknown

Alcoholic John

*N*obody knows Alcoholic John's surname or nationality, not even him, and he likes it that way "Because I'm not much good at remembering things".

An absolutely top bloke, Alcoholic John thinks he served in the armed forces at some point, and there are rumours that his membership fees are paid from a generous soul whose life he once saved whilst taking heavy gunfire. The truth is that the club just doesn't bother charging him because you don't fuck over someone who is dropping £2k on booze each month.

Alcoholic isn't actually a bad golfer, and despite his name he doesn't even drink much before 10:00am other than on weekends and Club Night. His chosen tipple at the club is Bells whisky, but at home he drinks vodka which he acquires at a bargain price from his Polish next-door neighbour who just happens to drive articulated lorries throughout Europe.

He once attended an AA meeting, but only the once, because "It was full of pissheads". In 1996 he did give up the drink for a couple of weeks but soon got back on it because he didn't enjoy being sober. Loved by all in this world and will be loved by everyone in the next one too. A legend. End of.

Plus:
Rose Lubworth (63)
Full Member
Nationality: English

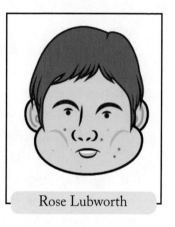
Rose Lubworth

Lubworth claims she got ousted from 'Bucks Fizz', just before they got chosen to represent the UK at Eurovision, and despite constantly saying "It's A dark time of my life I don't want to talk about" she'll tell anyone who'll listen every fucking detail. "The things I could tell you about Bobby Gee" she drunkenly dribbles whilst nursing often nursing a 'heart starter' vodka and lemon.

Most agree that Lubworth is both bitter and twisted, which is ironic as, like Sidney Waters, she had polio as a child. A fact that has led many to question whether she could have stayed standing during that skirt ripping move on stage in Dublin back in '81. She's not what you'd call a looker either, and it didn't help her self-esteem when she once heard Tank McAndrew describe her as having "a face like a failed soufflé".

When it comes to golf, Lubworth really isn't that fussed. She's a full member but would rather spend her time "supporting the clubhouse" until she falls half-conscious onto the bar, babbling on about how "…that Cheryl Aston woman ruined my life"

Martin Wagstaff shagged her at the '98 summer ball.

We begin…

For some people there are two kinds of hours, sleeping hours and opening hours, and whilst sleeping is pretty much the same for everyone, the demon drink can turn people into bitter bitches, loveable legends, or all colours of the beer rainbow in between.

On this particular morning at Russet Grange one person from each end of that rainbow found themselves at the bar, 10:00am sharp. Rose Lubworth (the bitter bitch end) and Alcoholic John (the loveable legend end) exchanged glances, they knew of each other, but they didn't really know each other. Glances which both followed with a respectful nod as Andy Biggs raised the shutters, logged into his own till account (quite the rarity among staff), and greeted his first customers.

Draught beer taps flickered into life, brands of *'Whitbread's'* finest glowing proudly against a backdrop of sparkling optics and wines from all corners of the wholesale warehouse, a magical moment in anyone's book. Indeed, had

Charles Dickens been seated in the corner, penning a novel whilst observing the scene unfold he would certainly have written *"It was the best of opening times, it was the worst of opening times"* - Yep, I wrote that entire paragraph for that one gag. Wasn't worth it but this is a very average chapter, *'Joke Index'* of 15 I expect. (Confirmed).

"Usual John?" Biggs didn't really need to ask, but to assume that Alcoholic John was still on the Bells Whiskey and hadn't become teetotal overnight would have been rude. Two politely raised fingers signified that a single measure was not a consideration. Rose Lubworth chipped in *"Same for me Andy"*. An unusual tipple for the self-proclaimed *'Bucks Fizz'* reject (Or *'Fucks Bizz'* when the drink took hold), but Lubworth fancied a change from the rum and this simple act gave Biggs a chance to deliver a joke he'd had ready for the best part of a decade:

"Eight forty please". He looked at John, then he looked at Lubworth, and asked *"For whom the Bells toll?"* Not a smirk at what might be the third best joke in this entire book. Dickens in the corner would have got it.

"Stick it on mine Andy." replied Alcoholic John. An act which brought his bar spend into four figures for the month. Impressive for February, incredible for the 9th.

"A quick winter warmer before a few holes". Asked Lubworth as she smiled at her drinking companion. Whilst there was little doubt that an early tipple would keep out some of the morning chill, the tipple was more importantly playing the role of *'hair of the dog'*, and it really was a fucking big dog. The polite enquiries continued: *"You going out as well?"*

"Still making my mind up." replied Alcoholic, blissfully unaware that he had effectively just ridden a Derby winner of a gift horse into the bar. A racehorse which was wearing a *"Tell me the Bucks Fizz story"* sash, one that Lubworth was now staring squarely in the gob.

Sure enough, tales of bitter rejection, skulduggery and outright deceit were forthcoming, almost every one of them the figment of an imagination ravaged by time and clouded by years and years on the drink. The tales left Alcoholic John in no doubt that this was a woman with issues. Doubles all round became trebles all round, and if Lubworth could have decided which of the eight shoulders she could see was a real one, she would have cried on it.

"Never mind love, they did fuck all else after winning in Brighton..." (yes I know that was ABBA, give me some credit), *"...let's go and play a few holes".*

Lubworth smiled at each of John's four heads in turn, she'd become a little less bitter over the last hour, she liked this gentle man. She'd found a friend who understood what she thought she went through during her early days of not being a major player in the music industry.

Like most golf clubs, Russet Grange provided a practice putting green. Kept in near-identical condition to the greens on the course so that people could miss short putts with consistency, it was an essential stopping off point on the way to the first tee. Both Lubworth and Alcoholic felt the need to partake, not because either of them gave a shit about practice, but because the freshness of a February morning might help their vision to return to near normality, offering perhaps a 50/50 chance of hitting the correct ball down the first fairway.

Ten minutes of putting helped, not a great deal, but the first tee was clear, and golf wasn't going to play itself. Lubworth had the honour. Mulligan (aimed for the imaginary ball, missed both). Second mulligan (aimed for the correct ball but hit the imaginary ball).

The demons resurfaced as a tirade of cuss words, blaming all four members of Eurovision's answer to *'The Beatles'*, turned the crisp morning air blue.

Alcoholic John was more successful, he actually hit his ball, but as he fell over onto an arse numbed by glass upon glass of Scotland's cheapest, he watched his effort soar wayward into the land of *'bacon in waiting'*.

Lubworth felt a murmur. Half a bottle of Bells and last night's Asda *'Essentials'* Chicken Bhuna had long since become gastric bedfellows, and as the stiffening breeze wafted in the stench of some of *'Peppa and Friends'* finest faeces across the fairway, she came to the swift conclusion that golf was best left for August.

They were a sorry pair indeed, but they laughed (Lubworth in a rather restrained fashion because she had no desire to see yesterday's budget curry once again). Then they laughed some more.

Alcoholic John got to his feet on his third attempt. *"I think that's enough golf for one day, let's have another little drink and then you can tell me a bit more about the time they kicked you out of The Nolans."*

A Tale of Portaloo Waterloo

Chapter	Par	Length	Joke Index
30	5	2,564 Words	2

Introducing:
Dimitri 'Pudding' Pavlova (44)
Full Member
Nationality: Romanian

Dimitri Pavlova

*D*imitri Pavlova, otherwise known as 'The Brickie from Ludnicki' came to England in the Summer of 2010 to work on building the Olympic Stadium in London .He aimed to put a few quid in his pocket as well as sending some to each of his wives back home in Romania. (Neither wife knew of the existence of each other, which is probably just as well for all concerned).*

On one fateful day in August, and following the antics of a drunken Russian who claimed he could juggle with a chainsaw, Pavlova left work with one less arm than he had arrived with. Because said Russian should have been nowhere near a chainsaw, let alone be pissed at work, a six figure compensation package was swiftly agreed upon. The Russian was on the next flight to Minsk, cargo hold class, and Pavlova treated himself to a little place in the countryside, right next to a golf course.

It's not easy to play golf with one arm, but Pavlova is a big bugger, and despite having one sleeve too many on his golf shirts, he still smashes his driver 220 yards, playing off a single figure handicap.

He is loved by all at Russet Grange too, especially the finance director, who noted that his average vodka spend in a year covers the club's utility bills.

And also
Lee 'Majors' Willis (48)
Full Member
Nationality: English

Lee Willis

*E*very club has one of *these characters too, the ex-soldier who doesn't like to talk about his past, but wears a polo shirt with his regiment crest on it and gets pissy if you don't ask him about his time in the armed forces.*

Willis likes to think of himself as a real-world John Rambo but the reality is he spent a total of nine weeks on active duty, four of them as a commis chef in Afghanistan and five doing the same job in Bosnia. The nearest he ever got to danger was a chip pan fire that he started in a mess tent over 90 miles from the front line.

On return from active duty he moved into his mother's flat, losing his right arm below the elbow in a moped

*accident whilst out getting the both of them a fish &
chip supper. (Yep, we've got two people who are lacking
in the limbs department in the same chapter. Weirdly,
this has no relevance to the story).*

*Little sidenote: Willis' mum used to post about his
"wartime action" on Facebook, though when someone
pointed out that one of his lasagnes resulted in more
British casualties than the Afghans, the posting stopped.*

*He's known as 'Lee Majors' at Russet Grange on
account of his prosthetic limb, and when he walks out
of the bar members have been known to do that slow
motion thing whilst saying "We can rebuild him…"*

*Willis was going to be a Social Member but then I
realised that I needed him to play golf in this chapter.*

We begin...

I t feels like we haven't had any so-called *'toilet humour'*
for quite some time, so let us hop back a couple of
weeks to a Ladies' Golf Committee meeting and,
ironically, item number two on the agenda: *'Unisex Toilets'*.
Some readers will have already worked out where this is
heading and that it isn't going to end well for the ladies,
so badly in fact that *'Portaloo Waterloo'* might be the most
memorable chapter in what must surely be the book about
golf that contains the least about golf ever written.

Author's note: I don't think we've established who sits on
the Ladies' Golf Committee, so let us elect Debbie *'Bambi'*
Watts as Chairperson, she seems like a fairly decent sort.

Rose Lubworth can be on the committee too, she'll have sobered up by 6:00pm when meetings start, just in time to get back on it again. Bless her.

Sophie Pasquale can add a bit of youth/glamour and Pam Cleaver can make up our final committee member because she's got the hots for Pasqualle (you'd know that if you'd paid attention earlier). Also at this meeting is Carol Brittan, she's Ladies' Captain (remember?) so she's allowed to come along and annoy everyone. The good news is that we've met all of these people before (thank fuck for that.) so we're good to go. (Worry not, Willis and Pavlova will appear later in the chapter, I haven't forgotten how it works).

"Item number two – unisex toilets on the course". (I told you). Watts spoke with a sigh in her voice (Not quite a line from *'Song Sung Blue'*, but it's worth a mention), forced as she was to bring up the one and only item that Rose Lubworth had ever requested to appear on a meeting agenda.

"Rose has suggested that all three Portaloos should be made available to both sexes, rather than the current arrangement, which in my opinion has worked perfectly well for the last forty years". Watts couldn't hide her disdain for the idea. The proposer however wanted to make her case:

"To be honest the blokes just piss in the hedge, or, mentioning no names, take a number two on the fairway when they think nobody who cares is watching". Lubworth had clearly thought about this. *"Unisex just means three portaloos for us girls…"* (Pasqualle resented the *'us girls'* phrase, the only thing she had in common with Lubworth was a pair of X chromosomes). *"…seems like a sensible suggestion to me".*

Lubworth was happy, Brittan didn't care, Cleaver agreed with whatever Pasquale thought, Pasquale didn't care. Brittan didn't get a vote (though deep down she thought it was possibly the most stupid thing she'd ever heard). Thus, and I really didn't want to write this, the motion was passed. The existing door signs denoting which bog was allocated to which sex would come down, and one which featured some kind of bloke in half a skirt would be fitted instead. A few words to note the change would go in that week's newsletter to the members. Job done. (Honestly, this stuff writes itself),

We now move to the present day, a busy day, a Saturday, and a packed course for the Professional's Fourball Betterball (Look it up if you don't know, I can't be arsed to explain, the chapter is already too long). A day, as fate would have it, followed Lee Willis' birthday, an occasion which had seen him and nineteen of his golfing buddies, including Dimitri Pavlova out on the piss, followed by a curry. There was only one curry house in the nearby town, and you know those food rating things… well this establishment had just had an inspection and been downgraded to a mere one star out of a possible five. The one star was generous, earned by the fact that the chef vaguely knew that food hygiene regulations existed, and because most of the raw meat was stored fairly close to a working fridge.

So twenty mates out on a golf course, mates who had booked the first tee times of the day, mates who would most certainly be in desperate need of the on-course facilities on each of the three occasions they passed them.

"How are you feeling my friend, it was a good night yes?".
Obviously this is how Romanian bricklayers generally speak, and we're not making any exceptions for Pavlova, despite him only having one arm.

"Bit of a jippy gut to be honest mate…" replied Willis, *"…must have had a bad pint last night"*.

"Twenty bad pints, and a Vindaloo. Ha! You thought you were in a Chinese takeaway and wanted free prawn crackers. You are a funny man." To be honest Pavlova wasn't feeling all that great either, and there were some tell-tale rumblings felt as he smashed a drive straight into a section of the pig farm that, well let's just say it is where piggy ends his days and a few days later, bacon begins.

Willis would have to score the points on the first, he did so, three of them, despite regurgitating a quite grotesque cocktail of Kingfisher Lager and Prawn Bhuna at 200 yards from the pin. (He knew he was at that distance, as much of the putrid mix actually landed on the big white disc in the middle of the fairway, signifying just how straight he had hit his drive).

Behind this fourball were three other groups, all of whom had been out with the birthday boy. None were in what you might call good shape, with many of them having partaken of the most ill-advised of hangover cures, the Full English Breakfast. Thus there were payloads-a-plenty that would be looking for a home by the sixth. And, because it's that kind of book, behind this choice section of humanity was a group consisting entirely of ladies.

Indeed, they were four ladies from the golf committee, a group of people who not just two weeks earlier had been instrumental in the approval of the *'woke bogs'*. Four ladies who were a few holes away from falling tragically foul of the law of unintended consequences.

Feel free to imagine the course layout if you wish, but the trio of toilets, a bog battalion, were ready for impending action, situated as they always had been on the ground between the sixth, eleventh and fifteenth greens.

Willis had never been so pleased to see his seven iron approach to the sixth green fall well short and into the duck pond, a pond which hadn't seen ducks, or any kind of wildlife other than bluebottles and the occasional mosquito, since 1997. (This being the year that a former greenkeeper earned himself the nickname *'Slick'*, and then dismissal a few days later, when he overturned a tractor and dumped almost 100 gallons of diesel into what was at the time a thriving habitat for wildlife).

"Up to you mate, I need to pay a visit". Willis began a desperate sprint to the bog, knowing that he was not a million miles from a round-ending trouser incident.

"Same here." laughed Pavlova, hoping that he could manage to keep himself contained for a few more minutes.

Mike Flowers and Adam Bobble made up the first quartet of hungover sportsmen, and they too were desperate to use the on-course facilities. Bobble drew the short straw (though it was nothing like as short as that drawn by those in the following groups), and had to wait for Willis to offload what Kipling would surely have called *'faecal cargo'*. Willis left *'Woke Bog One'* and gave a quick glance to Bobble, one which conveyed both relief and abject apology.

"Holy fuck." a muffled cry of despair before Willis had taken two paces, a muffled mumbling of misery as Bobble took a lungful of fetid oxygen and looked on in horror. The stark reality that whilst the Portaloo flush was a miracle of science, it was not designed to cope with a gastric outpouring of such magnitude. Four men left the Bog Batallion in a very, very bad state and it would only be ten minutes before another four would follow in their wake. And then another four, and so on…

Twenty men, five groups of players, with the leading group of Willis, Pavlova, Flowers and Bobble arriving back at the *'Portaloo Waterloo'* via the eleventh green with military precision, moments after the last group of this band of merry men had paid their first visits.

The scenes were like some kind of twisted Japanese game show. Open a random door, in fear of what might await due to the all-pervading stench, courtesy of a southerly breeze that you'd picked up before playing your second shot on the fifth. Look inside, wretch, try two more doors and then pick the least disgusting of the three cubicles. (Readers might like to avail themselves of the *'Monty Hall problem'* via a quick Google, there is a certain similarity here).

As the day progressed the Bog Battalion gradually succumbed to the horrors of war, with the aforementioned *"least disgusting"* (but still absolutely horrific) progressing to something beyond belief. *"Christ I've got to go again".* Willis knew what awaited him as he putted out on the fifteenth green.

"Same here, but in the bushes this time. I cannot stomach the toilets again". Pavlova grabbed a branded golf towel, which proudly displayed the message: *'Scotland's Finest'.* Not to clean a club with, but for a more rudimentary use, one which it was certainly not churned out of an Indonesian sweatshop for. More laughter ensued and took a cheek-clenching shuffle to his self-designated *'drop zone'* (That could be my favourite metaphor of the entire book, though again, the standards are not high, relying as I do on smutty one-liners and toilet humour).

He thought he had hidden his massive frame pretty well, but the Ladies Golf Committee fourball, all of whom had had the good sense to have a wee before playing, were chatting their way down the eleventh fairway. They had not yet needed the one-course facilities, and Pavlova was not as well hidden as he thought. Four ladies of a certain age were horrified to see a six foot four inch Romanian bricklayer taking a dump among the Azaleas. A man struggling to clean himself up with two square feet of golf towel, lacking as he was in a full complement of limbs, desperately trying to balance, with his trousers and boxers around his ankles, lest he tumble into something terribly, terribly bad of his own making. (It's not exactly *'Great Expectations'* is it?)

One by one the ladies caught on, having already felt that there was a certain stench wafting its way around the course. Not the piggy smell that all members were used to, but something more…. human. (One for us die-hard *'Star Trek'* fans there).

Lubworth needed to go. Just a wee, but the specific nature of her toiletry situation was irrelevant, and as she approached the blue soldiers of relief the horrors of *'Portaloo Waterloo'* began to become all too clear. Her eyes started to water as she got within chipping distance and at putting range she saw what can politely be described as *'seepage'*.

Picture the scene that greeted Rose Lubworth when she tentatively opened the door of her chosen unisex toilet that day. If that is too much of an intellectual challenge, which it might well be for my chosen demographic, please do this: Imagine filling an industrial food blender with lager, mutton dansak, prawn vindaloo, lime pickle, fried eggs, baked beans, sausages, black pudding and a decent glug of stomach acid, giving it all a good blitz and then removing the lid in a confined space whilst the blender is still blending.

Lubworth screamed and threw up in an instant, slamming the door as she did so, taking *'Woke Bog Three'* past its tipping point and sending it to the floor, spewing forth gallons of flushed and unflushed ordure. Her three playing partners ran over as the last battle of *'Portaloo Waterloo'* unfolded. It was a scene they would haunt each and every one of them for the rest of their days.

It was also a scene which, of course, determined item one on the agenda of the following month's meeting of the Ladies' Golf Committee: *"Separate toilets for men and women, clearly labelled and placed a minimum of 100 yards apart"*.

A Tale of a Man Who Knows More About Greenkeeping than the Greenkeepers Do

Chapter	Par	Length	Joke Index
31	4	1,657 Words	30

Introducing:
Martin Wagstaff (81)
Full Member, Former Club
Captain and Chairman
Nationality: English

Martin Wagstaff

*E*x-club captain,
ex-club chairman,
ex-rugby player,
ex-company director, ex-
copper, still a twat. One of
those annoying old bastards who reckons he's better than
everyone else because he played rugby for his university.

*Martin Wagstaff thinks nothing of squeezing the arse
of any passing barmaid, laughing it off as "just a bit of
fun", in the mistaken belief that being a pensioner and
dysfunctional in the cock department gives him licence
to grope. Currently the subject of a disciplinary hearing
and swollen bollocks having referred to Jacqui Fletcher
as a 'MILF' in hearing range of Jenny McCulloch .*

*As an ex-copper he should know better, but he thinks he's
above the law when it comes to drinking and driving.
However, he's been done twice, once when clocked at
134MPH on the M1. In that instance he claimed he was
rushing to his wife's hospital bed but was too pissed to
remember she was in the passenger seat. On the second*

occasion he was given a six month suspended prison sentence, claiming he got off lightly because "...the Chief Super was a fellow old boy at Rochester."

Wagstaff is another one who is creative when it comes to golf scoring, and also a master of outright bullshit. He claims he was a consultant on the first series of 'The Apprentice' and that his mother helped crack the Enigma code at Bletchley Park. This is highly unlikely as she died giving birth to him in 1939.

He was the shortest-serving Chairman at Russet Grange, being in the role less time that Brian Clough was at Leeds United. He resigned after being caught taking a dump on the 14th tee. (In the sequel I won't fall back to toilet humour quite as often).

And also:
Brian 'Tex' Hanley (47)
Clubhouse Manager
Nationality: Not American

Brian Hanley

*B*rian Hanley is about as American as a Paella Biryani served in pitta bread but our Clubhouse Manager desperately wants everyone to regard him as a bit of a cowboy, a gun-totin' redneck, born and raised in the deep south. Well the last bit is true, he's from Paignton.

A TALE OF A MAN WHO KNOWS MORE ABOUT GREENKEEPING THAN THE GREENKEEPERS DO

Even if you don't spot the Dallas Cowboys Baseball hat, or the sticker quoting the 2nd amendment on the bumper of his Nissan Micra, you will certainly notice the cowboy boots as 'Tex' wanders around the clubhouse collecting glasses. It has to be said that he's a good bar manager though, welcoming all and sundry with a cheerful "Howdy", delivered in an accent that slips from South Carolina to South Devon as the day passes.

Hanley lives on a caravan park in a trailer which he refers to as his 'Winnebago'. He was financially cleaned out by his ex-wife who finally got sick of the American thing. Ironically, whilst on a singles cruise to Bermuda, that her ex-hubby paid for, she met and subsequently married a bloke from Nevada.

The bottom line though is that Brian Hanley is likeable, honest, hard-working and good at his job. A shame then that behind his back, more than a few members refer to him as "Butch Tragedy".

We begin...

Martin Wagstaff had a bit of a grump on, to say the least. His Thursday morning game with fellow twat and current President Timothy Bleauchamp (who we met earlier) had not gone well. Three holes down at the turn, knees covered in mud having slipped into a ditch laden with duck faeces trying to retrieve a ball he found on the previous hole, and reeling from the news (delivered with a matter-of-fact text message) that his *"filthy slut"* of a daughter had got herself knocked up again.

"She's already got four fucking kids with five different fathers, she only speaks to me when she wants something. Total fucking slut, just like her fucking mother".

"How can she have five fathers of four kids?" asked his playing partner, slightly bemused, but also pleased that the resulting mental anguish would surely put him even more firmly into the driving seat of today's game.

"She shagged identical twins on consecutive days during her gap year in Cancun". Wagstaff had a well-practised look of resignation in his eyes. *"Would need the two of them to wank into a test tube to find out who's the real father, but you try convincing a couple of Mexicans to knock one out over a well-used copy of El-Razzle at their local clap clinic. Not going to happen, so little fucking Schroedinger Rodrigo's got two dads".*

"Shame Jeremy Kyle got scrapped, she could have gone on there, he loves that kind of stuff." Beauchamp was only half jesting.

"She'd already been on it, whilst working as a stripper at the time. Show was called 'My boyfriend thinks I work in the Co-op', so she strolled on stage and got her tits out. Ended up in a mass brawl involving more than half of the audience". Wagstaff shook his head and looked to the sky, *"Surprisingly they wouldn't have her on again."*

The relationship between Wagstaff and Beauchamp had always been a fractious one, because despite Wagstaff's outward appearance as being someone who thought he was better than everyone else, he knew all too well that Beauchamp was the person he desperately wanted to be. Someone slightly wealthier, better connected, and also not tarred with the *"Took a dump on the 14th"* brush (the low-point of his time at Russet Grange that had featured few, if any, high points).

Beauchamp was well aware of the envy that bubbled below the waterline of their relationship, with occasional mention of his *'charity work'* (Wagstaff had never been invited to be a Rotarian and Beauchamp was certainly not going to invite him), plus the occasional not-so-subtle hint of the power he wielded on the local planning committee. *"Young couple wanted double glazing on a grade two, just because we agreed to a dual carriageway at the back of their place. They were lucky we didn't sue them for wasting our time".*

Anyway, Wagstaff had indeed been rattled by the fact that he was going to have to go to *"Another fucking Christening, would have been cheaper to buy her a church."* and he lost the match five and four (if you're not a golfer, just know that he got soundly beaten, and please accept my thanks for reading, you're not target audience but I appreciate the seven quid I made if you bought the book).

Anyway, hands shaken on the 14th green, around 100 yards from where Wagstaff had gone for a poo.

"Mind if we skip the last few and just walk in Martin, I've got to go and tell some chancer widow she can't build a granny annexe?"

Wagstaff agreed, he had no desire to play a few pointless holes, and as Beauchamp wouldn't be joining him for a post-humiliation pint, it would give him a chance to tell anyone who would listen that his loss was entirely due to the poor state of the course.

Brian Hanley (finally he gets a mention) was on duty at the bar. With Marge Simpson on a day off he could get away with wearing his cowboy hat, and listening to *'Smokey and the Bandit – The Soundtrack'* on the clubhouse music system. He was in a good mood, and a well-intentioned *"Howdy"* greeted Wagstaff as he drifted into the spikes bar, still wearing his *"Chinos with a hint of Mallard crap"* having left his change of clothes in his hallway.

"Good game Mr President?" Hanley's choice of referring to former Russet Grange Presidents as *"Mr President"* was as tiresome as it was embarrassing, but as you know he's a decent sort. Indeed, not since a visiting golfer, at the rough end of a nine-pint bender, had given him both barrels: *"You're not American, you're just some sad fucking twat who lives in a caravan"*, had anyone else mentioned the tragic nature of his adopted nationality.

"Fucking awful mate, fucking awful. Whoever looks after those greens should be sacked. Too slow, pins in the wrong place, surface water, snails, thatch, bumps, crudge weed all over the place, the fucking lot".

"Did you win?"

"Did I fuck. Tiger couldn't have putted out there, fucking disgrace." Hanley's question was not well-received. *"Freddy West reckons they had five weeks of rain in five hours. Said he'd kill for a few dry days, I told him to get the fuck on with it, he can start with that prick Beauchamp. Not a clue those greenkeepers, too busy wanking over lawnmower catalogues and chainsaw calendars".*

A TALE OF A MAN WHO KNOWS MORE ABOUT
GREENKEEPING THAN THE GREENKEEPERS DO

"Well nobody else has complained Mr President, most reckon the course is in good nick." Hanley had removed his hat and also took the trouble to turn down the music, just as Jerry Reed was in full flow on the second verse of *'Eastbound and Down'* (It's a decent tune, have a little listen now because you're only a few pages from the end of the book and you probably need a break. Then later on you might like to watch *'Convoy'* or maybe just the first five minutes of *'The Cannonball Run'*).

"Ah fuck it, give me a Guinness and a little heart-starter to wash it down with". Wagstaff had often turned to alcohol in times of need, and heaven knows he'd had plenty of those.

As the Guinness flowed slowly from the tap, Hanley walked away from Wagstaff and then slid a large glass of Bell's along the bar. (Why simply pass it to a customer when you can risk making a complete twat of yourself by misjudging the angle and smashing a glass on the clubhouse floor?).

The drink helped, and another couple helped even more, and sure enough a slight smile found its way onto Wagstaff's face. Perhaps things weren't so bad after all, because whilst the victor of the day's game was sat in a meeting with people who regarded the Daily Mail as the new New Testament and deluded with the power of his authority over double-glazing, he was going to have a few more beers and enjoy Hanley's unbridled respect for authority.

"Same again please Brian, one for yourself"

"That's very kind Mr President, I'll have a Budweiser with you. Oh, by the way, I've been meaning to ask how's your daughter doing these days?"

*On the way home from defeating the
Armada, British Ships burned timbers from
Spanish Ships to fuel their engines.*

*With a following wind and a fair tide
they could achieve almost forty miles
to the galleon.*

*We've just turned down the opportunity to
host the 2027 Ryder Cup.*

*Russet Grange would have been the ideal
venue but our members come first and hosting
the tournament would have meant cancelling
the Chris Cridge foursomes competition and a
ladies' coffee morning.*

Not going to happen.

A Tale of a Pro-Am (Part Two)

Chapter	Par	Length	Joke Index
32	5	2,720 Words	18

Introducing:

Claire Tingleford (45)
Full Member
Nationality: Chubby

*A*nother character for whom the cake was invented. *Claire Tingleford has the intellect of a piece of flat-pack furniture and genuinely believes that in some way, Diet Coke absorbs the*

Claire Tingleford

calories from a catering pack of Terry's chocolate orange. She won a place at the 2013 Pro-Am, and having done two golfers' mega-breakfasts before her 8:30am tee time she still managed to stuff a six pack of Mint Club biscuits into her fat gob before stuffing her tee shot into a pond on the third.

Tingleford has been, rather cruelly but fairly, described as "A Slimming Company's Dream" having gradually raised her target weight from 11st at the turn of the decade to something just shy of 22st as old father time ticked into 2020. Week in, week out, she has enjoyed a collective "well done" from a bunch of equally delusional chubsters as she piles on the actual pounds, whilst simultaneously meeting her conveniently continuously increasing target.

In the last two decades Tingleford has been through three husbands, four wedding dresses, two past captains and an entire Asda shelf full of Mars 'Celebrations'.

On the plus side, she's bloody good fun, she doesn't care, and she know that there's more chance of Arnold Palmer winning again at Augusta than she has of seeing her 50th birthday without a gastric band welded to her substantial frame.

And also:
Chris 'Trip' Hazzerd (62)
Full Member
Nationality: English

Chris Hazzerd

Chris Hazzerd is a bit of a 'Jack the Lad', who by his own admission has "Seen more pussy than a vet doing overtime at the Cats Protection League". To look at him you can't really imagine how he manages it, but despite his unremarkable appearance, and advancing years, manage it he does.

In his mid-twenties he worked as a TV stuntman, though to be frank, he was never very good at it. By his own admission he "Almost killed the lovely Glynys Barber when I wrapped a Sierra Cosworth around a tree during Dempsey and Makepiece, and let's just say I'm not on Eddie Shoestring's Christmas card list."

Hazzerd soon left the glamour of TV and made a few quid in the mid-1990s selling houses on the Costa Brava to gullible Daily Mail readers, who then wrote to the very same newspaper when the houses didn't actually materialise. He blames the Spanish government, and to be fair, there is now an eight lane highway where Hazzerd once promised, via a huge roadside banner "You're [sic] dream home from home in the glorious Spanish sun".

With the proceeds from selling non-existent holiday homes he bought himself an XR3i and a hair transplant. His current 'official' squeeze is a 58-year-old hairdresser who Kevin Pudgett described as looking like: "...the wrong end of a Bulldog, plums and all".

Hazzerd idolises Guy Potton, spending much of his spare time in the Pro-shop showing him WhatsApp messages he's received from some of the old tarts he's been treating to a bit of 'stuntman love' that week.

We begin...

R ight then. Having re-read part one of the Pro-Am story it's clear we should have a short recap. In summary, very few people paid to enter a team, a local drainage firm is the main sponsor, there's a fuck load of free booze, prizes of many standards are up for grabs and some shit cars adorn either the first or second tees. (I can't be arsed to check, it's not as if it matters).

The big news from the early starters is that one of the visiting professionals (Ryan Framley) went round in 59, smashing the course record, and then just a few hours later smashing Sophie Pasquale. Bless.

Other things? Well many of the golfers didn't have one of those handicap things, not being members of an actual golf club, but Russet Grange needed the entry fees so these rebels/non-conformers were allowed to play and given a 28 handicap. This turned out to be quite generous as among their number was a county amateur champion, three people who had played off of single figures a few years previously and, I shit you not, a former tour professional whose career ended in the kind of disgrace that would not be fitting to describe in this book. (Which really is saying something).

So let us dip into the action, we might as well have a bit of golf so we join the lovely Claire Tingleford on the third tee. Yes, she's a 'curvy' girl, but she's a fucking good golfer too.

Seven iron to within eighteen inches of the pin. *"Oh you beauty, you absolute beauty."* Chris Hazzerd was well pleased with his playing partner's shot. There was a team prize for nearest the pin on this hole, and although it was early days in the competition, nobody was going to beat Tingleford. All three playing partners were near certain to be picking up vouchers for 20% off four Michelins, courtesy, weirdly, of a local Chinese takeaway. (There's a *'rubbery'* joke here I'm not doing it).

"The 'Weapon' needs new tyres, what a result." Hazzerd hugged Tingleford as best he could, getting perhaps 80% round, thrilled at the automotive saving she had probably just won.

(Yes, Hazard referred to his car as a *'weapon'*, peak-twattish when you drive a Porsche, unforgivable when you drive a nine year old Toyota Corolla).

"Got a bit of luck Chris, but glad you're happy". Tingleford rather enjoyed the near-complete hug. *"See if you can return the favour on the 13th, year's supply of Ben & Jerry's"*. The little smile she gave to Hazzerd was rather cute, he reciprocated with one of his own, desperately hoping that his playing partner didn't mis-interpret the gesture, because whilst he was not particularly choosy when it came to matters of the flesh, he was never going to be interested in someone whose day would be made by winning 52 gallons of ice-cream.

"I'll do my best love, I'll do my best". (Spoiler alert, his best wasn't even close to being good enough, the ice-cream was won by Ricky Blower, one of the single figure players, enjoying 28 shots whilst representing the family firm, *'Blower's Ice-Cream Wholesalers'*.

Over on the 10th hole the Men's Golf Committee team were having an absolute nightmare with a very miserable Graham McMagnussonson, (I'm taking no risks with this one), a professional whose mind was elsewhere, Spain to be precise. A place where he should have been enjoying his debut on the professional tour had he not missed a nine inch putt in a qualifying competition. A competition won by his assistant pro, a kid of just 19 years of age, with chronic acne and personal hygiene issues.

"Nine inches. Nine fucking inches". McMagnussonson was still raging a week after missing the crucial putt. *"Spots Boy is sunning it in the Costa Brava, surrounded by suntanned fanny*

and sangria, I'm in this shithole where you can win a thirty quid Asda voucher or a fucking meat hamper".

As you can imagine the committee representatives didn't take kindly to this admittedly harsh but fair critique, spoken quite deliberately in their earshot. Ron McAndrew, never one to mince his words, responded in a way that did nothing to restore any kind of harmony: *"You're shit anyway mate, you'd never have made the cut."*

Things were hotting up on the eighth, where the always-popular *'Nearest the Pie'* competition was forcing golfers into tough decisions. Should you go for prime position on the fairway, giving yourself a great chance of setting up a double bogey, or should you play a little shorter, and try to stick your tee shot within a few feet of the magnificence of a *'Fray Bentos Meat & Potato'*, winning a dozen tins of this *"Foodstuff of the lesser Gods"* in the process?

Currently with his eyes on the prize was Clive Rush (we'll meet him in the final chapter, he's one of the good guys), in a rare venture onto the course: *"Greg, I'm going for the pies, I bloody am you know".* Greg Norketh nodded, if anyone deserved to win an on-course prize it was Rush *"Good luck mate, good luck".* (We're never going to meet Norketh, feel free to let your imagination run wild, you'll probably come up with far better characters than I've managed).

Rush's drive travelled some forty feet, never getting further from the ground than when it was on the tee. Our man just laughed, Norketh made a mental note to send him a dozen pies, accompanied a *'thank you'* note for being invited to join his team.

Meanwhile, the complimentary burgers/sausage baps, served with no consideration for basic hygiene procedures by a 20 year old lad, on his day off as a team leader at Halfords, were going down very well. I say *"down"*, but *"through"* is more appropriate. Leave the 6th green, shove something that was made from the very worst bits of a cow or a pig down your gut, and then choose the least disgusting on-course convenience as you leave the 11th green some 55 minutes later.

"Do you have any vegan options?" asked Simon Babbage to the young bundle of enthusiasm. *"Well the rolls aren't made of meat so you could have one of those with some chutney. They didn't tell me there would be any bacon-dodgers".* (Babbage was playing on a freebie due to serving on some committee or other, it really doesn't matter. I've assumed he's a vegan, in fact let's go the whole vegan-hog and assume he's a celeriac or whatever they call it).

Babbage took a couple of beefburgers, suspending his most heartfelt of beliefs that eating meat was tantamount to murder, as he was quite peckish. A decision he would regret precisely twelve minutes later when he shat himself and had to take a half mile walk of shame back to the clubhouse to clean himself up as best he could.

Let us do one more little tale before we head back to the clubhouse, this time we hop over to the 9th where the Ladies' Golf Committee were making professional golfer Dunk Frisbee wish he was dead, having endured eight holes where the conversation drifted from hot flushes to *'Love Island'*, and then to that show with Ant and Dec where people eat wallaby cocks. To him it seemed that ladies played golf to give themselves a chance to talk about television or the menopause somewhere other than their local Costa. (Dunk is a token American golfer, he's part of an exchange program where American golfers bring their remarkable names to the UK and in return we send them professionals with normal names like *'Brian Benson'* in the hope that they learn the error of their ways).

Despite his three human handicaps, Dunk was playing out of his skin, not well enough to break the course record that had been set earlier in the day, but certainly in with a chance of almost covering his petrol costs by finishing in the top three. Four consecutive birdies was impressive stuff, and under normal circumstances (not playing with people who were more interested in what was being discussed on *'Loose Women'* that day) he would have received some praise for his efforts. As it was, none of the ladies were that bothered about Dunk's scoring, though Debbie Watts was rather enjoying looking at his bottom.

"Mind if I ask you something?" Watts observed in awe as Dunk struck an absolute peach of a three iron straight onto the green of this pathetically short par four. *"Do you watch Bargain Hunt?"*

3pm, many teams back in the clubhouse, a few still on the course but getting a bit bored with it all. The late starters tended to be the ones who had paid nothing to enter, but having said that they were blessed with getting two goes at the buffet. Stuff your face before you go out, stuff it again five hours later. What's not to like? (other than the buffet, which was frankly shocking for something that the chef had been allocated twenty quid per player for).

Furthermore, it was becoming clear that the on-course free alcohol had flowed all too well. Most at Russet Grange weren't used to such hospitality, and various members were reacting in various ways. One senior member fell asleep whilst changing his trousers and Billy Heron saw his pre-game bacon roll again, this time soaked in a tasty mix of Vodka and Red Bull. Brynn Morgan wet himself whilst taking part in the charity putting competition and Claire Tingleford wandered aimlessly around the place, absolutely bollocksed, asking *"Where's the fuck is my stuntman, he promised me some ice-cream"* before planting her well-cushioned face into a bowl of Eton Mess.

New-course record holder Ryan Framley was slouched in the corner on a sofa that looked like it could have been used for forensics training. He seemed surprisingly miserable given his golfing and sexual achievements of a day that was still relatively young.

This misery was probably due to the fact he was almost certain to win first prize and was thus contractually obliged to stay hang around to the bitter end, where he would pose with the boss of a third rate drainage business and the club captain, for a photograph that might make page 80 of the local rag, captioned in all likelihood with him name wrongly spelt. He'd have to make a short speech too, something along the lines of : *"The greens were in top-notch condition, the food was excellent, and thanks to all of the sponsors and the clubhouse team, it was a great day"*.

He wanted to add *"Also, the place didn't stink of shit quite as much as usual and it was good to see so many prizes that the club professional was given by the sales reps."*

This seems to be a very long chapter, but we do need to get in something about that stalwart of any Pro-Am, the evening *'entertainment'*.

A three-piece band, *'Seventies Stardust'*, had been booked to provide musical merriment from 5pm to 8pm. Hanley was impressed with the modest £100 fee so he checked out a few of their performances on Youtube, liked what he saw, and signed them up right away. It was only when the three souls who turned up looked nothing like the five people of Youtube fame that he realised his mistake. *'Stardust Seventies'* (subtle difference in name, huge difference in ability) were so called due to them all being in their seventies ten years ago. A musical repertoire of *'Sweet Caroline'*, *'Hi Ho Silver Lining'*, *'Yes Sir I Can Boogie'*, a reprise of *'Sweet Caroline'* and then a tragically inadequate rendition of *'Bye Bye Baby'* being the backbone of their act.

That's pretty much it. I can't be bothered to write any more about the Pro-Am, these chapters are getting longer and longer. Suffice to say that it all ended in typical style with a couple of fights and one or two of the more accommodating ladies enjoying some personal attention from the young bucks who made up the some of the teams from *'Biddies Drain Company'*. Also, a car from *'Brain's Autos'* ended up in a pond due to handbrake failure. (A Citroen Picasso which had suspiciously passed its MOT the day before).

A TALE OF A PRO-AM (PART TWO)

Ryan Framley took first prize, actually mentioning the stench from the pig farm and one or two other home truths in a drunken speech. The American bloke got third place, enjoying a net profit of almost ten quid, and even the kid year old who ran the burger van got his end away during late afternoon. He posted something on social media about his exploits, but as he couldn't spell the word *'meat'* there was quite some confusion about what was supposed to be a double-entendre.

By 7:30pm the proceedings drew to a close. By 7:45 the clubhouse had emptied of golfers. The only people who remained were either asleep, throwing up on the patio, sat in the clubhouse waiting for leftover roast potatoes, or members of *'Stardust Seventies'*.

"Shall we call it a day Brian?" asked their lead singer. *"Will you fuck."* replied a typically enraged Handley, *"I paid you for three fucking hours, you've done two hours and fifty minutes, play 'Sweet Caroline' again or you don't get a fucking penny"*.

Unfollowed a few people this morning who kept posting shit like "170 yards to the pin, strong crosswind, which club are you using?"

If you cannot phrase a question correctly, you're gone.

Followed Stormy Daniels instead.

Like everyone else we're aiming for #NetZero. In our case, members, not carbon.

All they ever do is moan so we'll be 'Societies Only' in 2025. Forty blokes on a coach and on the piss spend more in a day that the members do in a week.

They smile too.

A guide to our menu:

"Local Produce" – Came from this planet
"Organic" – Wasn't grown in a laboratory
"Seasonal Vegetables" – Potatoes
"Ethically Sourced" – We didn't steal it
"Sustainable" – Always stocked in Asda

A Tale of Comedy Night Going Horribly Wrong			
Chapter	Par	Length	Joke Index
33	4	1,986 Words	25

Introducing:

Norman 'Banksy' Naylor (71)

Honourary Member and Finance Director
Nationality: Anglo Scottish

Norman Naylor is one of the club's most popular members. He never has a bad word to say against anyone (except Les Hamill of course) and was given honourary membership in 2005 following 50 years at Russet Grange Golf Club.

Norman Naylor

He's never been married though has a reputation of being a ladies man, which he rather enjoys, particularly because he's gay.

Naylor earned his nickname 'Banksy' during a particularly raucous Seniors AGM, when one too many brown ales put him into an artistic mood. A trip to the greenkeepers' sheds provided some white paint and a brush, and ten minutes later he had painted a rather stylish cock and balls on the side of Hamill's Volvo, complete with jiz and an authentic bell end.

Naylor was club captain in 1994 and raised £20k for local charities, £100.00 of which came from a bet with Ray Pullman where he ate an entire card of 'Piggy Nose Best' pork scratchings in under 30 minutes.

Naylor got a GCSE (grade 4) in Money Studies whilst at secondary school, and is the club's Financial Director.

And also:
Maureen Welsh (61)
Social Member
Nationality: Anglo Irish

Maureen Welsh

*I*f Maureen Welsh were to appear in an episode of 'Friends' it would be called 'The One with the Doormat'. Everyone loves her, but nobody would ever invite her to a barbecue. She's single (natch) and whilst she has never told anyone that she has at least 10 cats living with her, it is widely assumed she does.*

If you need badges sewn onto 30 golf shirts or someone to act as a starter on Pro-Am day at 6:00am in the pissing rain, it's Maureen you should ask. She would do anything for anyone and the world doesn't deserve her.

Our hero says she "struggles with her weight" (yes, another one, sorry). What she actually means is that she struggles to walk past Greggs, and let's be honest, buying one doughnut is foolhardy when five are much cheaper.

She's another one who has been a member of a slimming club for years, her huge bulk and frankly shocking BMI would suggest that her membership hasn't been what you might call successful for her. On the other hand it has been a Godsend for them.

The lovely Maureen has been on the club's social committee for 20 years, she doesn't play golf for health reasons, all 27 stones of them. (I think I've done this line before. Never mind).

In 2012 she got stuck in a lift at a Travelodge in Sunderland for over seven hours. When her rescuers asked why she didn't press the alarm button she replied "I didn't want to make a fuss."

We begin...

One of the lesser chapters, a one joke wonder, but I've written enough in the rest of the book to stop people rejecting it on the grounds of it not having many pages for twelve quid (plus postage unless I'm signing copies at your own club which isn't going to happen).

Anyway, as you'll have read earlier, the unlikely pairing of Eric Wibble and Charlotte Sheen have organised a comedy night at Russet Grange. They share a hatred of the *"morons on the social committee"* (Wibble's words) and they also shared a love of comedy.

Today's event takes place on what was to be a twenties night, but only eight tickets had been sold to that particular extravaganza, so it was cancelled via an email to all members. (Obviously all members are on email, there's absolutely no chance that one or two who were almost alive in the nineteen twenties don't have email. No way will they turn up, suitably dressed for an evening of Irving Berlin music, *'Dave Glubb is Fred Astaire'* and whatever crap they ate in that particular decade).

Wibble's comedian friend Dick Frenzy has been booked as the headline/only act and advised to keep things a bit *'family'*. He explained that there would be a mix of age groups attending, and they really didn't want a repeat of what happened when *'The Village Person'*, a one-man *'Village People'* tribute, left the stage in tears after a drunken Bob Cheese called him a *"bummer"*. An accusation which Brian Cooper took exception to and therefore giving Cheese what Billy Hollworth described as *"a fucking good hiding"*.

Last minute, Frenzy catches leprosy (he didn't really, but honestly, it doesn't matter). Luckily he had got in touch with Mike *'Honky'* Best and asked him to do the gig instead. Wibble was mighty relieved at this, had he fucked things up he would have felt obliged to sit on the social committee, having established that he was one of their own.

You know what's coming don't you?

An almost-packed clubhouse hadn't been told of the change of personnel. Wibble decided it didn't matter, and his co-conspirator, Sheen, wouldn't have known the difference if good old Eric Morecambe had risen from the grave and turned up on stage. Wibble had also made the fatal assumption that Frenzy had advised Best to keep things fairly clean, rather than deliver the two hour tirade of filth that formed his typical set.

Eric Wibble took to the stage. We say *'stage'*, but it was basically a six inch platform that one of the greenkeepers had knocked up from pallets a few years previously - ironically the same greenkeeper also knocked up the ladies' club champion some days later, but that's yet another tale for the sequel, which is almost writing itself).

"Ladies and gentlemen....." Words that were barely audible, the bloke hadn't checked the batteries in the radio mic. (Some people never learn do they?) New batteries inserted. *"Ladies and Gentlemen, many thanks for coming along this evening. It's good to see more than eight people, which is what you'd have got if 'Twenties Night' had gone ahead, and that's in the unlikely scenario that nobody died since buying tickets."*

Wibble got a polite laugh, and continued: *"My old mate Dick Frenzy couldn't make it this evening, but we've pulled out all the stops and got one of clubland's finest here tonight, ladies and gentlemen, Mr Mike 'Honky' Best…".*

Best rose to his feet, surrounded by polite applause, and also as it happened, a feeling of terror from one or two in the audience who were well aware of the reputation of the man who was about to do a turn. John Conrad recalled the Daily Mail headline *"So-called 'Comedian' gets two years for inciting racial hatred"* and Ray Pullman knew only too well that Mike Best was, well let's just say *'opinionated'* in matters of race, sexual orientation, general life choices politics and pretty much everything else to be honest.

Most members had no idea though. They knew that the twenties night had been replaced with some wholehearted comedy, it might get a little *'risque'* in places but Eric

Wibble had never let them down before (probably because he had never organised so much as a *'Guess the Number of Sweets in the Jar'* competition), so why should he now?

"Fuck me, did the crematorium kick-out early today? You lot wouldn't look out of place on the slab in Silent Witness". Best's opening line didn't get a lot of laughs, it has to be said. *"Barman, there's one here who's already dead. If the widow asks say the show had started so no refunds".*

An awkward silence descended. Sheen and Wibble exchanged a look which conveyed just two words: *"Oh fuck".*

Best spotted Edna Troggle in the front row. *"Alright love, do they still burn witches round here? Probably best to pay your membership monthly, just in case like."*

Lionel Darcy was seated next to Troggle, desperately hoping that this was as bad as it was going to get, terrified that his rather dapper outfit of a velvet jacket, pink shirt and silk cravat would go unnoticed. It didn't.

"Hello beautiful, you probably remember when 'LGBTQ' was just a fucking awful hand in Scrabble." Darcy was mortified, and it didn't help that there were more than a few laughs around the room. *"You're not the one who stuck a roll-on deodorant up his arse are you?"*

It was at this point, in a moment reminiscent of the Wake/Wedding chapter, that a conga burst into the room, led by Norman Naylor (finally he appears) and Maureen Welsh. They and the other six elderly members they'd brought along apparently knew nothing of the twenties night cancellation and were determined to make an entrance, dressed as they were in dicky bows, evening suits and flapper dresses.

"La la la la Conga, la la la la Conga, la la la la..". Welsh led the singing with gusto, completely pissed, having chucked countless cocktails down her gob at Naylor's pre-twenties night gathering. Naylor himself was equally hammered, *"Nah nah nah nah nah nah, nah nah nah…. oh, Maureen, I think we've got the wrong night…"*. Wise words spoken before he decorated the carpet with a brace of tequila sunrises.

Welsh carried on regardless, she could have walked into an exorcism and not known any different, such was the state of her. *"Nah nah nah, don't stop Norm you twat, they'll be a pile-up… Nah nah nah, Conga Co…. Jesus Christ, I'm going over….."* Naylor had stopped dead, Welsh's momentum kept her going, dragging with her an octogenarian couple, pissed as parrots, managing to conga whilst using walking frames. Eight bodies tumbled to the floor, some at speeds greater than they had moved in a decade.

"Christ on a bike…" quipped Best, *"…are there any doctors in the house, or better still, any there any welders?"*

A tragic pile of shit-faced pensioners formed at the back of the clubhouse, walking sticks, walking frames, even an artificial limb became detached and more than one set of false teeth formed part of the general detritus.

Naylor finally dragged himself to his feet, aided as he was by a dozen people who had decided to leave rather than sit through any more of Best's routine. *"I think my false arm is under one of the tables, it's probably holding a hip flask"*. A bit of mild concussion had perhaps set in but he was otherwise in decent spirits. (Not sure if he had a false arm before this chapter, do you honestly care?)

Welsh brought her ample frame back to a near-vertical position, and with no apparent broken bones and still attached to a chain of geriatrics, she saw no reason not to pick up where she had left off following Naylor's unexpected emergency stop. *"La la la la, la la la la, Conga, conga….."*

Such enthusiasm from one so morbidly obese was surprisingly uplifting and those heading for the exits decided that perhaps the evening wasn't lost after all, so they joined in the merriment. The conga grew, twenty, thirty, forty people and more, singing their little hearts out as they snaked around the room, conveniently passing the buffet table, wisely sneaking a few prawn vol-au-vents as they went their merry way.

Wibble, Sheen and even Mike Best, who would later treat the attendees to a rather more socially acceptable set of jokes about immigration, food banks and the Labour party, put on their dancing shoes. An evening that had transitioned from an unwanted twenties night, to a blue comedian delivering a routine of highly offensive material, back to some kind of comedy/dance/demolition derby/ oldies piss up, ended up as a rip-roaring success.

As the front of the impromptu conga twisted and turned around the bar, to meet with its tail, Eric Wibble couldn't help but throw a passing comment to the still shit-faced Welsh: *"I bet you're glad you didn't know twenties night was cancelled Maureen"*. Welsh turned to reply, slipped on the slowly spreading pool of tequila puke, and cushioned by her own bulk simply bounced a little and nodded off to sleep.

A Tale of Kindly Men and the Good Old Days			
Chapter	Par	Length	Joke Index
34	3	1,451 Words	27

Introducing, as our final character:
Clive Rush (68)
Full Member
Nationality: English

Clive Rush

*C*live Rush is the Handicap Secretary at Russet Grange and possibly the nicest bloke anyone could ever hope to meet. He's worth a few quid but gives almost all of his considerable income to charity "Plenty of others need it more than me, and giving helps me sleep at night".

He lives in a very modest house, drives a ten-year old Mondeo and shops for clothes once per year in Sainsburys."I do like a nice pair of 'TU' chinos, and they do some lovely socks". He holidays in the UK, claiming that he likes flying even less than Mike Parris does, rarely mentioning that he flew a Vulcan bomber during the Falklands War or that there's a lounge named in his honour at Nottingham Airport.

Rush has been proposed for Club Captain on more than one occasion, but has always declined, preferring to stick with the job he knows he's good at, leaving the limelight to others at the club.

We begin...

Our final chapter should be visualised like that scene in Dirty Dancing where the two gentlemen reminisce about the good old days. It features *'Uncle'* Andy Biggs, who we have met on a few occasions already. It is fitting that he appears just one more time. I hope your golf club has an Andy Biggs, but if it doesn't, you should employ one.

Also appearing here, for the first time, is Clive Rush. As we've just discovered, a wonderful chap who, along with Biggs, is going to make this a far more gentle chapter with hardly any cuss words or talk of a sexual nature. I think we all need a little breather from that don't we...?

"Six fucking nil, SIX FUCKING NIL. Wankers. Not a fucking clue. Six fucking nil.". Rush was not happy on this otherwise perfectly fine Monday morning, a morning which followed his beloved Blackburn Rovers' exit from the FA Cup just sixteen hours earlier. His irritation was directed with precision, and in truth a bit of a knowing smile, towards Andy Biggs. He knew this great friend and club stalwart would lend a sympathetic ear, like he had done on countless previous occasions, to all and sundry over two decades.

"Yeah I saw that..." smiled Biggs. *"Your lot were a decent side once, and then along came the invention of the bicycle and the world changed forever."*

Rush smiled in agreement and grabbed himself a coffee. As a volunteer at the club, someone who worked more hours than most of the staff, he was perfectly entitled to free soft drinks and hot beverages, but he always paid. Always.

"We weren't too bad in the 80's as you well know, those were the days, bit like this place really." Rush was referring to what older members generally agreed was the *"Golden Age"* of Russet Grange when the paint wasn't peeling from the bog walls, the pig farm was yet to open, and a criminal record was a rarity amongst members.

"Those were indeed the days. There was a joining fee, a thousand quid a year for membership, and black ball for anyone who wasn't a barrister, heart surgeon or an Air Vice Marshall." Biggs was only too aware of how things at Russet Grange used to be, a time when being a member of what was once a prestigious club was reason enough to join because most would not get past the application process. (A selection process which involved little more than the club committee deciding if you had either a shit load of money, shot wild animals for pleasure and/or regarded the law of the land as something for simple plebs to comply with).

Rush gave a knowing smile. *"No idea how the likes of us got in to be honest. The membership committee turned down the Grand Poobah from the local Freemasons because his wife drove a Japanese car".* Rush wasn't joking.

Biggs chipped in (not literally, these boys are in the bar, right where they should be). *"Remember Admiral Westerforth? Paid a grand to join, plus subs for over a decade, played nine holes during his entire membership."*

"Yep, Captain the year after he joined, Chairman the year after that, President for a five years". Clive Rush remembered all right, the man was a club legend. *"They reckon it cost him three hundred quid for every shot he played. Decent bloke though, spent*

more at the bar in '78 than the Scottish fans did at the World Cup, and he was only here every other Wednesday".

The buds of reminiscence came even further into bloom as our kindly men chatted about an era long since passed.

"There was the bloke who built the new clubhouse extension. Local chap, trade prices for everything, did it all in his spare time, labour never cost us a penny." It was all flooding back, like the taps had been opened on a barrel of dubious history. *"He raised half a million for a cancer ward at the local hospital, applied to join, got five black balls. Basically got told to sling his hook because he actually worked for a living".* Biggs shook his head in disbelief.

"Yes, I remember him, Colin Mathers. Bit of a double-whammy for the bloke if I recall, the day after his application got turned down his missus left him for the Club Chairman. Poor bastard".

Rush winced, recalling what was certainly not one of Russet Grange's more proud moments *"They let her join though, another right old kick in the plums for the bloke".* More tales resurfaced as these two stout and rather wonderful fellows continued their conversation.

"There was a convicted international drug smuggler too, don't recall his name… (wise move by the author), *….normally he wouldn't have got within five miles of the place but he was Lord somebody or other and his wife owned most of Holland. Andy* Biggs continued: *The President proposed him, the Chairman seconded him and they say a brown envelope to pay for a new boiler for the central heating sealed the deal".*

Clive Rush remembered this all too well, shaking his head in mutual disbelief. *"Five weeks later he was back to his old tricks and got sent down for ten years. That was nine years and sixth months longer than the boiler lasted".*

Biggs recalled another tale from The Golden Years: *"Back in '81 the waiting list contained over 100 people. Five years to even get an interview and you had to have paid a few hundred quid in cash to get on the list in the first place. Spaces really only came up when someone died ".*

Clive Rush knew where this was going, Biggs smiled.

"They only let you on the list if you were in your seventies, and there were no refunds for widows. The club made thirty grand that year from people who died waiting for others to do the same. Nice work if you can get it."

At that moment Australian John appeared, he'd played three holes and despite the clear blue skies and temperatures in the high seventies, he wasn't going to risk getting caught in the rain, especially when the bar was open. His newly found golfing buddy Rose Lubworth followed, the two of them absolutely shit-faced having shared a vodka-based breakfast before setting out on almost forty minutes of golf.

Lubworth was slightly confused as to why Andy Biggs and two of his twin brothers were working behind the bar, so she smiled at the middle one, ordered a *"Todka and Vonic for me and my good friend Johnnie"* and fell over. Australian John fared slightly better, managing to hold things together long enough to recall some sporting action from the day before: *"Nine fucking nil, Stoke got fucking stuffed yesterday didn't they Rushy? Eh, eh? Nine fucking nil"*.

He down his *"Todka and Vonic"* like the professional that he was, forgot what he was laughing about, and then slumped into a clubhouse sofa, fast asleep before his head hit the lager-stained cushions.

Biggs looked at the golfing buddies that adorned the otherwise tidy clubhouse, and found himself loving them for what they were. And then in a brief moment of reflection he realised that feeling extended to all of the members and staff at Russet Grange Golf Club. *"You know what Clive, I think this here right now is the Golden Era for our club. You can keep your joining fees, your dead man's shoes, your blackballing of builders and your bent barristers, I like it this way, I really do."*

Clive Rush smiled a gentle smile and nodded in agreement with his good friend, *"Me too Andy, me too."*

Yes, the club logo is meant to look like a pair of bollocks.

Those are the tales so far, I hope you enjoyed them.
There are many more tales to be told...

Acknowledgements

To the Staff of Wetherspoons in my home town, every little *"How's the book going?"* meant a lot. Thank you guys.

To Kev P and Steve J. They read just the intro and their kind words at that very early stage were hugely encouraging. I owe both of you many beers.

Thanks to my brother too. I knew I could trust him to be honest, and he loved what I wrote: *"Very good so far, just get the thing written".* So I did (though it took three years).

To beer. I doubt I'm the only author who gets those words onto a laptop more easily when there's a pint on the table.

To Baz and Kev, yet more encouragement. Such things really mattered and helped me reach the end.

To a certain group of women in a certain local school. They wanted the book to be *"racy"* but they bought it anyway. Maybe in the sequel...

And finally to my wife Jan and my son James. Neither were anything less than entirely supportive, and as a golfer and a golfer to be, they laughed too.

About the Author

After a career in broadcasting, Crispin Aldrin
(a pseudonym), published *'Tales from Russet Grange'*
at the tender age of 59, having spent a casual three years
writing the book.

His inspiration for the events and characters came
from time spent as either a member, a member of staff,
or a freelance worker at a number of golf clubs in the
south-west of England.

Despite the book's theme Aldrin is not a keen golfer,
playing no more than three or four times each year. By his
own admission he finds that golf takes up too much of his
time, time that he would rather spend in Wetherspoons.
He did play off of 13 once, but it was a long time ago.

Whilst *'Tales from Russet Grange'* is his first
book, he is planning a sequel in 2025 to be titled
'More Tales from Russet Grange'.

Aldrin lives in darkest Somerset,
he is married to Jan and has a son called James.
This book is dedicated to them

One day he will buy a boat.

ISBN 978-1-80352-399-6

Printed in the United Kingdom

ISBN 978-1-80352-399-6

9 781803 523996 >